Also by Scott Geisel

Miller Knew

Jackson Flint series
Fair Game
Water to Bind
Wheat Penny

Praise for

Fair Game

"Strong series launch... Assured prose matches the credible plot. Fans of realistic PI fiction will look forward to the sequel."

– Publishers Weekly

Readers say

"I loved this book. Fast paced and hard to put down."

"Makes you feel like you are in the story"

"This book is as good as anything else you'll find in this genre"

"I recommend it to everyone"

"Well-written page turner doesn't disappoint"

"Keep them coming!"

Water to Bind

"Original plot with fully fleshed-out personalities...this lead can easily sustain a long series"

– Publishers Weekly

Readers say

"Jackson and his crew are so easy to relate to...Can't wait to read more"

"I read with gusto"

"I highly recommend...cannot wait for the next"

"I enjoyed every paragraph...action, adventure, and a good story"

Wheat Penny

"Twists, thrills, and the usual humor…something for everyone"
— Yellow Springs News

Readers say
"Well-plotted mystery…good companion to the earlier books"

"Another good story…it's a fun read"

Miller Knew

"An unexpected — and shocking — meeting with two men out in the woods…sets off a chain of dangerous events"
— Yellow Springs News

Readers say
"This story grabs you and you can't lay it down…one of my favorites now"

"It's been a while since I've read a book in one sitting. Greatly enjoyed this."

"The story grabbed me in the first chapter and held me to the end. It immerses the reader in the Appalachian culture."

"You, too, may find yourself like me holding your breath as you read"

"Absorbing thriller with rich character development that kept me turning pages"

"Very enriching"

ORCAS' CALL

A
NILS & BLY
NOVEL

Scott Geisel

Fox&
Possum
PUBLISHING

scottgeisel.com

Printed and published in the United States of America.

First edition: August 27, 2025

Cover art and book design copyright by Pam Geisel.

ISBN 978-1-7350183-6-2

This one is for Pam. She said other people go on vacation and get a t-shirt and photos. She gets a mystery novel.

Also, thanks to Dan Rudolf and Dennis Moore. (You know why.)

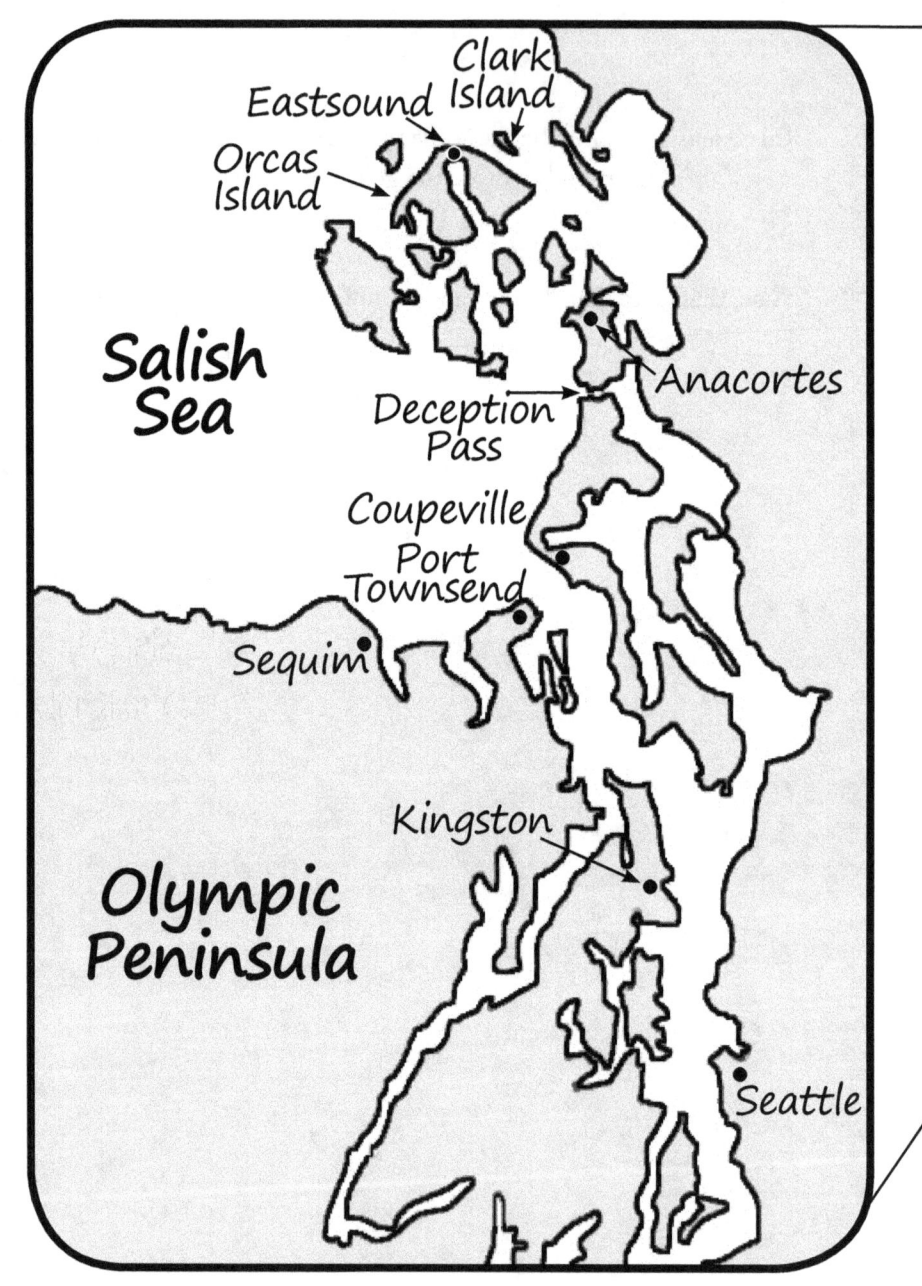

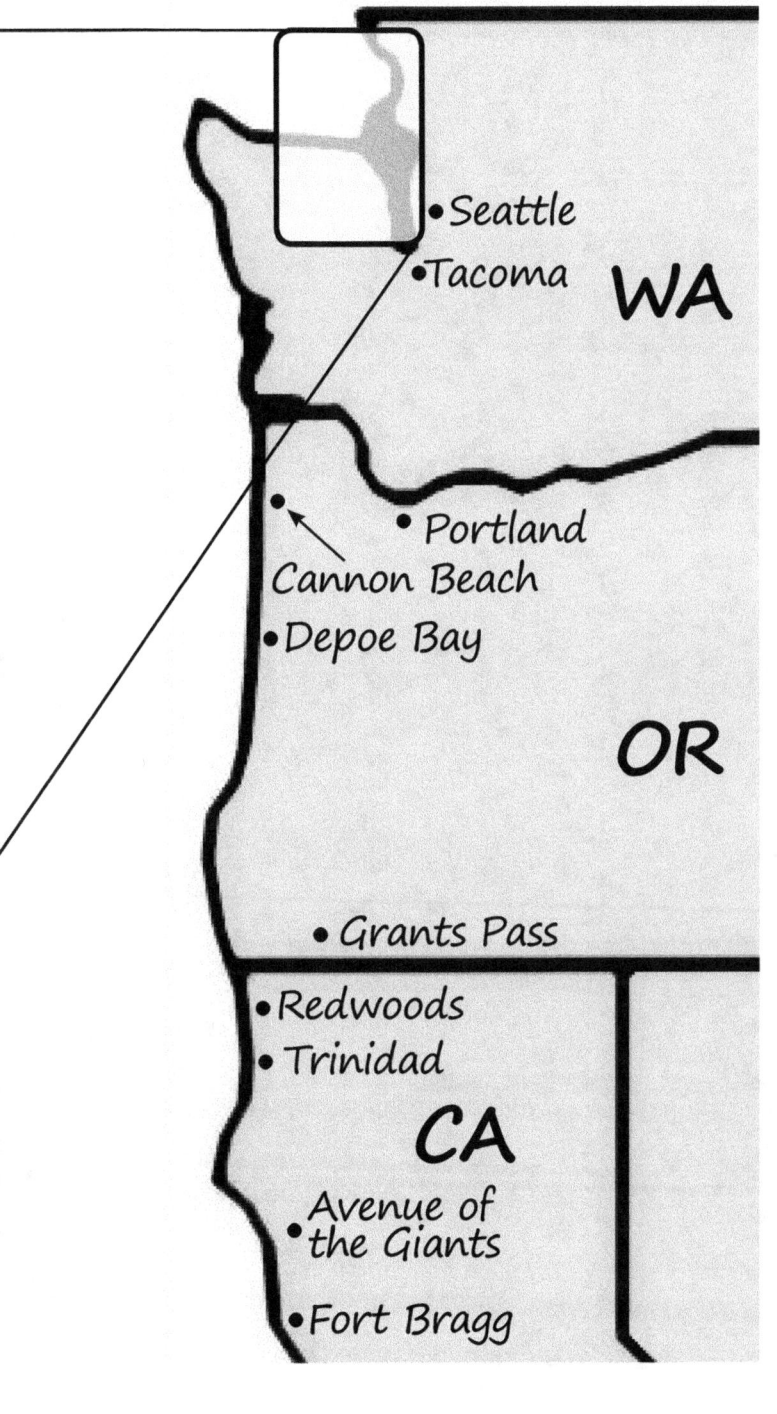

Seattle

Tacoma

WA

Portland

Cannon Beach

Depoe Bay

OR

Grants Pass

Redwoods

Trinidad

CA

Avenue of
the Giants

Fort Bragg

1

NILS GARNER DANGLED by his fingertips from the flange of a steel I-beam that supported the upper deck of a Washington State ferry. He was alone. Above the beam was an empty observation area that jutted from the hull of the ferry into a chilly and blustery June day. Below the beam, Nils was getting a workout.

The top deck of the ferry, devoid of passengers, provided Nils the solitude he wanted. The beam provided the lift he needed to get in some muscle work. From Nils' feet hung the backpack he'd carried with him these last ten days—days spent alone and wandering in something of an existential crunch. It wasn't his first grappling with who he was or what he thought he might become, but it had been his toughest. Alone time had helped.

Nils tightened his fingers against the flange and pulled. The muscles in his forearms, back, and shoulders responded and lifted his chin up toward the beam. Now that his eyes came level with the painted steel, the beam looked more like an *H* on its side than it did an *I*. It was a Nils thing to think. Another existential musing.

Nils released that thought as he released his pull and lowered from the beam. Focus was good, not thinking. Just feel the muscles and the lift. He paused to listen and scan the deck. Still empty. Good. He didn't care for an audience.

Nils twisted his feet tighter into the straps of the pack he'd been carrying. The pack had been home, and now it was extra weight for the lifts. He bent his knees, raised the pack, then raised himself again by his fingertips.

The pack swayed at his feet, and Nils slowed his rise and dampened the motion to isolate the muscles he wanted. It had been a long ten days of wandering, and workouts had been improvised and hard to come by. This felt good. And needed. He lifted again, and again, focused only on the control and the burn. Thinking nothing and being alone.

Just beyond the ship's rail in front of Nils, the hull dropped into the cold waters of this unnamed part of the Salish Sea. Behind the ferry to the East lay the Rosaria Strait. To the North lay the Strait of Georgia. South, the Strait of Juan de Fuca and the Olympic Peninsula. And here where Nils was lay the San Juan Islands, breaking from the water in dark clumps like ancient creatures rising for breath.

The ferry slipped now between Shaw and Orcas Islands, cutting a path to the Orcas terminal at the bottom of West Sound. Soon, the horns would blare to announce the ferry's arrival. Nils lowered his arms fully and hung from the beam, tilted his feet to twist free the pack that had provided ballast, and released his left hand. With his right arm he did a quick one-armed pull-up, followed by a slower and more difficult second ascent. Without allowing himself time to think, he switched hands and powered through two pull-ups with the left arm. The burn in his muscles carved a singularity of focus through Nils' thoughts that felt good.

The engines sounded and reversed, and the ferry slowed. Water churned beneath the hull, and Nils felt pressure thrumming through the bones of the vessel and into his arms. He rested for a few seconds, then raised himself again with both arms. When his chin reached the level of the bottom of the beam, he thrust himself upwards, released both hands into the air, flung his arms around the beam, and caught a slim purchase with his fingers on the far side of the *I*, which Nils now thought of as an *H*. He inched his fingers in for a better hold, then descended and began raising himself in a series of chin-ups that would work different muscles in his chest and biceps.

The slope of Orcas Island rising from the water appeared in the view between his forearms as he lifted and descended. Almost there. Soon he and the other passengers would be called down to disembark, and Nils would have to intermingle again with the population of the ship. This time alone would help prepare him for that.

The engines continued to slowly work the ship toward the dock, the starboard bow cutting an angle into the wind. Cool air raised the hairs on Nils' forearms. He welcomed the sensation. Nils liked the chill and the dark. He always had. Low skies and gray drizzle closed the world around him and made him feel whole and centered and alive.

He struggled through a final chin-up, pushing his muscles toward fatigue and failure, that familiar place where performance ended and growth began.

The ferry had nearly stopped. Nils released himself from the beam and bent to retrieve his pack. In that movement, something caught his attention. He stopped and listened. There was a sound on the deck. Halting footsteps. The snick of a door.

The spell was broken. Nils was no longer alone, though it seemed odd to him that someone would come to the top deck now, when the ferry was about to dock.

From behind him he heard a voice. "Mister."

He wanted not to turn. To remain alone. To stay in that place of inner privacy. To keep others out. To put behind him what he had set out to put behind him.

"Mister, will you help us?"

Us? Nils turned. It was human nature. And it was Nils' nature. He turned and saw a woman.

She was small but not petite. Dressed simply. A skirt that was modest but revealed her knees. Long socks that covered her calves. A light cotton jacket that would help against the chill. Her complexion was light like his, but tinged with a look of weathering that was beyond her years.

Something about her was vaguely familiar. Nils knew that thought must be an illusion, but something about her hair, or her eyes, tugged on a memory. It was as if from a dream or a painting, something abstract and unreal that he couldn't place.

Nils knelt, slowly, silently, and slipped the pack back onto his shoulders. The woman watched Nils without moving, holding her place rigidly in front of the door to the lower decks. A breeze teased the trim of her hair against her shoulders. Then the woman's eyes narrowed, searching the deck. Memories of images clicked rapidly through Nils' thoughts as if in a movie sequence. Faces of women. Where had he seen this one before?

The deck juddered as the engines pushed the ship into its final position against the dock. The woman shifted her feet with the change in momentum. The movement revealed a young girl standing behind the woman, the girl's head at hip level, her long, loose hair blowing against watery eyes. The girl was thin and wore a summer dress and a ragged sweater that draped to her knees.

The child's eyes went up to the woman, then over to Nils.

Nils straightened, the pack's straps stretching against his shoulders. The child completed an image that snapped together in his memory. A TV screen. Playing in the ship's lounge when he'd walked through, the volume louder than he'd expected and drawing his attention. The woman and the child. The woman's hair was shorter now than in the photo on the TV screen, and there was a general demeanor and look about her that was somehow changed. But the child looked much the same. This was them.

Nils' memory called up more details. It had been a news alert. There was an abduction. A woman and child missing. This woman and child. Family was involved, a brother-in-law or someone close. They were activating the amber alert. Imminent danger.

The alert had been flashing across the screen. Armed and dangerous. Do not approach. Alert authorities immediately. Nils tried to remember if there had been a photo of the abductor.

The woman stepped from the door behind her, one pace closer to Nils. "Mister." She put an arm to the child and moved the girl with her, as if trying to wrap the girl beneath the hem of her skirt. Her voice grew more desperate. "Help us."

For a fraction of a second, Nils considered what he should do. No, for a fraction of a fraction of a second. The time it takes for a stroke of lightning to descend. And it pained him that he took that long to decide. Because he knew. He knew he would help this woman and child, with abandon, no matter what.

Nils took a single step toward the woman. As he took another, footsteps rang behind him, clanging on another set of stairs to the aft. Fast, heavy steps.

The sound startled Nils into making what he would soon know to be a mistake. He paused to assess. In that pause he turned toward the sound. The aft stairs opened directly onto the deck with no doors. That configuration and Nils' pause allowed the footsteps to become a head, then shoulders and a man rising and running from the stairs.

Nils processed, perhaps making his second mistake. Savior or sinner? Was this man the abductor from the amber alert or someone come to save the two?

The woman cringed and pressed the child into her hip, turning as she did to scrabble for the handle on the doors behind her. Now seconds that had passed exceedingly slowly sped up to fractions of seconds flashing exceedingly fast. Nils moved to intercept.

The man ran hard, his dirty and mottled Seattle Seahawks jacket whipping from his shoulders, stringy hair tangling in his beard. Nils ran to catch the man. As he neared, the man veered from the woman, lowered his arms, and hit Nils with an upward blow like a tackling dummy. The impact drove an elbow into Nils' ribcage and he tumbled backward onto the deck.

Instinct took over. Nils rolled. The backpack dug into his vertebrae and he flipped to his feet and squared for the man, who had been flung from the hit into the deck chairs. Nils ducked his head and came at the man with his hands up, wanting to get to the man before he could rise.

The man kicked and crawled backward through the tumbled chairs and fled for the stairs he had come up.

Nils then made what might have been his third mistake. The woman and child had disappeared down the stairs to his right. The man had run down the stairs to his left. Nils' thoughts fast-switched from chasing the threat to protecting the two. Neutralize or protect.

He chose to protect.

Nils ran to the doors and down the stairs, swatting behind him in vain at the backpack to try to reach his phone inside. He emerged onto the passenger deck into sparse groups of people moving toward the exit.

Nils ran through the deck and the people and searched for the woman and child. "911! Someone call 911! The amber alert."

Startled faces turned. Nils pushed through, pointing at the TV. The news story had ended, but the alert still crawled across the bottom. "They just came through. Somebody call."

Someone swiped a phone. Another phone came up and was recording. Nils ran through.

He reached the open observation deck and scanned passengers offloading on the pedestrian walkway. He leaned over the rail and looked to the cars directly below, idling and waiting for the vehicle ramp to open.

Nils did not see the woman and child. A breeze riffled his hair.

People and walkway to the right. Cars below.

He listened, watched, breathed.

People, cars. Which way did they go?

Breeze.

People, cars. Where?

A shout came from below. Nils looked down. Directly below him through the open air, two cars idled side by side at the front of the line of vehicles waiting while a worker in a yellow jacket secured the ramp for exiting.

On the left, a man and woman in a dark blue BMW convertible with the top down sat in jackets and sunglasses, looking surprised. On the right a gray, rusting Honda Civic crouched under clear plastic sheeting that was taped over an open sunroof.

The rear driver's-side door of the Civic flew open and the man in the Seahawks jackets scrambled out. He was followed by legs that kicked and wore the long stockings that Nils had seen above.

The woman shouted from the back seat. "No! Chelsea! Let her go!"

The man withdrew as the feet kicked and forced him back against the BMW. The man in the BMW frantically tried to raise the top.

Nils shouted down. "Stop them!" He pointed to the man in the Seahawks jacket. "Stop him."

The ferry worker in the yellow jacket had a phone out. The man and woman in the BMW sat frozen as the car's top slowly worked to cover them. The man in the Seahawks jacket fought to push the stockinged legs back into the car and close the door. Nils leaned farther over the railing, grabbing at the air that separated him from the man below.

A line of shadow entered from the left, and a man in a tight black sweatshirt emerged, running between the rows of cars. The newcomer had his fists raised and shouted. "Stop."

The abductor pivoted and brought up a hand with a pistol. The man in the black sweatshirt skidded and backpedaled, his hands opening to palms. "Whoa."

It was close quarters. The top of the BMW clicked into place, covering the riders inside. The would-be rescuer scrambled away from the pistol. The worker in the yellow jacket had disappeared. And Nils stretched down over the rail, leaning down but out of reach of the fight below.

The man with the pistol shouted. "Anybody come at me, motherfucker, and I'll blow your head off." He did not look up and see Nils above him.

The pistol pressed against the Honda's window, pointing at the woman inside. "You try that again and I'll blow *your* head off."

Testosterone soaked the air. Nils calculated the time it would take him to run down to the vehicle deck.

The man pressed himself into the driver's seat of the Civic. Nils swung a leg over the rail.

The Civic revved, a belt squealing like the high-pitched whine of a child. Nils swung the other leg over. His backpack pressed him away from the rail. He hung on with one hand and leaned out over the Civic. How far was the fall?

Below Nils, the vehicle deck's exit ramp locked into place. Muscles and instinct and resolve took over. He stepped from the railing and aimed his feet for the plastic on the sunroof.

The drop was swift, the landing fast and clumsy. One foot ripped through the plastic sheeting. The other jammed into the roof and sent needles into Nils' leg.

The gate blocking the vehicles' exit lowered. Both of Nils' feet were through the sunroof opening, and the Civic lurched forward.

The motion tossed Nils onto his back. His knees bent and caught the edge of the sunroof opening.

The Civic jettisoned from the ferry. Nils was compressed against the Civic's rear window.

Nils might have recognized this as his fourth mistake, but he chose instead to think of it as commitment. Once he decided something, he was capable of a fierce and sometimes unsensible loyalty. That surfaced rarely. When it did he could seldom control it.

The dock landing flew by, Nils pinned on the rear window and watching. Grocery market, ticket office, road, cars lined up to board. And Nils' thoughts turned from whether he'd made a mistake to how he'd gotten here.

Nils in his thirty-two years, nearly half of them as an adult, had rarely committed to anything for more than a short time. He had expected to. He'd made a go at college, a year and a half undecided at the state university until his parents died in a car wreck just before Christmas of his sophomore year. There had been no one to help. No family, no relatives, no childhood friends to turn to.

He'd gone home, collected a meager life insurance policy, and dealt with arrangements for his parents' remains. There was no way to pay the mortgage or keep the house, so he'd sold everything and cashed out. He moved on, and soon he tried to forget.

Nils bounced around the Northwest coast, mostly sticking to small towns that suited him better than the larger cities. Sometimes working and making money, sometimes spending down the funds from the insurance and what his parents had left.

Nils believed in the value of a good friendship, but he had no friends from high school or college who he was close enough to that he wanted to reconnect. It was easier to forget and start fresh. No one asking him how he was or how he was doing. Just Nils finding himself without history attached.

He believed also in the value of a good relationship. He'd dated a few women, but nothing lasted long or hinted at the depth of commitment he'd seen his parents share.

He believed in staying in shape, keeping his face clean shaven when he could, and cutting his sandy-brown hair when it threatened to reach below his ears. He liked a good meal early in the morning. Beyond that, he mostly just let things happen as they would.

For reasons he couldn't explain, Nils just didn't connect. Through his early twenties, that hadn't bothered him much. Into his later twenties and now beginning his thirties, he'd simply come to accept it. He liked being alone. He liked moving around.

Jobs stuck until they didn't. Working as a kayak guide for a private company was better than the construction or landscaping jobs he'd found. Temp jobs in factories or on the loading docks were boring and made him itchy to do anything else. A summer stint keeping bees in the foothills of the Idaho mountains held sweet memories for him, but seasonal jobs always fell away after a time. And again for reasons Nils couldn't explain, he never went back to them.

His most recent gig had sealed that thought into his brain. He'd signed on as a wilderness guide for a small company that took elite clientele to very remote locations. Some clients were ready enough for the rough experience of the wilds. Others found that the stories they wanted to bring back from the trip weren't worth the inconveniences they had to endure to get them.

Nils had begun that gig several months before in the spring, and Nils being Nils, he'd already thought of moving on when his last excursion ended disastrously. It took a toll on his psyche and he'd given his notice, turned off his phone, drawn a pile of cash from his savings, and set out on this trip up the coast to the San Juan Islands.

Until landing through the roof of the Civic, Nils had committed to nothing, not so much as a sit-down meal, in the last ten days. So why jump now, literally, into something from which he had no way to extricate himself?

It was just his way. This type of rashness was seldom and fleeting for him, but when it surfaced Nils felt it impossible to escape from.

Now, as the Civic bore a hard left onto Orcas Island, the pressure in Nils' legs increased as he struggled to cling to the sunroof, and he revised his previous thinking. This was not a commitment. He was right that it was a mistake. He could do nothing better pinned to the roof of this car than the authorities who would have already been alerted could do. But he was committed now, with no exit route.

The Civic slipped through loose gravel on a curve, the wheels skittering and the man twisting the wheel to try to gain control. Nils strained to pull himself up from the rear window to a seated position in the sunroof, kicking his feet into the man's shoulder and head.

The man punched Nils' legs and pounded the roof. "Get off my car, motherfucker."

The car jerked sideways and skidded and slowed. Nils stepped hard onto the man's head and shoulders, trying to keep him from regaining speed.

The man had the pistol in his hand and was trying to raise his arm. Nils kicked to keep the hand down and the pistol away. The car had nearly stopped. Nils shouted to the woman and child in the back. "Out! Get out! Jump!"

Nils heard the woman throw herself against the door. "It won't open. Child locks."

"Kick it."

"It won't open!" Her voice was frenzied. "Don't shoot us! Don't let him shoot us."

Nils and the man tangled, Nils pressing and kicking down through the sunroof, the man trying to raise the pistol and get the car going.

The Civic nosed to a stop. Nils tried to reach down outside the car to a door handle, but he could not.

The movement allowed the man to gain leverage, and when Nils fought back, the pack on his back wrenched from his shoulders and slipped away.

A shot banged out and the front passenger window splintered. A shriek pealed from the back.

Another vehicle emerged from the blind curve, swerving to avoid the Civic with the bullet hole in the window and the man sitting through the roof.

Another shot rang out, the bullet exploding the dash, and the Civic began to move again.

Nils kicked harder against the arm with the gun. With the pack gone from his back, he could squeeze down through the roof.

The Civic accelerated erratically. The driver shouted and punched as Nils squeezed in on top of him. "What. The. *Fuck?* Get off my car."

They were squeezed tight, no room to move gun or arm or wheel or legs. The Civic slipped and fishtailed toward trees beside the road. The man frantically tried to correct.

Nils forced his hand down beside the man to the door handle. His fingers found a grip, and he pulled.

The door lurched open, Nils kicked, and the man spilled into the open door frame. Nils kept one foot against the gun and stepped down on the wheel with the other. The car spun, Nils pushed, and the man dumped out onto the road.

Then Nils was in the seat, the gun was on the floorboard, and the man was in the gravel. Nils jammed the shifter into park and the Civic jumped and stalled and stopped. He reached for the pistol on the floorboard. "Everybody okay?"

He saw them in the rearview mirror, the woman clutching the child so tight it seemed she might disappear.

"Anybody hurt?!"

The woman whimpered. "Don't shoot us."

"I'm not going to—" Nils saw the gun in his hand and dropped it. He got out of the car and checked on the man. The abductor was a crumpled shape limping away on the shoulder.

Nils went to the rear door of the Civic and opened it. "He's gone."

"Don't hurt us!"

"He's gone. I won't hurt you." Nils put a hand out for the woman. She recoiled.

Nils stepped back from the door. "Are you okay? Anything hurt?"

The woman looked at her daughter. The daughter looked back. "He didn't shoot me."

The woman locked her gaze on Nils. "Why'd you do that?"

"You asked me to help."

"But that's crazy. He could have…"

Nils felt heat. "I made it worse. I put you at risk."

The woman's voice was a tremor. "No. It would have been worse if you hadn't. It was worth the risk."

A car stopped down the road. Nils wanted his phone, but it was lost with his backpack. He called into the car to the woman. "Do you have a phone?"

She didn't seem to understand.

"A phone. Can you call 911?"

She shook her head. "He took my phone."

The man who had taken them was gone around the curve. Nils knew that whoever sat in the car that had stopped would have a phone. He waved for the vehicle to come forward. It didn't.

Nils put his head inside the car. "You call to them."

The woman understood and came from the car, waved her arms and shouted. "Help! Please help us. We need help."

The car inched forward. The woman waved and called again.

And Nils stepped back.

The car approached more quickly. A siren started up in the distance.

The woman turned to Nils. "Where are you going?"

"These people will help you." He took another step away and with a finger motioned to the sound of the siren. "You'll be okay now."

"Don't leave us. Why would you leave us?"

"I have to go."

Her stare was almost unbearable. "What is your name?"

Nils moved back. "I'm sorry. I have to go." His feet began to move. He didn't want to run, to leave this woman and her child, but he couldn't stay. A crushing feeling of closeness descended on him like a strange, dark mist. He wouldn't face the sirens, the questions, the explanations. He wanted space. He wanted to be away, alone, now.

And as the woman watched Nils and hugged her daughter, her arms wrapping the little head and shoulders, Nils began to run. He ran into the trees beside the road and faded away into the foliage.

2

THE ADRENALINE was wearing off, the synapses between Nils' axons and dendrites burning up and flushing out the neurotransmitter chemicals, the binding receptors on his cells settling once again to normal functioning.

His breathing slowed and evened, his heartbeat softened and quieted. Now, standing in the dappled shade of the trees, Nils felt his blood sugar drop, the epinephrine no longer telling his body to produce glucose for quick energy. The buzz was gone.

He felt a tremor from the low sugar and hungered for a granola bar or dried fruit, something to carry him through the crash. But his backpack was lost, and with it everything Nils had been carrying—food, water, clothes, wash kit, some outdoor gear. He bent at his waist, inhaled deeply, and quietly held onto his breaths as his body worked to even out.

Bird song came to him through sunlight and leaves, and he felt salt air on his pores.

He exhaled, straightened, and took stock. Stupid, jumping onto the car. He should have left well enough alone and let the local authorities intervene. That was easier to think now than it had been in the moment, but still it ate at him, making rash decisions. And maybe the woman had been right. Maybe things would have gone badly for her and her daughter if he hadn't jumped. He would never know, and he couldn't go back now. He listened to the birdsong and tried to redirect his thoughts.

Backpack. What he needed now was to look for his backpack.

Nils knew the island and knew he was on Orcas Road. Probably close to the turn toward Turtleback Mountain. The pack had fallen away to his left, toward the water. There had been trees along the road. He closed his eyes and tried to remember seeing where the pack had gone. Was it on the road, where someone might stop and pick it up?

Sweat trickled on his brow, and he gave up. He couldn't see it. His attention had been on the car and the man driving it and the gun.

He assessed his options beyond searching for the backpack. Eastsound, the main and only significant town on the island, was a half dozen miles or so to the north. He'd planned to catch one of the island shuttles at the ferry dock, get to Eastsound before dark and find a place to stay, then rent a bike for a few days.

Nils had no plans beyond that. He had no home to get to. No job. No vehicle. He had a few things stashed in a tiny storage unit in Sequim. After his last gig had gone sour, Nils trolled online want ads for a driving or delivery job that would take him up the coast. He could have rented a car or booked a flight, but that wasn't Nils' style. He wanted a cheap and mindless distraction, something to help get his mind out of the churn he'd sunk into.

He found a guy who wanted someone to drive his truck up to Sequim. Turned out, the deal was to drive both the truck and the guy. The truck owner was recently paroled, and his brother-in-law had promised work in his garage if the guy could get up to Sequim. But the man, who Nils knew only as Mike, didn't have a license and didn't want to break parole by driving. Nils hadn't asked if crossing state lines would be a problem. Driving the truck was the distraction he wanted, and he took the job and was paid fifty dollars and two meals to drive a quiet, skinny ex-con up the coast.

After they arrived at the garage in Sequim with the truck, Nils had paid the garage owner's teenaged son to drive him to a storage unit where he stowed a few things, then take Nils the couple of hours up to Anacortes. He'd paid the kid the fifty he'd gotten from Mike plus gas money, and the kid didn't even ask for a meal. Nils got dropped at the ferry terminal and found the restrooms and a sandwich while he'd waited for passage to Orcas.

He had with him now his wallet and ID. Some money. A credit card he rarely used. Not much else. He longed for a bottle of water. Granola or nuts, some snacks from his backpack. He could replace what else was lost later—the tent, sleeping bag, clothes. But what he wanted right now was sustenance. Something to eat, and to keep his head down and not have to answer any questions about what had just happened.

Faint pink lights flickered through the trees where Nils stood. He walked to the berm of the road and looked. Emergency vehicles had arrived where the Honda sat in the road.

He stepped again into the trees and made his way slowly back toward the scene. He would have to pass the Honda and the responding vehicles to go look for his backpack, but the trees ended and there would be no cover. Nils watched from a distance.

The sirens had quieted, but the scene had grown. An ambulance and police cars blocked the lane, EMTs and officers moving about, and a few gawkers stood by with phones. One of the gawkers was taking a lot of video and trying to get close to police or the woman from the Civic. Nils wondered how long it would be before recordings got onto social media or a local news source.

He walked deeper back into the trees. Was there something in the backpack that could identify him if the authorities found it? If the pack had skipped safely away into the trees, he'd be better searching for it later when the scene had cleared.

He turned and walked north instead, up-island, staying off the road and close to the trees where he could hide in shade and shadows. The sun was nearly down, and when it sank lower Nils ventured to the road and jogged along the shoulder, running into the dark, longing to reach Eastsound where he could get water and something to eat.

It was harder than he expected. The day had been long, it was late, and it was several miles to Eastsound. Nils grew tired and plodded. His focus narrowed to keeping his feet moving, with only a few headlights to remind him of the outside world, until he reached the edge of the quiet and sleepy town.

He walked the short main street. Lights dotted the interiors of closed shops and eateries. The tink of glass bottles sounded somewhere

in the distance as they were dumped into a can. Nils turned onto North
Beach Road and walked directly to Village Green Park and the water
fountain, and there he slurped several long and luxurious drinks.

The jog had syphoned off his nerves and softened his mind with endorphins. He walked the empty street to the little crescent beach behind
the waterfront stores and lay back on some driftwood. The stars winked
down on him and Nils listened to the water.

An undetermined amount of time later, Nils shivered and woke.
The stars were oriented differently and the moon had gone. Pinpricks
of light peeked through ribbons of dark sky. The faint sound of what
he believed to be orca song drifted across the water to Nils. He sat
up and listened closer, but the singing had gone. Probably just tin in
his ears.

He shivered again and rose from the driftwood and climbed back to
the street. He walked again to the park, drank again from the fountain
and peed, then huddled against the shelter of the amphitheater and tried
to sleep more, waiting for sunlight and warmth.

When Nils woke again, long shadows stretched across the green. He
moved into the warm shafts of sunlight, marking time until the town
began to stir.

When the town did stir, Nils went straight to the Island Market and
picked out a cap with the longest bill he could find. He purchased the
cap and left with a vague hope that images and video captured at the
ferry the day before would not have drawn much attention and no one
would recognize him.

Nils cleaned up in the public restroom and was surprised how satisfied he was with the cap. He found himself at the door of Olga Rising
when the café opened for business.

He kept his head down, paid in cash, and received nary a strange
look nor a sideways glance. And he ate voraciously in the corner of the
café garden, a frittata, overnight oats, and coffee, and he was still hungry.
But his worries faded as his stomach filled.

Forty-five minutes later, Nils had purchased a day pack, water,
snacks, peanut butter and a box of crackers, and a couple of sandwiches.
He added an extra t-shirt, shorts, sunscreen, and a lightweight jacket. No

replacement phone. He hadn't touched his for more than a week and still had hopes of finding it and his backpack.

A young woman at the register when he bought the clothes smiled at Nils when he pulled a bill from his wallet. He dropped his head beneath his cap and the bill onto the counter.

The woman's hand hadn't moved to the cash. "Credit is better for me if you have it."

Nils kept looking down.

"I'd have to give you change in fives. They don't give us much cash to start. Unless you have a smaller bill."

Nils didn't. He pushed the bill back into his wallet and fished for his credit card.

The woman smiled again. "Thanks. I hope it's no trouble for you."

"No trouble." He tapped his card against the reader and it beeped.

"I guess I shouldn't have asked you. Hardly anybody pays with cash anymore anyway. You wouldn't believe what people will put on a card. Little thing for a dollar or two." She shook her head. "Hardly worth it after the swipe fee."

Nils grinned. Small talk was good. It meant nothing memorable was happening. Either the hat was working, or nobody cared and yesterday was already forgotten. He nodded his sympathy. "I hear you."

The woman reached for a bag. "Receipt?"

Nils put his hand on the clothing. "Thanks. I don't need a bag. Or a receipt."

Now the woman looked up at Nils.

He kept his head down. "If it's OK with you, I'll just put them in here." He hefted his new day pack.

Her smile came back. "Sure." The receipt had already spit from the machine, and the woman casually plucked it away and dropped it into a waste can.

Nils pushed the shorts and shirt into his pack.

"You visiting Orcas?"

"Yeah."

"First time?"

Now Nils hoped to clip the conversation. "I've been before."

She looked a little disappointed that he wasn't a newbie. "You came for the parade tomorrow?"

"Parade?"

"Solstice parade."

Nils zipped his pack shut. "Sounds interesting." It did. But he didn't plan to see it.

The woman brightened now. "Oh, you have to go. Lucky that you're here now for it. Coolest thing ever."

Nils turned. "I'll bet."

She called after him as he exited. "Right down Main Street, then up Beach to the park. Then the festival. It's a big deal here. Everybody goes. Very cool!"

Nils raised an arm to the voice behind him. "Thanks." The bell on the door tinkled as it closed.

Nils followed that by getting in and out of the bike rental shop without any chit-chat. Just a bike, a helmet, and he was ready to go.

The small talk came while he was adjusting the bike seat in the alley behind the shop. A man in an aloha shirt and sandals scratched his belly while he waited for a miniature dog on a leash to investigate beneath some shrubbery. He pointed to Nils. "You're going to need that helmet, mate."

The helmet dangled from the handlebars. Nils finished adjusting the seat height and didn't look at the man.

"You heard about the crazies?"

Nils leaned away and strapped on the helmet.

"Ran someone off the road. Jumped right into her car."

Nils got on the bike and cocked a foot on a pedal.

"I'm just sayin', mate. Crazies out there. Watch yourself."

"I will." Nils began his motion, but the tiny dog jumped out from under the shrubbery as if it had been slapped or stepped on, and the line on the retractable leash zipped out and pulled taut in front of the bike. Nils jerked the brakes.

The man laughed. "He'll do that. Run at anything."

The man made no effort to reign in the dog, so Nils maneuvered around the line.

"Here for the parade?"

Did Nils have a sign on him that said visitor? Or did all the locals just know everyone? "Uh, no."

"Where you headed?"

Nils pressed down on the pedal and glided away. "To the mountain."

The man called behind him. "You're going to want an e-bike. That's a long ride."

Nils pedaled.

"Watch out for the crazies!"

He would.

Nils skirted the village, picked up Lover's Lane, then swung onto Orcas Road to go look for his lost backpack. The trip was much quicker by bike than when he'd run it the night before. He felt loose and strong and free and made good time.

When he reached the spot near where he thought he'd lost his pack, the sun had risen higher above the trees and threw a broad arc of shadows across the road. There was no traffic. Birds sang, and a light breeze wafted in from the water. Nothing belay the tranquility to suggest what had happened here the day before but for a set of long, black rubber tire marks on the pavement.

Nils drank from his water bottle and ate some trail mix, then he searched in the trees and open areas around the road for his lost backpack.

Failing that, he traveled down-road and searched again. And failing that, he traveled up-road and searched more.

Failing that, and as frustrations began to settle in, he wondered if someone had found the pack and picked it up. With no way to know and only worries if he thought about it, Nils tried to settle into the feel of the new, smaller day pack that had already grown familiar on his shoulders.

He itched to get back on the bike and onto the mountain. Moran State Park and Mount Constitution were a long way from where he was. He'd have to ride back up the island, around Eastsound again and over the thin strip that connected the two lobes of land, then down the other side of Orcas Island. Nils walked back to the bike where it leaned in the shadow of some trees, stepped from sight, and took a sandwich from his backpack. Something in his head as he ate told him it would be better to get off the island now, but Nils wanted to do what Nils wanted to do. He wanted to climb that mountain. Then he'd get off-island.

Nils rode. There were hills and there was sun and cool shade and there were cars and other riders. Nils paid attention to no one, and no one paid attention to him. When he reached the park and the trailhead for Mount Constitution, Nils locked the rental bike to a tree, refilled his water bottles, and began the ascent.

The forest invigorated him. The trees, the water, the steady climb. Everything invigorated him. This was Nils' element. Something basic in him came alive and heated up.

The route was familiar, four and a half miles out and two thousand feet up. A solid climb. No one else was within sight or sound. The trail was his. Nils took a deep breath and started up at a brisk pace.

The first feeling that he wasn't alone touched Nils well into the trek. He slowed to look at the hollow black opening of an old mine shaft on a bluff above the trail. The digger had hoped for gold but come away only with pyrite. A fool's journey.

Nils paused and drank some water. A dull, quiet sound tamped through the forest. He turned downslope and listened. Footsteps?

But he saw nothing moving below through the trees. The sound faded, and Nils began his ascent again.

The sound returned as he climbed, haunting and intermittent. Then at a tight switchback where the trail carved upward around a ledge, Nils caught sight over his shoulder of a dark, slim figure moving behind him through the terrain. A runner. Moving faster than he was.

Fine. Nils liked a challenge.

He increased his pace, running to keep ahead of his pursuer but not burn himself out too soon. There was a long way left to go.

Nils sweated as he timed his breathing with his pace. The rhythm felt good, and he picked up more speed. He figured the runner wouldn't be able to stay with him for long.

He reached the Cold Springs shelter, still moving fast. Beyond that where the trail crossed the road before the final length to the top, Nils ventured a look back.

He no longer heard the footsteps behind him, but the figure was still there, coming through the trees sleek and fast. Closer now, and closing as Nils had slowed to look back. Not more than twenty-five yards behind. Close enough that Nils could see the figure was a woman.

His pursuer saw Nils gawk, reached the road he had just crossed, and shouted. "Nilson!"

Nils' mind spun. How had they—

"Nilson Garner. Stop!"

He did not. Nils pitched forward onto the path. He caught a root with a toe and stumbled and righted himself. The woman behind him drew closer.

"Nilson, people are waiting for you. At the top. You don't want to go there. Stop."

Nils did not. He ran.

"People you don't want to find you."

She was very near now, Nils sweating and breathing and running and confused. "Who are you?"

"I can help you."

What did that mean? He ran on.

The woman behind him was strong. Ahead the trail ran the edge of some bluffs. He would need to slow there to navigate the ledge. If she hadn't caught him by then, the woman would be on his heels when he reached the cliffs.

Nils called out again. "Who are you?" He twisted left and right as the trail zagged up through the trees and scrub. "How do you know my name?"

The woman's footsteps answered for her, moving swiftly behind him. Staying with him.

Nils ran but could not gain any distance from his pursuer.

"Stop and I'll tell you. Nilson, stop running. You don't want to get to the top."

The trail turned sharply then and narrowed as it traveled the length of the bluffs. Views of the Salish Sea opened in the distance. Green islands loped from the water and split the line between blue water and bluer sky. Other flatter islands swam on the water like oddly shaped pancakes. Farther out, thin and hazy clouds mixed and fused with land and water in a blur that stretched to Canada.

Nils stopped. Beautiful.

The woman glided to a stop beside him and turned with Nils to look out over the view. Her breathing was labored but not heavy. She was slim and very fit and her hair was very dark but caught shades of more than black in the sunlight. She looked about his age, but a touch younger. Thirty at most. She was sweaty and dressed all in black running clothes and her hands rested lightly on her hips.

"Nilson." Her voice was gentle, barely more than a whisper.

"Caught me."

They looked out over the land and sea together. Nils' breathing slowed. He could hear that the woman's had also.

She reached to a compact runner's belt around her waist and released from it a water bottle Nils hadn't noticed before. She drank from the bottle and wiped a forearm across her brow. "Very nice view."

Nils felt oddly relaxed. Endorphins, probably. He stretched his back. "Totally worth the climb."

The woman drank again and re-holstered the water bottle. She moved with grace and kept her gaze on the sea below as if she had come up here for the view, and not to chase Nils.

The woman broke the quiet that surrounded them. "You didn't make that easy."

She said no more, so Nils filled in the gap. "How did you know..." What did Nils want to know? "How did you find me?"

Her eyes were dark and enigmatic. "That's not the most important question right now. Do you want to try again?"

Did he? "What's at the top? Why don't you want me to go there?"

"That's a much harder thing to answer."

"Okay, let's get this over with. It was me. I jumped into the car."

The woman's mouth twitched. "Everyone who watches the news knows that, but that's not what we're here for."

Nils stepped back. "*We're* here for?"

"*They* are. The people at the top."

"I thought you weren't with them."

"I'm not." She stepped in to close the gap he'd opened. "And they're not on your side."

"Okay, I admit it. I caused the crash. I left them there. I shouldn't have jumped into the car."

"I don't think you understand."

"They could have been really hurt."

"They almost were. You stopped it."

"It was my fault."

"Nilson." The woman's hand went out. "You don't understand. That's not what this is about."

"Nils." It came out reflexively. He hadn't meant to say it.

A question came into the woman's dark and quiet eyes.

"I go by Nils."

"All right." Her hand hovered, still reaching toward him but not touching.

"You didn't have to make such a big deal about this. You could have waited at the top. I just want it to be over."

"No." She kept her eyes carefully on Nils'. Her features were soft and tinted with a complexion Nils couldn't place. Mediterranean, maybe. It was alluring.

Then the woman's hand came forward and she lightly laid two fingers on Nils' wrist. "I'm not with the authorities."

He tingled where the fingers touched him. But her words took him back.

Her whole hand took his wrist now. "There's not a lot of time to explain."

The tingling that emanated from the touch of the woman's hand traveled all the way up to Nils' brain.

"There's something I need you to understand. It's very important."

A sound began to hum in the distance, wavering quietly across the sea and sky.

"Your government is very interested in a man who was on your last trip."

A tiny surreal wave washed through Nils and he felt as if something in him had become loose and tilted. "My…what?"

"You were a guide. You lost someone."

"Lost…" The humming grew louder and resolved into a thumping. Nils recognized the sound. He tried to pull away.

The woman held his wrist. "Nils, stay with me. Listen. The man who disappeared from your party was very important."

"But why…"

"You vanished."

"I…"

"After the trip. After the man was lost. You were gone."

"There was an interview. I talked to someone with the sheriff's."

"This is bigger than that. Your government—"

The sound exploded above them now, helicopter blades pounding waves down on them. A cockpit drew into view and swept past them and out over the cliffs.

"I can give you an alternative."

Nils shouted above the thud of the receding chopper. "I didn't do anything wrong."

"I know that. They don't. It won't be easy to convince them."

"But—"

"There's not much time. You have to decide. I can give you an alternative. Come with me."

"Alternative to what?"

The chopper looped back toward them. The woman pulled Nils' arm.

"You're Homeland Security?"

"Nils."

"NSA?"

"I can't—"

The chopper exploded above them again. Nils yelled over the din. "Who *are* you?"

She was trying to pull him back down the trail, into the trees and away from exposure on the cliffs.

"What's going on?"

"Nils! Let's go. It's complicated. There are competing interests. I can make things easier for you."

Nils' head felt as if it had expanded and might erupt or float away.

The woman was mesmerizing. But the scene was absurd. The chopper swooped again, closer, louder. Nils heard shouting from a bullhorn, mostly garbled but he could pick out his name.

Everything grew louder. Nils' cells hummed. He hadn't done anything. He could explain it to them. To anyone. He just wanted this to be over, whatever this was.

The woman moved so quickly and with such strength and leverage that Nils wouldn't have been able to stop her even if he'd seen what was coming. She flicked his arm down and slipped behind him, coiling her body strength to push Nils away from the bluff.

The woman was good. She'd obviously had training. But Nils was strong, and he vibrated with energy and instead of fighting her motion, Nils moved with the woman's push and her momentum kept her going. The motion surprised the woman, and Nils spun and broke free and ran.

3

HE KNEW SHE COULD CATCH HIM. The woman had done it once already. But the top of the mountain was close, and Nils hoped he could outrun her on the short, steep slope. He'd take his chances with whatever waited above.

He didn't have a lot of gas left. The past couple of days had been hard and without a lot of sleep, but the helicopter overhead and the woman behind were motivating factors to push him up the trail.

He heard the woman behind him, her footsteps coming through over the sound of his own breathing and the thrum in his ears as blood pumped hard through his carotid artery.

"Nils!"

She was wasting good breath.

"Nils!"

The trail grew steeper, twisting through sharp switchbacks around trees and over roots. Nils dug in, and now the woman fell back. If she called to him again, he didn't hear it.

Nils cleared the steep climb and the trees thinned on a wide, gentler expanse. The top of the stone tower at the peak flickered through the foliage.

He ran toward the parking lot and the gift shop. The woman behind him was gone. Nils could hear the faint thrum of the chopper blades in the distance.

It was too quiet. No tourists on the paths, at the gift shop, or lingering at the restrooms and water fountain. No vehicles moved through the parking lot. Only bird song and a big black SUV parked on the sidewalk. Orange tape and barriers across the lot entry.

Two men in dark clothing came from behind the SUV and looked toward Nils. He stopped. A glint of light splintered down from the direction of the tower. Sunlight on binoculars.

Maybe the woman on the trail had been right. Maybe she was a better option.

One of the men at the SUV lifted a hand to Nils in a gesture to halt. The other had a phone in his hand and shouted. "Nilson Garner. You are ordered to stop. Halt and raise your hands above your head!"

The man hadn't identified himself. Nils didn't like that.

Then the man's hand went to his belt. Nils liked that even less. He didn't halt and he didn't wait to see what the man was reaching for.

Nils turned and ran.

"Stop!"

He ran back down through the open expanse between the trees. The thud of the chopper blades intensified behind him.

"Nilson Garner!"

Nils wanted this to end.

The chopper reached Nils as Nils reached the trees. He flew under the cover of the foliage, flinging himself down the narrow path. Limbs and leaves churned above as the chopper passed low.

The trail dropped and Nils skittered and worked hard to keep his footing. He high-stepped over roots and used the trees to swing through the sharp switchbacks.

He could detect no men running behind him. The chopper buzzed in the near distance, probably readying for another pass.

Nils' mind went to the woman. An image of her appeared in his head. In the same instant, the real woman appeared ahead on the trail, poised and waiting among the hemlock and red cedar.

The trail pinched there, and Nils ran forward with his hands up, expecting an encounter like before. But the woman simply stepped aside and let Nils pass.

Nils ran, and the woman fell in and ran behind him. They did not exchange words but he felt her, tight behind him.

The chopper grew louder again. Nils thought ahead. The bluffs were coming. After that the trail crossed the road. Then it made the long descent to the trailhead and the parking lot where he'd left the bike. How was he going to get through?

Nils called over his shoulder. "You going to tell me what's going on?"

"Love to. Kind of busy now."

"This isn't funny."

"Well, I don't think so either."

Nils' foot skidded in the dirt. The woman skidded behind him. "I told you you wouldn't like it."

He didn't.

"There will be others ahead."

"I've thought of that."

"You won't be able to get through."

He'd thought of that too.

"So what are you going to do?"

Nils stopped. He stopped so quick the woman jolted into him. "Look, I don't know what any of this is, but I want out."

"I know you do."

He glared. "What does that mean?"

The woman steadied herself on the grade, reached up and held a branch for leverage. The limb came down and draped over them, drawing them tight together.

"Tell me what's going on."

"First you have to choose. Me or them?"

Not them.

"We don't have much time."

The chopper neared. Nils started down the trail again.

"You have to say it."

He didn't.

The woman followed. "Me or them?"

Neither.

"I can't help you if—"

"I'm going with you, aren't I?"

Then the woman elbowed around Nils. "Okay then. We're getting off this mountain."

"How are we going to do that?"

They'd come to the bluffs. The woman stopped and pointed down. "We're going to climb."

Nils stopped beside her.

"Then I'll explain things to you." She reached for a tree at the edge of the drop, roots holding to the rock and limbs dangling out over air.

Nils crossed his arms. "Explain now."

The woman pinched the bridge of her nose as if she was deciding. "Those people are with your government. And they—"

"*My* government?"

"*Our* government. The short story is they believe you were involved with the man who disappeared on your outing. He had something very important that they want."

"I didn't even know the guy."

"I believe that. Someone may have lied to them. Regardless of whether you knew him or not, they want to know what happened to that man."

Nils stared at the woman. The chopper hummed above them. "I don't know anything."

"That's why I'm here."

"I don't understand." He had to talk louder over the sound of the chopper.

The woman eased out onto the tree limb. "Come with me."

The chopper neared. Nils looked down. The entire drop wasn't sheer. Some rock faces were long, clean edges straight down, as if a giant hand had sliced off some of the mountain like butter. But the terrain was broken at the edge of this slice, with slopes and trees and duff and faces that dropped several or dozens of feet but offered limbs and rock handholds.

The treetops shook and the chopper blades thudded.

The woman disappeared over the edge, into the limbs and leaves. Nils went with her.

They clung just off the trail to the underside of the tree as the chopper thumped overhead. Dirt and grit swirled and the limbs swayed. The chopper circled and they waited while it passed again, farther away down the mountain.

Then the woman began their descent. They worked slow and were careful to keep under cover when they could, moving limb to limb, rock to rock. Finding their next hold before they released their current grip at the most precipitous spots.

The climb down seemed impossible, but the woman moved steadily and surely as if she'd done this before. But Nils guessed that no one had.

The chopper was audible occasionally now, circling down the mountain. Nils had some questions, but the descent was tricky work and they had to concentrate. He kept his mind on climbing, not falling.

The horizon opened and the Twin Lakes appeared in the distance, and beyond those flatter ground and the shoreline. They continued downward. The woman was strong and moved with a fluid precision that looked both innate and born of training and activity.

Nils' instincts were sharp, and he felt somehow as if they were heightened by the woman's presence. He knew that feeling probably came from the chemicals cruising through his brain, but he liked the idea of a shared heightened ability. It allowed them to navigate together what had seemed unnavigable.

Nils realized the absurdity of believing an unspoken union existed between him and the woman, yet at that moment it seemed no more absurd than what else had happened since the day before.

They reached a level where the grade lessened and there were stretches of trees and loam they could scamper down stiff-legged. Nils didn't hear the chopper anymore.

The woman seemed to sense his thoughts. "They're moving farther away. Didn't figure we'd come this way."

No one would.

The topography flattened again and they entered woods and undergrowth. They picked up speed.

Nils had been figuring their location, searching for a place to make a break. Ahead, a thinning in the canopy told him they were near the Twin Lakes.

Nils slowed and let the woman drift a little farther ahead of him.

He slowed again.

The woman turned. "What are you doing?"

"We're near Twin Lakes. There should be a trail ahead." And that might give him a way out.

She shook her head. "No."

"There." He pointed to the lightening in the tree canopy.

"I don't mean no, that's not the lakes. I mean no, that's not where we're going."

"I think we should look for the trail to the lakes."

They'd stopped, and she closed the gap between them now. "We need to get off the mountain."

"We're off the mountain. Let's take the trail."

"Just follow me."

The woman walked. Nils did not. "Where? You have people waiting?"

"People?"

"You know, people. Who you work with?"

She stopped. "Not now. We've been through this."

"Where's your phone? Why aren't you calling for backup?"

"Stop."

"Are you carrying a weapon?" He scanned the woman, running shoes to shorts to runner's belt and water bottle to top. "It doesn't look like there's room for a gun."

"Nils—"

"DEA?"

"I'm not with the DEA."

"Homeland Security?"

"I already said—"

"NSA?"

"That's not even—"

"I know you're with someone. You're not working alone."

The woman drew in a long breath and sighed it out. "We've come so far. And it's been so hard. I didn't think we'd even get this far." She rubbed her eyes. "But I told you. Right now, I'm alone. No one knows I'm out here, and I'd like to keep it that way until we're more clear and I have time to explain."

"You've had time."

Her gaze hardened.

Nils stood his ground. "I've come all this way with you. You haven't said a thing."

"I've been concentrating."

"Me too. Who are you with?"

The woman neither moved nor spoke.

"If you'll tell me, I can understand better. I might be able to trust you more."

"I'll explain, but not now."

"Call your people. Have them meet us at the lakes. Or anywhere."

"I told you." The woman's stance shifted, squared facing Nils, feet planted, hands resting at her side. Ready. "We have to go. *Now*. Don't make me do this the hard way."

A gear slipped in Nil's psyche. The ribbon of fondness he'd imagined for the woman dissolved into a cloud of gray reality. He didn't know her. He didn't know what was going on. He didn't know who he could trust.

Nils dropped his eyes. "Okay. I'll follow you."

The woman watched him for a few seconds, then turned and continued picking a path through the woods.

He let her go. The woman walked and Nils didn't. Some space opened between them. Nils waited until it was enough, guessing when she would be farthest away before she turned, give him the most space before he ran.

She gave him more than he expected. Exactly when the woman slowed, Nils turned and sprinted.

He ran, and the woman's footsteps behind him were angry rebukes. "We don't have to do this the hard way."

But they did.

Nils found the Twin Lakes trail and veered on that toward what he believed would be the trailhead and the road. He didn't look back over his shoulder, but he believed he had opened some distance between himself and the woman.

He ran, ducking and pushing branches from the way. But there was too much water coming into view, too much lake. He'd gone away from the trailhead, not toward it.

The roofline of a house appeared through the trees. Nils left the trail and ran toward the house. There would be a road.

He emerged at a modest structure with a weed-and-dirt drive. Nils skirted the house and ran down the drive.

The drive dumped him onto a single-lane deserted road. A mailbox in the distance signaled another home. Nils ran toward that.

He listened. No chopper thudded overhead. He could discern no footsteps behind him. No voices. No one shouted. No cars or people.

That road took him to another backroad. He followed that, descended yet lower toward the open water, and turned yet again onto an even narrower single-lane.

The feel of salt air reached him. Nils passed a mailbox mounted on a flimsy post and beyond that a house, then he was at rocks and the sea. On the jagged shore he spied the bright red bottom of an overturned kayak.

The kayak was unfettered and looked seaworthy. A paddle lay tucked underneath.

Nils flipped the craft over and dragged it to the water. Then without looking back he plunged with the kayak into the Salish Sea.

4

NOTHING RAINED DOWN on Nils. No chopper circled the sky. No one called his name. Nobody ran down from the road or the house, and there was no sound of cars. No men in dark clothes with holsters at their hips. No glint of binoculars from the trees. The woman was not behind him.

Nils glided quietly onto the water and everything behind him receded. It was as if he could close his eyes and none of the events of the last two days had happened. He was simply in a kayak paddling alone. There was no mysterious man who had disappeared from his last excursion, and there was no reason for anyone to want to find him.

If only it were true.

Nils dipped the paddle into the briny water and pulled. The kayak was narrow and sleek and moved forward steadily under his stroke. The boat was built for open water, but there was no spray skirt to secure to the coaming. If there was chop, he would take on water.

He nosed close to the land, near as the rocks would permit, looking. A gulp of cormorants eyed him from their perches in a barren tree jutting over the water. Then in a sudden collective decision, the birds clamored together from the branches and plunged out onto the waves into a mass of bobbing heads.

It was like turning a page. On land, Nils had been submerged in the chaotic human world. Here on the water, only a few feet from land, he'd left the human world and entered a more ordered natural one. Nils like this better.

A little beyond the cormorant tree, tide water backwashed against a small gravel shoal. Behind the shoal a cove not much larger than the kayak curved into the land. And from the back of that cove emerged a narrow and marshy stream cut between the trees. Runoff from the lakes, Nils guessed.

The stream was shallow and bordered by brush and thickly leaved trees. Nils pulled the kayak into the narrow waterway and grounded the boat. He sat in the shade and waited. For what, he didn't know yet.

Time passed mysteriously in a way that Nils couldn't decipher. He knew he'd waited a while when he grew hungry. He took a sandwich from his backpack and ate it. It was the eve of the solstice, and the sun would be up late into the evening. He drank water sparingly and considered his options.

In his pack he had more water, another sandwich, peanut butter and crackers, and some snacks. He also carried an extra t-shirt and the jacket. It would be enough for what he had vaguely in mind.

He had a strong urge to get off the island, and a sense that if he could get some distance from whatever was happening he might be able to find a more sympathetic party to explain it. Maybe get back to Sequim, find a burner phone or somewhere to make an anonymous call to the local authorities or the FBI. Slow things down and play this out on his own terms, rather than running.

He regretted leaving the rented bike behind and taking the kayak. If he could make amends, he would. But for now, Nils needed to rest and save his strength.

He willed himself to try to sleep sitting in the kayak seat. It seemed impossible, but he was still keyed into flight mode enough that he didn't want to leave the craft.

Nils' mind quieted. Tree limbs creaked. Cormorants called in the distance. Water ran gently past the kayak. Nils waited.

He dozed, woke, dozed, woke in the seat. Eventually he got out and stretched his legs beside the streambed.

When the sun had finally set, Nils took the kayak from the stream and out onto the moonlit Salish Sea.

He had paddled these island channels before and knew of the

currents that could chop the water or drive a kayak off course. He'd felt the winds that could bring you to a stop. And he knew it was unwise to paddle alone at night with few supplies, no lights, no skirt to keep the water out, and no one who knew where he was. But the water was calm and the current was slow and with him. His stroke was strong and the kayak moved swiftly.

The low, dark shape of Clark Island cut a line on the water in front of him. Nils figured he was about a mile and change away.

He could see no other craft in the channel. As he neared the middle of the passage, Nils eased his stroke and let the kayak drift. This was alone. The moon and the islands were there, and dim lights from Orcas Island spotted the water, but none of them could reach him. For a moment it was just Nils, and he relaxed.

Something carried on the air. The sound he'd heard when he sat alone on the little beach in Eastsound. The sound he believed was orca song. That singing grew louder and more clear.

Then a black fin knifed from the water near his starboard side. The water rippled and the fin sliced in front of the kayak.

Nils drifted. A blunt, black-and-white nose lifted from the sea. The kayak gently bobbled.

There was more singing, Nils drifting, turning in the wake of the big mammal.

More fins broke the surface. Another shape rose and became a nose, and another. The orcas sang and swam and Nils drifted.

Then the water quieted and Nils was alone again. He dipped his paddle in the water and resumed his journey.

He bypassed the state park campground at Clark Island and the lights and moorings and other boats there. Up the shoreline in the thin gray light he found a short, empty stretch of rocky beach and landed there.

Nils drank water, ate a couple of granola bars, and shrugged into his jacket. Then he lay back on the pebbled rocks and tried to sleep.

When Nils next saw the sky, the half moon had dropped. Time had passed, and he must have slept. The remote island beach was quiet but for an errant wave out on the water.

An intermittent breeze brought a chill. Nils got up and pulled the kayak farther from the water, flipped the craft onto its side, and set the nose against a rock. He lay behind the lee side of the craft to break the wind and tried again to sleep.

Again when next Nils looked up the sky had moved, stars trading position and brightening against the dark. He got up to pee and his eyes told him he saw a small shape out on the water. An orca, maybe, or a craft or other animal? Or an imagination?

He squinted and the shape wasn't there. And again he lay behind the kayak and tried to sleep.

When next Nils looked up, the sky was littered with pinpricks of light and he had no idea if time had passed. There was a sound like a prow gently striking gravel. It couldn't be, and his mind pulled him back toward sleep.

Then came the whisper. "Nils."

An eye dragged open. A shape blocking his sight. Hair falling around a face.

The whisper again. "Nils."

The other eye opened and he made it to one elbow.

"Did I wake you?"

Of course she had. "How did you…?"

"Do you have anything for the mosquitoes?"

Nils closed his eyes and opened them, and she was still there. "Mosquitoes?"

"They're killing me." She held an arm out in the dark and pulled up a sleeve as if to verify.

The arm didn't make sense. The woman didn't make sense. "I don't— they don't bother me."

She pushed the sleeve back down and sighed. "Lucky."

"What are you doing here?"

"I came for you."

"I…"

"I know what you wanted. But I'm giving you another chance."

"Another…?"

"You seem a little groggy. I guess I woke you."

Now Nils made it to both elbows.

"I know I woke you. I guess I meant to. I didn't want you to be surprised in the morning."

"Surprising me now is better?"

"I guess we'll never know. Stay here. I'm going to bring my kayak."

Nils stayed. He really couldn't think of anything else to do.

A moment later there was scraping, and the woman dragged a kayak and lined it up with Nils'. She sat behind the craft positioned away from the water as Nils had done and slapped at her forehead.

"Be better if you get on the other side."

"Huh?"

"If you're in the breeze. It will help keep the mosquitoes away."

"It will?"

Why was he helping her? "It'll be colder in the breeze, but fewer mosquitoes. One or the other."

She seemed to consider it for a second, then dragged the kayak around in an arc so hers was offset from Nils' and the two crafts faced each other. She zipped her jacket up over her neck.

Nils stared. "How did you find me?"

The woman leaned down onto the sand and rocks. "I'd like to tell you that I'm very good, but it was luck."

He didn't ask for details.

She offered them anyway. "I saw you go toward the house. Then you disappeared—that's not where the luck comes in." She scooted and adjusted and lay down. "I came back with a kayak and looked around. It was late and dark and I didn't see anything except a little shape way out on the water. I didn't want to give up, so I followed the little shape instead."

When he'd been out in the channel. Listening to the orcas.

"And eventually I found you."

So if he hadn't waited. If he'd struck out for Clark Island sooner, she might not have found him. But. "Don't you find that…a little hard to believe?"

She was maybe fifteen feet away, facing Nils and his kayak. Close enough to feel like a little camp, far enough that she was only a shadow in the dark. "Yes, but here we are."

Nils wasn't groggy anymore. He thought back. "You fell?"

"Hmm?"

"Back at the lakes. You fell?"

"When you ran away after you said you were going to follow me? Yes, I fell. How do you think you got away?"

She was trying to be funny? Nils let a moment elapse. "You said you'd tell me what's going on."

"I said I'd explain if you came with me. You didn't come with me. I don't have to explain."

"I climbed off the mountain with you."

"Well, there's that."

Nils thought she might leave it there. "I went with you."

"Until you didn't."

He got up and walked to the water. Nils had a vague sense that she'd followed him, but when he looked back the woman still lay beside her kayak.

He considered his options.

The woman offered one up to start. "You can run again."

He'd been thinking that. Wait until she was asleep.

"You won't lose me. I'm very lucky."

Nils walked back. "You're going to have to explain what you want sooner or later. Why not now?"

"It's a long story. It's complicated. Better in the morning."

It was lame. Nils knew that she knew it. "Start with something simple then. Tell me your name."

He didn't think she'd heard. Then from across the little camp came her answer. "Bly."

Nils returned from the water and lowered himself beside the kayak and silently tried out the name. Bly.

"You're not going to tell me it's unusual?"

"No."

"No jokes about Captain Bligh?"

"No."

"A pirate joke? Ask me if my middle name starts with arrrr?"

"Have you heard these before?"

She nodded. "You wouldn't believe it."

This was weird. Really weird. "What are we doing here?"

"What do you mean?"

"You're joking like…"

The woman's shadow levered up onto an elbow. "This is awkward." She pointed, from herself to Nils, and back. Lightening the mood makes things a little easier."

That made sense.

"And I can use that right now."

Maybe so could he. Some time passed. Not long.

"Nils?"

"Yeah."

"Why does the breeze keep the mosquitoes away?"

"They're not strong fliers."

"Okay." Bly's elbow moved, and she lay back down.

Nils wanted to lie down too, but it seemed too comfortable. "You say my name."

"I do?"

"Most people don't do that. When there's only two."

"I guess I just like using it. It's unusual."

So they had that in common. Uncommon names. But that wasn't what he'd been after. "You have to give me something."

"I know."

"Tonight. Before we sleep."

"Okay. It's short for Warbly."

"Warbly?"

"W-A-R-B-L-Y."

"What does that mean?"

"My daddy said he could hear me before I was born. He would put his ear to my mother's stomach. No one else could hear it, just my father. He said the sound was beautiful, like a bird warbling. So when I was born, he named me Warbly."

Nils said nothing.

"It's a fantastic story, I know. Only daddy could hear it."

Nils thought it was a good story. But not the story he was after.

"That's not what I meant."

"I know."

He waited.

"How about this? My middle name is Alexa. When I got a little older I tried going by Lexy. But everyone kept calling me Warbly. I gave up. The best I could do was Bly."

"That's not what I meant either."

There was movement, Bly adjusting herself on the hard ground. "First let me tell you that I want to be on your side. I want you to know that."

"Why is that important?"

"It's important because—look, this is going to get complicated."

"It already is. But only one of us has any idea what's going on."

Nils waited. When that seemed to be the end of the conversation, he was just about ready to get up and walk away again when Bly spoke. "I'm going to need something from you."

"I don't know what that means."

"That guy who died on your guide trip? He had something important, and I have to find it before anyone else does."

Nils hadn't known the guy had died. He only knew he'd disappeared. "I don't know anything."

"You know where you took him. You were with him."

It didn't make much sense. "What did he have that's so important?"

"That's where things get more complicated. I can't tell you yet."

Nils didn't like it. At all.

"Look, if I tell you more now, before I'm sure we're clear of the others, it could compromise things."

"Compromise?"

"Poor choice of words. It could make things more difficult."

"You mean if whoever that was back there gets to me, I could tell them what I don't know. Instead of telling you."

"Even if you don't know anything, they'll make you talk."

"What good would that do?"

"No good." Her words were as hard as the message.

"And you're telling me my only alternative is…"

"Me." She rolled over. "Now is that enough so you can sleep?"

He didn't have to think about it. Nils lay down and lied. "I think so."

"Good."

Bly grew quiet. Nils grew quiet. Their little stretch of the island was quiet.

When Nils next saw the sky, he hadn't just awakened. He hadn't been sleeping. He'd been waiting.

He waited longer. Listened. Eventually he rose as slowly and quietly as he could and neared Bly.

Nils waved a hand over her, testing. Bly didn't move.

He bent and looked closer. That's when Nils saw the holster and the gun.

It was a surprise and not a surprise. He straightened very quietly. Nils didn't like his chances with whoever had been in the helicopter and the van. Bly was certainly much better company. But he liked his chances best on his own. When he could decide who to turn to.

Nils inched back to his kayak. He exhaled and bent over and lifted as carefully as he could and hoisted the craft to his shoulder. Then with slow steps and breaths he moved away, up shore, until he was out of sight of Bly.

Then with equal delicacy he lowered the kayak to the water, stepped in, and paddled away once more into the dark sea.

5

THE CURRENT RAN faster now. Nils used that to his advantage, adjusting his angle to let the water carry him north. He wanted to be around the top of Orcas Island before sunrise, out of sight and hoping Bly's luck would run out.

He hugged the shore of Orcas as gray light became orange sky behind him. Other craft appeared on the water, dotting the horizon. Nils paddled toward the harbor channel. He had a plan.

He was going to slow this down. Find some local authorities, or call the FBI. Find a safe haven where he could make the calls and decide who to talk to, and when. He was tired of being chased. He might even hire a lawyer if he had to, god forbid.

Nils reached the breakwater barrier at North Beach. There he paddled into the harbor channel. Boats moored at long, thin docks in the narrow waterway. Nils pulled his paddle up and loosened his jacket. He'd gotten damp without a skirt on the kayak, and the morning sun felt good. He drifted and ate some crackers and peanut butter.

Nils exited the water at the south end of the channel and carried the kayak across a gravel lot where he stowed it near a road that paralleled the little island airport. From there it was a short walk, about a mile, to Eastsound.

When he neared the village, Nils took his cap out and pulled it low on his head. He was considering something else for disguise when it seemed he wasn't the only one with that thought. Ahead of him a woman crossed the street. She wore a red skirt, bright orange shirt, and knee-high orange socks. On her head was a large tiara that sprouted a sculpture of the sun. When the woman walked, the sun sculpture bobbed as if it was animated.

Behind her, a man in Bermuda shorts and a tall red cap pedaled a bicycle that pulled a homemade trailer stacked with pink flamingo lawn ornaments. The flamingos all wore bright knitted scarves, sunglasses, and bushy mustaches.

Nils passed down North Beach Road, and the strangeness escalated. Two young girls in bright skirts and tie-dyed shirts held hands with mom and dad. One of the girls waved a hand-held bubble machine that shot watery globes into the sunlight. The other girl held a long, sparkly wand that shed glitters as she waved it. Both wore ballerina shoes and long, red socks. Mom and dad wore tall hats with a sun and moon on them and brightly colored shorts and shirts.

No one noticed Nils or looked his way. He felt invisible, as if the events of the day before had never happened.

Nils paused at a woman who was rolling a rack of clothing from a store out onto the sidewalk. He looked at his shoes and addressed her. "Pardon me."

She stopped pushing the rack. "Yes?"

"Solstice parade?"

"Huh?"

Nils motioned to the street. "People dressed up."

"Well it's not Halloween." She glanced him over. "Help you with anything?"

"No, thanks."

She fingered a flowered shirt on the rack. The shirt was printed with orange suns. "This would be perfect for you."

"No, I…"

The woman held the shirt in front of Nils. "Make you look like a local."

He considered that. "Have you got sunglasses to go with it?"

"You bet." She jerked a thumb toward the door.

They went in and Nils bought the shirt, buttoned it on, and chose a large pair of sunglasses with reflective lenses. He topped that with his long-billed cap and walked straight down the street without so much as a second look from anyone, all the way down until he found himself in front of Darvill's Bookstore.

There he bought a paperback mystery novel that served the dual purpose of something to read and something to hide his nose behind if it came to that. Better than a mustache, he had a book.

Then Nils walked back up North Beach Road and made mental plans to get off the island. Get a burner phone, get an Uber, get to the ferry terminal. If he wanted to keep his conscience clear, he could square with the guy about the missing rental bike and make an anonymous call to the local authorities about the location of the misplaced kayak.

More people were showing up in colorful clothing. Solstice. Longest day of the year. By the time it was over, Nils intended to be off this island.

But first, sustenance. Back to Olga Rising.

Nils reached the café without incident and read from the menu as he ordered. "Tuna sandwich, please, and—"

"Nils."

"Yes, and—"

"Nils."

The voice had come from behind him. The voice knew his name. And he knew the voice. It couldn't—

An arm stretched out with bills in hand. Bly's arm. "I'd like a coffee. And the tuna sandwich too. My treat."

"You can't..."

The bills dangled. "Sure I can."

"But you can't..."

Bly looked to the woman at the counter. "And he wants a coffee too." She held up two fingers. "So two coffees and two sandwiches."

"You can't be here."

"I'll explain." She dropped the bills onto the counter. "Add two of your best pastries. Any two you choose."

"But you can't *be here*."

Bly took Nils' arm and guided him away from the counter and

toward the garden. She looked back to meet eyes with the woman work-ing. "Thanks."

Nils pulled from Bly's touch and patted hands over his pockets. He reached to the back of his shirt collar and felt along the seams. He bent and felt along the tongue of his shoes.

Bly tried to steer him to a bench seat. "You look like you're dancing."

"Where is it?"

She took his elbow. "Come. Sit."

Nils swung his pack from his shoulders. "Where?"

"Nils, sit. I'll tell you." She got him to a bench under a tree.

Nils jerked zippers on his backpack and folded the top open.

Bly laid a hand over Nils'. "Stop. Here. I'm sorry." She reached into a pocket on the side of the backpack, dug her fingers in, and pulled out a small, black device.

Nils looked at the thing. "Air tag?"

"No. It's GPS."

"It doesn't matter. That's just wrong."

Bly touched something on the device. "There, it's off."

"You can't just track me."

Bly tucked the device into her pocket. "It seemed prudent."

"Prudent?"

"Based on the way things have gone, it was the smart thing to do."

It didn't feel very nice. "You can't just…"

"You keep saying that. But obviously, I can just… The question is whether you can get over it."

"Get over it?"

"Move on."

"I can move on."

"Then let's do that. Look—" She pointed. "The coffees are here. I'll get them." She got up, stopped, looked back. "Don't go away."

A moment later Bly set two coffees on the low garden table in front of the bench. "I didn't know if you wanted cream or sugar."

Nils picked up his coffee. "Little cream might be nice." He stood. "I'll get it. You want me to carry the tracker, or do you trust me to walk all the way over there by myself?" It was about ten feet.

She waved him on. "You wouldn't leave before the sandwiches get here."

Snarky, but maybe true.

Bly watched Nils when he returned and sat. "Look, I'm sorry, okay? The tracker made things a lot easier. We'll relax and eat. I'll explain."

"I don't want you to explain."

"You were begging me to tell you last night."

"I have a new perspective today."

"What does that mean? I—"

"Look." Nils pointed. "The sandwiches are ready. I'll get them."

He came back with the two sandwiches and the pastries and set those on the table.

Bly chose one of the sandwiches. "I owe you a story."

"I don't want your story. I want this to be over."

Bly unwrapped her sandwich. "It's not over."

Nils sat still.

Bly stopped unwrapping. "What?"

"I don't think I can eat."

She laughed. "Of course you can. Here, take this one." She handed it over.

It was a simple gesture. Handing him a sandwich. Nils wasn't going to take it, but everything seemed so simple and clear in that one gesture that he reached out.

Bly picked up the other sandwich. "So what's changed?"

"Changed?"

"Now you don't want to know what I have to tell you. You don't want an explanation."

"What's changed is me."

"That's it?"

"That's it. I haven't done anything wrong. I'll just explain that and be done with it. I'm tired of being chased."

"You'll explain it to who?"

He didn't correct her grammar. "Whoever. Anyone."

She didn't correct his grammar. "I don't think you've been taking me seriously enough."

"Seriously enough? You chase me up a mountain. There are men and helicopters. You chased me across the channel. In a kayak. At night." He breathed. "You planted a tracker on me. And I have no idea what's going on."

Bly set her sandwich down. "I just offered to tell you."

"No. I'm going to get off the island. I'll make a call. To the police. Or the FBI. I'll end this. I don't know anything about the guy who disappeared. And I don't care."

"You know where he left the trail."

"What?" Nils set his sandwich down. "How do you know that?"

"How do I not know?"

"What do you mean *how do you not know?* What the…?"

"You said you didn't want me to tell you."

Nils leaned back. "This is not a game."

"I agree."

"How do you know about the guy on my trip?"

Bly leaned in where Nils had leaned back. "I know this. I know that everyone you led on that hike has been interviewed. They were sequestered. I know that you were supposed to be interviewed, but you weren't."

"I didn't know about the interviews."

"You disappeared too quick."

Nils remembered. "I had to get out of there."

"That's exactly what it looked like, and it doesn't make you look good."

Nils rubbed fingers through his hair. "It's a misunderstanding. I'll explain it."

"Things have escalated a bit."

"I see that."

"You probably know that the item we're looking for is very important."

"You said that. I still don't know anything about it."

"You know exactly where the man disappeared on the trail. None of the others could pinpoint that."

"Who are you?"

Bly smiled. "We did this last night?"

"Who are you working with?"

"Nils, I told you. I'm independent in this."

"Who's looking for me?" Nils realized his voice had gotten louder. He wasn't sure if he cared.

Bly looked around, apparently satisfied that they hadn't drawn attention. "There's competition. It's not just one party."

"I'll tell them. I'll tell them where we were on the trail. Whatever."

Bly reached a hand over, set it on Nils' chin, and turned his gaze to her. "Listen to me. You have to tell the right people. There's a lot at stake."

Nils' pulse quickened. It was a bold move, Bly turning his head like that. Intimate but intimidating. And her hand was still there.

Nils stood. He didn't know why. Maybe to put some space between his face and the hand.

Bly's gaze followed him. "Nils, slow down. Listen."

He stepped back. He hadn't planned it, but his body was moving.

"They won't let you off the island."

"I've already been off the island. You followed me."

"You can't paddle all the way to…"

She didn't finish it. Nils didn't know if she'd meant the mainland or Canada. It didn't matter.

"It's a matter of national security."

"I'll call the FBI."

Now Bly's voice rose. "You can't do that. Listen to me. *You can't contact the FBI.*"

Nils heard the alarm in her words. It rang an alarm through his whole body.

"I can get you off the island. But if you go to the FBI I won't be able to help you."

He felt himself moving, ready.

"Nils, don't do this."

But he already was, adrenaline taking over. Fight or flight. It would be flight.

Nils ran. This was serious. He'd left his sandwich behind.

6

HE RAN STRAIGHT INTO the parade. Nils slipped through a string of watchers at the curb and jumped into the street. He was immediately engulfed by a set of giant puppet arms. The gauzy fabric held by paraders surrounded and hugged Nils. It was heady and surreal, and the arms hid him.

Nils walked in the puppet's embrace and stripped off his bright flowered shirt, grateful that he still wore the t-shirt underneath.

Bly was not there. No one shouted his name or tried to tackle him. Nils ducked under the arms, ran to the far curb, and plunged through the wall of watchers there.

He was pursued only by drum music, horns, and the chanting of dancers that rose up into the sky like smoke.

Nils cut left through people, potted sidewalk plants, and chairs. He stuffed the bright shirt into a trash can. Still no Bly.

Behind Nils a colony of mushrooms with large red, polka-dotted caps marched by. The caps sat atop dancing bodies with flowing clothes. Behind them, a giant globe sat watch over the proceedings, held up by a collective of little hands.

It was the coolest thing Nils had ever seen and he wanted to embrace the feeling, but the threat of Bly behind him pressed like the tide. He peered through the watchers into the street. On instinct, Nils recrossed the street, dodging a large mysterious puppet creature on high stilts. He regained the far side of the road, like a convict backtracking to throw off the dogs.

Still no sign of Bly.

Nils second-guessed now. Stay embedded in the crowd and move under cover, or break free and hope not to be spotted in the open?

What he wanted was his phone. Or a pay phone, if such a thing still existed. Anywhere he could make a call in private. If there was a dollar store, somewhere he could find a prepaid—

And then he saw it. An image, a recent memory. A package on a table. Where had that been?

The memory crystalized. When he'd bought the shirt and sunglasses. A minutes phone in the bargain bin. Why had that not registered before?

Less than an hour later, Nils had purchased the phone with cash, taken it to the Orcas Island library and charged it enough to use, and located an FBI field office on the mainland. There had been no sign of Bly or of any other persons pursuing him. Nils had worn the cap and kept to the corners and shadows.

He sat outside the library and called the FBI office. He reached an automated answering service, persisted through that, and eventually heard a live voice on the call. Nils said he had information about the man on Orcas Island.

There was a staticky pause, then, "Hold on."

Nils held.

"Where are you calling from?"

"Orcas Island."

There were sounds. Typing, maybe. Voices in the background either live or from a radio signal.

"What is your location on the island?"

"Near Eastsound."

More sounds.

"Can you give me a more precise location?"

"Not at this time."

There was a longer pause, filled with a variety of unidentifiable sounds.

"Can you confirm the number you're calling from?"

Nils didn't answer.

The man said a number.

Nils looked at the settings on his phone. "That's it."

"And who is that number registered to?"

"Me."

Typing. The voice Nils was talking to spoke to someone else.

"And what is your name, sir?"

"I have information about the man on Orcas Island."

The voices in the background intensified now.

"Stay on the line. Do not end the call. Hold on."

Nils held again. This went on for several more minutes, a slow cat-and-mouse routine, Nils waiting through muted voices and sounds, the man on the other end coming back a couple of times to tell him to wait. Finally the voice came back, more urgent. "I'm transferring the call. Stay on the line. Do not end the call."

Nils didn't end the call, but his nerves began to tingle. Bly had warned him. Maybe he'd made a mistake. Maybe the phone would run out of minutes. Not knowing things made him more tingly.

A loud and raspy voice came through the phone. "Garner?"

"Yes." He'd answered before he'd thought. He'd confirmed his name.

"Don't move."

"I'm not moving."

"You move your ass one inch, and I will come down on you like hell on a wildcat."

"I'm not moving." Whatever hell on a wildcat meant.

"Where are you?"

"Orcas Island."

"I know you're on the island. WHERE ON THE GODDAM ISLAND ARE YOU?"

"Whoa."

"Hang on."

Nils sensed a hand over the phone.

The man's voice came back. "Look, sorry about that. The wildcat stuff. You're doing the right thing now. You're calling. It's gonna be okay."

"All right."

"You need anything? Food? Water? A shower? We can help you."

"I'm okay." The man changing tactics. Buddies now. Good cop.

"It's been a long couple of days, all right? I'm sorry about yelling at you. We can work together now. Clear this up. But I have to know where you are."

Nils figured they probably already knew by now. The island was small. There couldn't be that many towers to triangulate from.

He rose from the library bench where he'd been sitting and scanned the grounds. "I didn't do anything."

"I believe you, son, and we'll clear all that up very soon. Just tell me exactly where you are."

Nils didn't like the son part. "You didn't need a helicopter to chase me." He hadn't liked that either.

"This is a serious matter."

"Your men didn't look friendly."

"I didn't say they were friendly. I said they were serious."

Nils heard voices behind the man speaking, then the man's voice came back. "Okay, look. Sorry again. Let's get this back on the right foot. We're on the same side here. But we need you to come in so we can clear this up."

"Come in where?"

"We'll come to you. Hang on." There were voices in the background again, then the man said, "They want to know how you got off that mountain."

So they didn't seem to know about Bly. Maybe like she'd said, she was alone.

Nils heard a new voice cut through in the background. "Twenty. Got him."

Nils scanned the area more intensely, almost expecting the dark cars and overdressed men to have materialized from thin air.

The man's voice softened now. "Listen, we can send someone to you. Just stay put."

"I can go to the island police."

"NO."

"You can meet—"

"DO NOT GO TO THE ISLAND POLICE. You hear me? Do. Not. Go. To. The. Locals."

"I hear you." But Nils didn't like it.

"Just stay on the call, and stay where you are and don't move."

He hadn't told them where he was. Nils tingled. It wasn't from the sound of a chopper descending or someone calling his name. He almost wished it was. Then he would know what to run from.

"Son?"

"I'll be here."

Nils ended the call and pocketed the phone. Bly's warning echoed in his head as he walked rapidly away from the library toward the Orcas Island police substation.

Nils passed through the remnants of the parade that had dissolved into a party at Village Green Park. A band was setting up on the amphitheater stage, and revelers lobbied for mayoral candidates that included a duck, a dog, and a cow. He pressed on.

Twenty minutes later as Nils walked an empty stretch of road that ran by the perimeter of the Orcas Island airport, a dark blue spot appeared ahead and took the shape of a van moving toward him. There were no other vehicles visible. No houses or businesses. Just the narrow road and the chain-link fence around the airport, beyond that grass and airstrips and hangars. A plane sitting on the tarmac. The far shoulder of the road was thick with trees and brush. Nowhere to go but straight ahead or back.

The van neared quickly. At ten feet in front of Nils it stopped abruptly and a man exited the passenger door and ran around the van with hands raised and a gun drawn. "Do not move."

Nils didn't move.

"Hands up."

They already were. Nils kept them there.

"Nilson Garner?"

He nodded, his throat dry like swallowing sand.

The man approached. His weapon did not come down. Nils' heart raced. He didn't like the gun that close.

Then the hand with the gun opened, the weapon palmed, and Nils wondered what was happening. The man's hand moved and the metal struck Nils, a sharp blossom of pain radiating from his temple. He stumbled but didn't go down.

Nils' vision and his thinking clouded. He felt the man behind him, pressure on his arms, twisting. His wrists were bound. The van turned around in the road.

Nils struggled to stay solid but felt nauseous and light. A black bag closed over his head. Nils tried to fight, but he tumbled into the van.

He heard the door close, and the van sped off. Nils tested his breathing in the bag. He could get air. His wrists chafed against the restraints.

A voice came from the front of the van. "Relax. I didn't hurt you."

Another voice came from the front. "You didn't have to put the bag over his head."

"He might yell. I don't want him to yell."

"The bag won't keep him from yelling."

"Whatever. I didn't want him to see us."

"He saw us. He saw *you*."

The van was going fast. It rose and dipped through a swell in the road. Nils felt his stomach drop.

The man who'd taken Nils spoke again. "It won't matter soon anyway. He'll see both of us."

"Take the bag off. He's not gonna be able to breathe."

"He can breathe. They make them that way."

"Just take the bag off his head. I don't want nothing to happen to him."

"Jeez, how often you get to try one of these things?"

"Just take it off."

"Okay okay."

There were sounds. Movement on a seat. A seatbelt being released. The van leaned into a turn. Nils rolled with it, unable to hold himself from slipping with his wrists bound. He tried to speak. "I'm going to..."

A hand reached him and lifted his head. "What's that, sweetheart?"

The bag came off, and the hand released Nils' head and he fell forward. "I'm going to be sick."

Then he puked, a hot stream of liquid that rose in this throat and ejected onto the van floor and the man in front of him.

"Je-sus H, buddy. You didn't have to do that."

Nils' stomach felt a little better. "You didn't have to hit me."

The man wiped his hands on the back of the seat. "You shouldn't have run. We went to a lot of trouble finding you. You think it's fun sitting around all day waiting for some shithead to—damn, this shit stinks."

Nils got himself sitting up against the van door. "You didn't find me."

"What?" The man's big head was coming at him again.

"I called you. You didn't find me."

"The hell you think just happened out on the road?"

His phone. "My mistake."

"For that, I'm going to put the bag back on."

Nils tried to lean away, but the bag went back on. It was hot and stank. He tried to keep more bile down. "I didn't do anything."

"You ran."

"That's not against the law."

"It is when an agent tells you to stop."

Agent? "So you're FBI?"

Neither of them answered.

The driver's voice came back. "Ask him."

There was some jostling. "You ask him."

"Okay, I will. How'd you get off that mountain?"

Nils was confused.

"We got a bet going. He thinks you walked out. I don't."

Nils got it. "What'd you think?"

"I thought you were dead."

"Why would I be dead?"

"We were crawling all over the top of that thing. We didn't find you. You must have fallen off."

"I didn't go off the top."

Nils heard movement and the other man's voice came back. "You giving lip? I'll come back there and shove that bag—"

"Calm down. He's not going anywhere."

"I didn't say he was going anywhere. I said he was giving me lip."

"Doesn't matter. He's not saying anything."

"I don't like the way he…" The van slowed. "What's that?"

The van slowed some more. The driver spoke. "Stalled car."

"Funny angle."

Nils instinctively turned his head, but he could see nothing through the bag.

The driver stopped. "Doesn't look right."

A hot moment passed.

The man in the passenger seat spoke. "There's nobody in it. Just go around."

The other man said nothing. Nils felt the van begin to move, then a jolt erupted from the front and there was a thud and the sound of glass breaking.

Even through the bag on his head, Nils could feel the light in the van dim.

"What the—"

A second thud pounded on the passenger door, followed by a click and glass cracking. More glass broke, and Nils heard the door open. "Hands on the wheel."

"You don't know—"

"Hands on the wheel or your head comes off. You too. Hands up. Now!"

Nils knew that voice. It was deeper and huskier than he remembered, but he knew it.

There was grunting and movement. "You don't—"

Nils heard a heavy, wet sound, then another grunt.

The van's side door opened behind Nils and he spilled out backward. "Get up, Nils. Now."

Bly helped him and he rose. She whipped the bag from his head and he saw that she looked bulked up. Heavy clothes or some padding stuffed under a long-sleeved black t-shirt. Black ski mask over her head and face. Tactical pants and heavy web belt. Black gloves. She looked like a man.

Bly pulled him toward a burnt-orange Honda CRV that blocked the road. Nils saw through the van's broken passenger window that the driver's hands were zip-tied to the steering wheel. The passenger's arms were zip-tied around the driver's.

The passenger, the man who'd hit Nils with the gun, shouted obscenities at Bly as they passed. She ignored him. A thick black blanket covered the van's windshield. A large sandbag cratered through the glass in the center of the blanket.

Bly had an automatic pistol in one hand and Nils' backpack slung over a shoulder. She spun Nils, ripped a folding knife from her belt, and cut loose the ties on his wrists. "Let's go."

He got into the CRV.

The car was running and Bly got in the driver's side and accelerated. She pulled the mask from her head and tossed it and another set of keys out her open window.

Nils tested his temple and the wound there. The blood had crusted. He watched Bly reach a finger into her mouth and extract a couple of large chunks of cotton gauze. "You look like a dude."

"Thanks. You look like shit." Her voice was back now without the gauze, softer and more natural.

Nils felt as Bly described, his head clearing but things still somehow watery and wrong.

Bly looked to the rearview, then tugged at her shirt. "Grab the wheel."

The wheel wobbled and Nils reached over, his shoulder reminding him of the twist that had been put there from the zip ties.

Bly pulled the long-sleeved shirt off, then a bulky sweatshirt from beneath that. "Phew." She reclaimed the wheel and shook out her hair. The long, dark strands fluttered in the wind. "Better?"

"You were trying to look like a man?"

"I was trying to look not like me."

"It worked."

Bly glanced over. "How's your head?" She touched Nils' temple. A thin bracelet hung around Bly's wrist, an odd thing with what looked like a dusty gray grommet suspended from it.

"What's that?"

"Breaks the glass." Her fingers came away from his temple.

"I've heard of those."

"I asked about your head."

"I feel a little off."

"Gonna puke?"

"Already did."

Bly put her eyes back on the road. "We have to move. This car is going to be hot soon."

Nils' head bobbed, either for real or from the thumping in it, he couldn't tell. "Would you really have shot them?"

"I didn't shoot anyone."

"You said you'd shoot them, if they didn't put their hands up."

"I didn't have to."

Nils looked out his window.

"You don't like my answer?"

"I didn't ask if you had to. I asked if you would have."

The car accelerated. "I'll do what I have to."

"That still doesn't answer the question."

"Best you're going to get." She reached for the shirt she'd discarded and tossed it to Nils. "Why don't you use that to clean yourself up? There's water in the back."

"I have water." He twisted in the seat to reach for his pack.

"Use the shirt, then toss it out."

"I don't like to litter."

"Oh, for godsake, Nils. This isn't normal circumstances."

He wetted the shirt with water from a bottle and pressed that to his head. "You got that right."

Nils cleaned the blood from his temple. When he was satisfied, he folded the stained shirt on itself and stuffed it into his backpack. Bly watched with steady, unjudging eyes.

Nils was feeling more solid. He watched the island go by out the window. "Those weren't real federal guys, were they?"

Bly flicked the wheel through a curve. "No—or yes. They're feds, but they're compromised."

"Compromised?"

"You really need me to explain it?"

"And so many things."

"I'd love to, but I need to know something first."

Nils didn't bite.

"I need to know if you're with me."

With her? "What does that mean?"

"You don't need me to explain it. Are you going to stop running? You want me, or do you want the guys in the van back there?"

Nils didn't say.

"It's got to be one or the other." Bly slowed the car. "Nils?"

He looked out his window.

She pulled to the shoulder and stopped. "I need you to say it."

"Say what?"

"If we keep going, you have to say it. Are you with me now? It's you and me?"

Nils stuck his jaw out. "Don't make me stop this car."

"This isn't funny."

"No."

"I can let you out. I can take you to the ferry. I can drop you where you want to go. Or it can be you and me. I have to know."

So Nils said it. "I'm with you."

She stared for a moment. Then, "As a show of good faith I'll tell you where the other tracker is."

"The—of course." He reached for his backpack.

"Nils."

He unzipped the top of the pack.

"Put the backpack down."

He looked over.

Bly pointed. "Shoe."

Nils took one off and felt inside around the sole.

"Other one. Down in the tongue."

He took the other shoe off and felt.

"Down in the laces."

He dug and found a dark round pod about the size of a quarter jammed down under the laces. How had he not seen that? A better question surfaced. "How did you get that there?"

"Have I told you that I'm very good?"

Nils dropped the device into a tray in the center console. "Any others?"

"Last one. I promise."

"We'll see."

Bly grinned. "Tell you what. I owe you that story. I know you said you didn't want to know, but now you're going to have to. I'll explain while you're in the kayak."

"While we're in the kayak?"

"I won't be in the kayak. Just you."

7

BLY DID MORE THAN EXPLAIN. She turned onto a side road, drove a short distance, and pulled to the shoulder behind a light gray SUV with a kayak on top. "Get your backpack."

Nils did, following Bly to the SUV and eying the kayak. "I don't know if I'm up to paddling off the island."

She carried some things from the other vehicle to the SUV. Her jacket, sleeping bag, backpack. "You're not. And you won't have to. You'll be on top."

"Instead of the kayak?"

Bly reached up now and loosened a strap holding the kayak to the racks. "I know you got hit on the head, but try to keep up. We're going to hide you in the kayak." She loosened another strap. "While it's on top of the car. Then we'll drive off the island onto the ferry."

Nils didn't feel good thinking about it.

She reached over the windshield and took hold of the prow. "Grab the back and we'll flip it over."

Nils moved slowly.

"If you're up to it."

"I can be."

"Or you have another idea."

He didn't have any other ideas, just a head with some cobwebs. He was thinking straight enough on one thing. "When did you have time for all this?"

She gave him a look.

"Two cars, the kayak." He gestured to indicate *and whatever else you have here.*

"I've been planning ahead."

"You haven't had any help?"

"If I did, we'd have a better plan. Now grab that end."

They swung the kayak off the car and exposed a large, opened sunroof on the SUV. Bly motioned to the shoulder and they flipped the kayak over and set it in the weeds by the road.

Bly knelt and felt around inside the cockpit. "We're going to need to get the seat out." She leaned and pressed on the edge of the seat, and there was a click. She did the same on the other side and the seat popped forward and came out. She handed that to Nils. "Set this in the back."

He placed it into the SUV. When he came back, Bly had slithered down into the kayak and was trying to arrange herself entirely within it.

Nils watched. "I don't suppose you could ride in there and I could drive?"

"That wouldn't really help us." She slinked out of the kayak. "You try."

He did, and it was a tight fit, Nils wiggling to get himself all the way down into the opening. His torso and shoulders stretched beneath the cockpit opening, his head tucked into the bow.

Bly said, "Okay," and Nils maneuvered back out.

"How'd it feel in there?"

"Not good."

She looked him over, reached up to move his hair and examine the wound on his temple again. "How do you feel?"

"I don't like it in there."

"But you can do it?"

"I can do it." But he didn't know. He knew he could try.

"It's going to be harder on the roof."

"That occurred to me."

"You'll be facing down, suspended over the cockpit opening."

Nils had thought of that too.

"Hopefully that won't line up too much with the sunroof. You'd slip through."

Nils eyed the alignment and tried to judge where the kayak cockpit hole would rest above the SUV roof. "We could leave the sunroof closed?"

"If we have too. I want to be able to hear." She looked inside the SUV. "Maybe if we stuff something under you at the hole. Give you something to lie on." She rummaged. "The sleeping bag, or maybe the backpack?"

"Sleeping bag."

Bly unrolled the sleeping bag, folded it, refolded it, trying to get a shape she liked. They lifted the kayak back onto the racks and pushed it forward and back until it rested solidly with the cockpit partially over the sunroof opening and the sunroof partially closed. It was the best they could do.

Bly stood back to look. "I guess we'll try it when you get up there. You ready? Day's getting long in the tooth."

Nils snickered.

"What?"

"Nothing. Long in the tooth."

"My daddy says it. Something to do with horses."

"Horses, yeah."

"It can be with other things."

"I guess."

Bly squinted at Nils. "Is this because you got hit in the head?"

"No."

"Then you must be feeling better. You ready to get up there?"

Nils pushed his hands into his pockets. "You think maybe this would work better if we waited until dark?"

She stared.

"Not to imply that you haven't thought this through."

Bly flipped her hair. "I thought it through. This just isn't the way I thought it." She took a phone from her pocket and swiped and tapped. "There's a late ferry. Reservations are full, but we can get in the wait line."

"That's what the wait line is for."

Now Nils pulled his phone from his pocket. Bly looked at it. "What's that?"

"What?"

"In your hand?"

"It's okay. It's a burner."

"Where'd you get that?"

"In town. What's the problem?"

"Have you used that to call anyone?"

"Yeah."

She rolled a hand. "So?"

"I called the FBI field office in Bellingham."

Her eyebrows went up. "That's how they found you so fast."

"I thought you knew. You showed up."

"I showed up *because I had the tracker on you*. I showed up because I was looking for you. I told you not to call the FBI."

"I thought you knew."

"No." Bly shook her head. "It's a miracle I found you in time."

Nils considered the phone in his hand. "About that."

"What about it?"

"I was already in the van when you stopped it. How did you know I was in there?"

"You need me to explain it to you?"

"I'd like that."

Bly gave him a hard look. "I was tracking you."

"Right."

"The tracker."

"Right."

"So I followed you."

"You saw me buy the phone? You saw me at the library?"

"No. And no."

"So when…?"

"I picked you up when you were walking by the airport."

"You saw me there?"

Her brows pinched. "I saw them take you. I couldn't stop that. It was too quick."

"That's why you did the roadblock."

"Stalled car. It worked."

"Okay." Either Bly was a very quick thinker, or the pieces seemed to fit. "When did you have time to get all this stuff? The sandbag. Zip ties. How did you know you'd need them?"

"Good questions, Nils. You'd make a good lawyer. And while I don't like being on the witness stand, I'll tell you if it'll make you feel better."

She waited for him to respond. Nils didn't.

"Most of that I already had. I got it when I first came to the island."

"After the news story—me on the car."

"Yes. It got everyone's attention. I thought I'd have to grab you. I thought someone might do something stupid."

Like calling the FBI. But it still fit. "So you didn't see me at the library, and you didn't find me until the men in the van did?"

Bly didn't look happy, but she had answers. "No. I knew you were at the library. I didn't know what you were doing."

"Where were you then?"

Her face screwed up. "I was eating the tuna sandwich, okay? Which was terrific. You missed out. And by the way, those pastries are *amazing*."

Nils watched Bly.

She watched him back. "What is it now?"

"You still have that other sandwich?"

"No. Now if you're satisfied and you don't have any more questions, we have to go."

Bly checked that the kayak was strapped down securely. "If your phone has location, turn that on. Then toss it, as far as you can, and get in."

Nils checked the phone settings.

"No wait. Make sure the location is on, then get back in the CRV."

"Uhm?"

"The other car. We're going to drive away, toss the phone, then come back and get this one with the kayak." She was already moving. "If anyone is tracking, the last thing they'll see is us heading away from the ferry terminal."

Nils followed Bly to the other car. "Don't you think that's being a little overly cautious?"

"You've already had a gun pointed at you, been hit in the head, zip-tied, and had a bag over your head."

It didn't answer the question, but she made a good point. Several of them. He checked the location setting on the phone.

Bly put them going back the direction they'd come from. "You know Turtleback Mountain?"

"Yeah."

"We're going to leave the phone there. Maybe they'll think we've taken to the trails to hide."

"You think they'd buy that?"

"They chased you up the mountain, didn't they?"

Good point.

"You know the way?"

Nils looked out at the landscape. There was a turn ahead. "Left up here, I think."

"Good."

Nils gave directions, and they made the trailhead in short order. Bly stopped near a trash can by the road. "Take the battery out of your phone."

Nils tried. "Looks like it doesn't come out."

"Then break the phone. We're going to do that anyway."

They were?

Bly reached over. "Here, let me have it."

Nils held tight. "I can smash a phone."

"Then do it."

He exited the car and dropped the phone to the pavement, stepped on it, and crushed the case until he could release the battery. He looked at the pieces in his hand. "I went to some trouble to get this."

"Trust me. You'll be glad it's gone." She pointed. "Trash can."

Nils deposited the pieces in the trash can and came back. "Happy now?"

"Relatively."

He clicked his seatbelt. "What now?"

"We go switch cars and get the kayak."

"Can we get something to eat? Some coffee?"

Bly leaned her arms on the steering wheel and sighed.

"Look, you had two sandwiches. I didn't have any."

Her expression softened. Less intense. "I guess we've got some time. You really must be feeling better."

"Tired. Hungry."

Bly smiled. It was the first time Nils had seen that.

She drove them back to the SUV and they made sure everything was out of the one vehicle and into the other. Then Bly got in.

Nils opened the passenger door and put his nose in. "What are you going to do with the other one?" He pointed to the burnt-orange car.

"Leave it. It's on a fake ID. They'll find it."

He didn't have an argument, so he got in.

Bly was cautious. She drove them all the way back up the island, over to the other side, and back down until she found a little store near Buck Bay. Nils had slept for part of the drive, and he woke when they stopped.

"Rise and shine, sleepyhead."

He groaned.

Bly held up some fingers.

"What are you doing?"

"You're not supposed to let someone sleep after a hit on the head."

"Now you tell me."

"How many fingers am I holding up?"

"Three. I'm fine. And you can let someone sleep after a concussion. You just have to keep waking them up to check."

"Check what?"

Nils rubbed his eyes. "I don't know."

Actually, he did know. That had been part of the training for the job as a wilderness guide. It had been a lightweight first aid course, but Nils didn't think he had a concussion. He was feeling sharper, just tired.

Bly was still examining him. "So how will I know if you have a concussion?"

"I won't act right?"

She laughed. "And how will I know *that*?"

Nils laughed too. "You won't."

"Okay, I don't think you have a concussion." She left Nils in the car and went into the store. She came back with fruit, salads, sandwiches, and coffee and handed them through the window to Nils.

He set the containers on the dash and the center console and dug into the fruit.

Bly got in the driver's side.

Nils opened a sandwich box and reached for a coffee.

Bly smiled again. Second time, in less than an hour. Maybe it could become a habit. She took the other coffee and leaned into her seat. "I'll give you some room. I don't want to lose a hand."

Nils ate, and Bly snacked on fruit. When it was over, she cleaned up. "Let's look for some out-of-the-way place to wait for dark."

"This is pretty out of the way."

"Out of the way-er." She started the car and backed out.

"You'll have time to tell me that story."

"I will."

But when Nils leaned back and closed his eyes, even the coffee didn't keep him awake. He drifted off and forgot about the story.

Bly found that quiet place to wait. Nils woke and found they'd stopped outside a campground. Bly unbuckled her seatbelt. "Pit stop."

They took the break, then got back in the car. Bly rested her hands on the wheel. "Probably late enough to head down toward the ferry."

"I guess so."

Bly snapped her seatbelt, and Nils saw a paperback novel tucked between the seat and the console. "Same book I'm reading."

"You loaned it to me, remember?"

He didn't, but that sounded like something he would do.

It was a bit of a drive back around the island. It was dark by the time they neared the ferry terminal. Bly found a gravel-and-dirt road and pulled to the weeds at the side.

Nils got out and loosened a strap over the kayak. "We'll have to tilt it up and you hold it while I get in."

Bly opened a door and stepped onto the sill plate.

"Then you'll have to strap it back down."

"I can do that."

"I'll be trapped."

Bly had the kayak on its side. "If there's anything you want to do before that."

Nils went into the weeds for that, then climbed into the kayak. It was as uncomfortable as before.

Bly strained to keep the tilt. As Nils settled, the kayak thumped down to the racks. "You okay?"

"Just do it before I change my mind."

Nils held himself suspended over the cockpit hole and the sunroof window, and Bly fussed with the window and the sleeping bag until Nils could slump down onto the bag and the window was open enough they could hear each other talk when she was in the driver's seat. Then Bly strapped the kayak down and got into the car.

She tapped on the roof. "I think that's as good as it gets. You okay?"

"Okay."

"You're not going to fall through? I've seen what you can do to a sunroof."

"If I fall through you'll know it. Let's go."

She started the engine. "I'm going to start slow and do a test run. Can you still hear me?"

"I can hear you."

She drove down the dirt road. It was slow and bumpy.

"How was that?"

He tried to give a thumb's up. Oh. "Try the paved road. We can go faster."

She did. It was louder and hard to carry a conversation but faster and smoother on the blacktop. They quieted and Nils let his mind drift, trying not to think about where he was. Not much later, they were in line for the ferry.

The SUV settled to a stop, and Nils settled with it, tight but not ready to scream yet. It was warm. He heard the window go down and then a male voice.

"Evening, ma'am. You're traveling alone?"

"I am."

"Destination?"

"Anacortes."

"After that?"

"Oh. I'm on vacation."

"A destination, ma'am?"

Nils heard shifting below, maybe Bly adjusting in the seat or reaching for something. "Of course I'm going to Anacortes, silly me. That's where the ferry goes."

"Of course."

"After that, I don't know. Down the coast. I haven't exactly decided yet."

"Free spirit?"

"You could say."

"I like that."

Nils could vaguely make out some flickering of light. He guessed a flashlight, maybe searching the interior of the SUV.

"Getting in some kayaking?"

"Yes."

The man tapped knuckles against the side of the kayak. Nils took it in the ear. "How long have you been on the island?"

"Less than a week."

"Sorry for the inconvenience, but I have to ask for your driver's license."

"Of course."

Nils heard some indistinguishable sounds, then "Everything looks fine. Sorry to bother you."

"No bother."

Nils heard the window winding up, but the voice broke in again and the window stopped. "We don't usually do this. It's just that, maybe you heard about some trouble we had here a few days ago?"

The window wound again. Nils assumed it was going back down. "I only heard a little."

"Some guy jumped into the sunroof of a car."

"Oh, my."

"Yeah, coming off the ferry. Turned out he was wanted by the FBI."

"Incredible."

"Yeah, craziest thing. We're helping out the agency. We'll find the guy if he comes through here."

It sounded like bragging, and Nils wondered if everyone in the line was going to get as much attention as Bly.

"They've sort of deputized us. Unofficially, you know, but he comes through here, I'll get him."

"I'm sure you will."

"No need to worry. You can feel safe."

"I do."

The window began to wind again.

"So? You're just driving down the coast, see what happens?"

The window stopped again. "That's the idea."

"You enjoyed your time on Orcas?"

"Immensely."

"Well if you ever come back… Or, if, you know, you don't find what you're looking for down the coast…"

Jeez. Nils had to be stuck in a kayak listening to this?

"Yes. Well. I hope you find your guy."

"Oh, we will."

The window wound again and Nils heard it tamp shut against the window seal. The SUV moved forward several car lengths then stopped, and Nils guessed they were queued for the ferry. Bly moved an edge of the sleeping bag to open a little more space in the gap of the sunroof window. "How you doing up there?"

"Sounds like you made a friend."

"Shut up." The sleeping bag slipped back over the window opening.

Not much later the line began to move, and they boarded the ferry. Bly stayed in the car rather than going up to the travel deck like most people did. After several minutes of sitting, Bly tapped the roof. "Okay, it's mostly cleared out now. Still warm in there?"

"I'm okay."

"I'm going to pull the sleeping bag out some. Just slink down a little more if you have to."

"You're not worried someone will see?"

"They won't see you. It'll let some air in."

"You don't suppose I could come out now?"

"Nils, I'm sorry, I don't think that's a good idea."

He squirmed. "Okay. Do it."

Bly adjusted the sleeping bag. More air flowed into the kayak's hull and it was a little better.

"Nils?"

"Yeah?"

"I really am sorry about all this. I know it's probably uncomfortable."

He could hear her better now. "Just let me know when I can come out."

"Not yet. I'll tell you what. I'm going to explain to you what I know right now."

He was quiet.

"Nils?"

"Captive audience."

8

"I'M GOING TO hold my phone up and pretend I'm talking on that."

"There are people around?"

"No, just cautious. You should keep your voice down. Only talk if you need to."

"We don't want anyone to hear the kayak talking."

"Yes."

Nils heard shuffling in the seat, some movement. Then quiet. What felt like too long passed. "Bly?"

Her voice was soft. "This isn't the way I wanted to do this."

"Do what, exactly?"

"Explain things. Actually, I didn't plan to tell you at all."

"I don't even know what you're trying to say."

Big breath. "Things have gotten more complicated than I expected. I need to tell you some things if we're going to go on. And if you don't like my story, I'll let you out of our deal."

"You mean if I don't approve of your story."

Long pause. "If you don't like what I tell you, we can part ways. But we both need something here. You're stuck in something you didn't play a part in. I have a different agenda."

And she was afraid he wouldn't like it. "Well, you'd better tell me."

"It starts like this: my daddy is a gangster."

Nils listened. There wasn't much else to do.

"I'm his only daughter. My mother is dead. There's no other family.

This is going to be important, okay?"

He listened.

"Right. You're being quiet. I'll take it for granted that if you don't say anything you're following."

Nils didn't answer.

"Right. Daddy wants me to take over the family business. It's a big business." Bly waited. Nils didn't know for what. She continued. "But I don't want to. That's important too. Okay?"

Okay.

"Someone stole daddy's books."

"I assume you don't mean his mystery novels."

"His records. His finances. And contacts. The businesses—the laundering and the legits. The dirty stuff."

Nils wondered how bad.

"Extortion. Protection. Gambling. Theft and trafficking stolen goods. Smuggling. Drugs, cigarettes. Some guns. The hits were—"

"Stop. That's enough. Your father did all this?"

"Yes. Does."

"I didn't think that kind of thing happened anymore. Just in the movies."

"And my life."

"And someone stole the records. For everything?"

"For enough."

"How could that happen?" Nils guessed he was breaking the don't-talk-too-much rule. Bly didn't stop him.

"It was daddy's number two guy. Jimmy Cheek. Jimmy didn't want the family business to go to me."

Nils turned that over. "But you didn't want it."

"Didn't, don't. But daddy was very insistent. Jimmy was not going to get the business. I was."

"So neither of you were going to be happy."

"Jimmy was very unhappy. They call him Jimmy Cheek because of a scar on his face, in case you were wondering."

Nils had been. He pictured the guy from his trip. He'd had a beard. Covering up the scar. "So Jimmy stole the files to get back at your father?"

"More than that. To take over."

"How was he going to do that?"

"Shh. Wait a minute."

Nils did. There was a voice.

"Someone is getting a jacket from their car. Wait."

He heard a door close.

"Okay. Jimmy was going to use the files to put daddy away. Turn him over to the feds. Here's the thing—and this is another important part. Daddy was doing business with the FBI. He had an agent on the payroll—at least one. Jimmy knew this, and he contacted the guy. He was trying to make a deal. Turn daddy in and get him out of the way. But Jimmy wasn't so smart. He should have just gone to someone anonymous at the FBI. Someone he didn't know. Who didn't know daddy."

"The FBI guy didn't go for it?"

"Worse than that. How was Jimmy going to run the business if he turned the files over?"

"You said Jimmy wasn't very smart."

"Daddy didn't keep him around because he was smart. He kept him close because he was an enforcer. Anything daddy said, Jimmy did. Until he stole the files."

"So your father didn't want the business to go to Jimmy because he's not smart enough to run it."

"Right. And he's not blood. Business goes to blood, and I'm daddy's only blood."

Nils listened. Old school.

"Okay, so daddy's mole at the FBI didn't go for it. Why would he? He had a good thing going with daddy. And Jimmy isn't smart. He'd just fuck things up. So they both went after Jimmy." Pause. "Nils?"

"Following."

"Daddy and the FBI guy both wanted those files. Daddy wanted to get them before his agent mole, and the mole wanted to get them before daddy. Daddy figured his mole wanted the files to get more leverage over him. Squeeze more money out of him. And what happened was, they both went after Jimmy and Jimmy got scared and ran."

Nils was starting to connect the dots. He didn't like where they were going.

"This is the part that involves you, so listen carefully, okay?"

He was listening.

"Jimmy was the guy who disappeared from your trip."

"Shit."

"You don't have to tell me he didn't register under the name of Jimmy."

Nils tried to remember the guy more clearly. Nondescript. Forties? Very quiet. Seemed out of place and kind of a ghost on the trip. Mostly stayed in the back while they were hiking, barely interacted with anyone. First one in his tent every night to sleep. Thick brown beard. That's all Nils could remember.

"Jimmy had the files on a flash drive. He had that with him on your trip. Then Jimmy disappeared out on the trail. Except he didn't, exactly. He left your group and made it out. He contacted daddy. He'd given up on the feds. Jimmy said he wanted back in daddy's good graces. He wanted forgiveness. He knew I didn't want to take over, and he thought he could talk daddy into taking him back. That he would run the business to provide for me."

"Provide?"

"But Jimmy was stupid. This is important to remember, okay?"

Okay.

"Daddy wasn't going to forgive what Jimmy did. He never would. When Jimmy came back after your trip, Daddy's men roughed him up. They wanted the flash drive. Jimmy wouldn't give it. It was the one smart thing he did. If Jimmy had given up the flash drive, they would have killed him." Bly took a pause. "It turned out that happened anyway. They roughed Jimmy up too much and he died."

The very close quarters inside the kayak seemed to close even tighter. Nils wanted out. He wanted to breathe and walk and think.

"And here's the part—you already figured this out, didn't you?— where you come in again. Before he died, Jimmy said he left the key to the files out on the trail. He said he gave you a clue. You'd know where to find it."

"No."

"That's what he said."

"I don't know anything. He never left a clue."

"And now you're the only thread left on this trail to follow."

"The trail dies. Jimmy didn't give me anything."

A long breath. "There's a lot at stake here. They want to be sure."

The walls of the kayak felt too close and too warm. Nils tapped on the side. "I have to get out."

"In a minute."

He twisted. The kayak shifted and strained against the straps that held it to the racks on top of the car. "Your father sent you for me."

"No. Daddy doesn't know I'm here."

"He sent other people for me."

"Yes. But I haven't seen any of daddy's men yet. The guys from the van who took you, they've got to be with the agent daddy was working with."

Nils tried to unwind, undo. Make this not be happening. "If the files are lost, Jimmy hid them somewhere and no one can find them. Just leave them lost."

"Daddy won't go for that."

"Everyone can just walk away."

"Look, I'd like it to be that easy. But it isn't. Daddy is very cautious. He won't take a chance that those files will turn up somewhere. He has to know if you can find the flash drive."

"I can't."

"That won't matter."

Edit undo. Edit undo. "Bly? Tell me why you're here."

"I don't want to hurt you."

"It's time to explain."

Breath. "You're my ticket out. If I can find that flash drive, I can get away from daddy."

"How?"

"He'll have to make a deal. There'll have to be a way."

"The flash drive is lost."

"If there's some way. I thought if I could find you, there would be some way. But now..."

"Now?"

"Now I don't want them to find you. I don't want what happened to Jimmy to happen to you. And I still want there to be a chance for me. We both have something we want here." Bly breathed. "That's my story. Now you're going to have to decide if you want to stay with me or not."

The car door opened. "I can give you some time to think about it if you want."

Nils twisted inside the kayak. He heard Bly loosening the straps. "Relax. I'm going to let you out now."

9

BLY STEPPED INTO the door frame and put a shoulder to the kayak. "Let's do this quickly while no one is here."

She pushed, and Nils forced cramped muscles to move. He wiggled and slipped through the cockpit hole, dripping into the open sunroof, and rolled himself off the car onto the ferry deck. "Uuungh."

"And quietly." She hurried to help him up.

He hobbled and stretched. "Don't ever want to do that again."

"Be weird if the opportunity came up." Bly scanned for watchers as she re-secured the kayak to the racks. "I think we're clear. Let's go up."

They climbed the stairs to the passenger deck, Nils happy to be moving and stretching things out. He headed for the restrooms, and when he came out Bly was holding a coffee in each hand. She extended one to Nils. "Cream, no sugar."

She remembered. Nils pointed to the other cup. "What's that one?"

"Same."

He filed that information away.

Bly sipped. "We've got some time. Let's go all the way up."

"As long as I keep moving."

They walked to the upper deck and found a spot on the rail. Bly cut her eyes to Nils. "How's your head?"

He touched the temple. "Forgot all about it."

"We've found the cure. Get hit on the head, you need a ride in a kayak."

Nils laughed once. "I'll put that with my first aid knowledge." He really had forgotten about the hit on the head, but the effects of the ride in the kayak were still with him. He stretched his legs and back.

"Nils?"

"Yeah."

"What I said, when you were in the kayak."

It hung there. "You finally got me some place I couldn't run away."

She looked down. "You know, I feel bad about that."

"But it seems to have worked. We're off the island."

Bly ran a thumb around the rim of her coffee cup. "I didn't know how you'd take it. When you thought I was an agent or something, I was kind of okay with that." The thumb circled some more. "Now…"

"Now you're waiting for me to decide."

"Yes."

"If I want us to stick together."

Moonlight dappled the water. Nils stretched and drank coffee. Bly stood and drank coffee.

"It's okay if you need some time to decide."

He stretched.

"I'm not going to chase you again if you say no. I'm done with that. This only works if we do it together."

The ferry churned. Mainland neared. Nils would have a tough go of it alone. He could try a different FBI office. He could try some local authorities, the news. He could find a way. He could go it alone, or he could go with Bly. Ten days ago it would have been a simple choice.

Nils looked at Bly on the rail, thumb on her coffee cup, wind pushing strands of hair around her face, biting her lip. Waiting.

It wasn't such a complicated choice. He came to the rail next to her. "I've decided."

The thumb on her coffee cup stopped. Biting her lip stopped. Hair kept blowing around her face, and she reached to push some back.

"Let's do it. Whatever we can to try to sort this out. You and me."

More hair blew. More hair got pushed back. "You sure?"

"Yeah."

"Thanks. It means a lot."

The coffee was gone. Nils was stretched out. He'd told Bly he would go with her. That's as far as he could see forward.

But he could see back. "This is where it started."

Bly turned.

"Up there, actually." Nils pointed to the beam overhead. "I was hanging from there, or that beam on another ship, when I saw that woman and her daughter."

Bly looked up. "Hanging."

"Doing pull-ups." He pumped his arms to demonstrate. "That changed everything. I didn't have to jump into that car. I could have just let them go."

"That's not when all this started. You just didn't know. You couldn't stay invisible forever."

"I wasn't exactly trying to be invisible."

Bly held two fingers up. "Two things. One." She pushed one finger down. "For someone not trying to be invisible, you were doing a really good job of it. And two—" The other finger went down. "No you couldn't."

Nils frowned.

"You couldn't have just let them go. You had to try to help that woman and her child."

On one level it felt to Nils like a nice compliment. On another level he realized she didn't really know him. That didn't matter. What mattered was what came next. "You have some kind of a plan?"

"Generally."

He waited a second. "You want to tell me?"

"We have to try to get that flash drive back. If we can't find it, we have to try something else. Convince everyone it can't be found."

"Wait a minute. You're telling me you do all this. You chase me across the island, to *another* island, you rescue me from—corrupt federal agents? All to get these files back, and you don't really have a plan?"

"My plan was to get you. I've done that."

"Now what?"

"We can start by looking through your gear. If there's anything you haven't gone through closely."

"Well there's the stuff in Sequim."

"Sequim?"

Nils held up two fingers. "First." He curled one finger down. "Little town at the top of the Olympic Peninsula. It's spelled s-e-q-u-i-m, but it's pronounced *skwim*. People there can be a little touchy about it." And second." He let the other finger fall. "I have a storage unit there."

"Why didn't you say so?"

"We just got to this part."

"How far?"

"Not far if we can get the ferry."

"We're on the ferry."

"There's another one."

They went down and got in the SUV, both of them inside this time. Bly was behind the wheel. When the ferry docked at Anacortes, she drove them off into the dark Washington night as if nothing unusual at all had happened back on the island.

Bly navigated through the dark streets. "So, Sequim?"

"Yeah?"

"Why there?"

"Why there what?"

"To leave your things. You bring them all the way up from California, then leave them in…*skwim*."

"Long story."

"We've got time."

Nils tried to sort out a good answer in his head. "It was handy."

Bly turned onto the road that carried them south out of town. "Not such a long story."

"I guess. I know some people near there. Own a little farm."

"Ee-I-ee-I-oh."

"Not like that."

"Like what then?"

"Lavender."

"Like the soap thing?"

"Sure. And other things. It's edible."

"If you say so."

They reached the state route. Bly turned, and that put them driving along Fidalgo Bay. "So you like lavender?"

"It grows well there. Right climate. Lots of little farms in the valley."

"So you know your way around."

Nils shrugged. "I worked the fields a bit, couple of times. When I was between things. Real nice up there."

"Sounds like it." Bly tapped fingers on the steering wheel. "Did you stop and see your friends when you passed through this last time?"

Nils slid his eyes over. Fishing. He went with it. How were they going to dig something up if they didn't try? "No. I put my things in storage and went to Orcas."

"So…"

"So you want to know how I got up the coast. How I got my things to Sequim and then got myself to Orcas."

"I'm wondering."

"To see if there's anything there. Anything useful."

"Had crossed my mind."

"There isn't. Everything's in the storage unit."

Bly drummed more fingers on the wheel. "Hmm."

So Nils told her. About the job and driving the truck and the guy and getting a ride with the garage owner's kid to the ferry.

"Okay. The guy, the truck, the kid. You leave anything anywhere someone could have…done anything with it?"

"No."

"You're sure?"

"I'm sure. The guy was an ex-con. Just paroled. On his best behavior. I put my stuff in the back. He never got near it."

"Okay."

"Guy at the garage and his kid never got near my things."

"I'm satisfied. We'll go to the storage unit and see what's there."

Nils jerked a thumb to the back. "And there's what's in my backpack. But you've already had a look through there."

It was bait, but Bly didn't take it. She said simply, "Light traveler."

"Little lighter without my paperback."

"You'll be all right. I'll give it back when I'm done reading it."

So that was it. She'd looked through his things while he'd been sleeping, and they weren't going to talk about it.

Nils looked out the window. They were making good time. "We'll be at Deception Pass soon."

"What does that mean?"

"Nothing. Just noticing."

"What's Deception Pass?"

"You drove over it on the way up."

"So a bridge?"

"Yeah, but it's the stuff below that's interesting."

"Like what?"

"Swirling waters. Whales, seals, sea lions, otters. Really rugged."

Bly drummed fingers on the wheel again. "I never get to see that stuff."

A few minutes passed. Bly's fingers drummed more. "It'll probably be too dark?"

"Too dark for what?"

"Deception Pass."

"It'll be closed."

"And we've been such rule followers."

"Well, I didn't litter."

Her eyes came over.

"The shirt."

She groaned.

"I don't mind breaking some rules. But we want to stay off the radar. No more helicopters or men in vans."

"I know that."

They arrived at the narrow bridge across the high pass and no one was behind them. Bly slowed and looked over. "Is there a beach?"

Nils pointed. "At the bottom." He couldn't see it in the dark.

Bly took them across the bridge to the parking lot. It was empty and closed. "How long?"

"How long what?"

"How long would it take to go down and see it?"

"In the dark?"

"Yes, in the dark."

"I don't even know. It's not going anywhere. Come back another time."

Bly squeezed the wheel. "I don't think I'm coming back."

She pulled onto the road and Nils figured that was that. Then the SUV slipped off the road into a spot in the trees barely large enough to hold it. Bly put the car into park and turned off the lights. "I know this is a bad idea, but if I get to do one damn thing before…"

She didn't finish it. She was out of the car. "You don't have to come with me, but I'm going."

Nils got out.

Bly walked back toward the trailhead. "We'll have to hurry."

He already was.

The trail was steep and dropped sharply at the edge into trees and rocks and water below. They descended quickly but with careful footwork. Bly was quiet and after some time she slowed. "Look, I realize this is a bad idea."

Nils watched his feet and didn't say anything.

"If this ruins everything. If we get caught…" She stopped on the trail. "We have to go back."

"Okay."

Bly turned. Nils didn't.

"What?"

Nils pointed. "It's right there."

They took a look. The trail opened from trees onto a narrow rocky beach and enough moonlight to reveal eddies in the water.

Nils found a flat stone and sent it out onto the surface of the water. It skipped once then disappeared.

Bly stood at the water and stared. Nils bent for another stone. He came beside Bly and looked where she was looking. The bridge was a shadow high above them, the water an enigma below.

Her shoulders dropped. "We shouldn't be here."

"I don't think anyone's going to find us now."

"If someone sees the car. If the locals run the plate."

"You used a fake I.D."

She sighed. "We need to be more cautious. Let's go."

"You don't like it?"

"I love it, but we have to go."

Nils didn't pretend to understand. He skipped the stone and it jumped once, twice until he couldn't see it. He wondered if it had sunk or if it was still out on the water somewhere, skipping.

Bly took them up the ascent even more quickly than they'd come down. They climbed in silence except when Bly called out a tricky step.

They reached the top and crossed the empty parking lot, and Bly hurried down the road to the car. The SUV was there, untouched and without a ticket or a car with lights swirling parked behind. She unlocked the doors. "I think we got lucky."

Nils figured so.

Bly drove them down the peninsula. "How far to Sequim?"

"Not far." He told her about the crossing from Coupeville to Port Townsend. "We can't get a ferry until tomorrow. We're going to want some sleep."

"We can tuck into the back of the SUV."

"Why don't we just get some rooms?"

Bly shook her head. "We got lucky once. We're going to have to be more careful now."

"What do you mean?"

"I don't want to use the I.D. if we don't have to. I don't want to be found."

"I'm all for that. But what are we going to do?"

"Cash. And sleep in the back."

Nils twisted to look behind him. "Going to be a little tight."

"It won't bother you if you're asleep."

Nils wouldn't bet on it.

Bly drove them to Coupeville, close to the ferry. She found a quiet road she liked behind some shops. She circled back to a gas station where they made pit stops, then back to the quiet spot and parked.

Bly turned off the dome light and folded down the back seats. She put all the gear except a sleeping bag into the front. Then she spread the bag out and rolled up her jacket for a pillow.

Nils stood outside of the SUV and watched.

"Get in here. You'll draw attention."

"I'll sleep up front."

"You can't sleep in the front. I put everything up there."

Nils reached in. "I can make room."

"The seat is pushed up."

"I'll move it back."

"Then I won't be able to sleep." Bly sat up against the back of the driver's seat so Nils couldn't push it back. "What is the problem?"

Nils didn't know exactly. Everything. He felt like the shy kid at camp. It was the closest he'd been to another person for a long time.

"This isn't a slumber party. It's a business transaction."

That helped.

"Get in here." Bly curled to the far side of the back of the SUV.

Nils briefly considered if he had options. Then he got into the back of the SUV and contorted himself against the side away from Bly.

He knew he wouldn't sleep much. He knew that very surely until he opened his eyes and saw daylight.

The air was warming inside the car. Nils sat up. Bly made a sound and did the same. She rubbed her eyes. "Already?"

Nils reached for his shoes. The road was still deserted, but they wouldn't want to stay sleeping in the back too long. He pulled the shoes on and opened the door. "I'm going for a little run."

"What?"

"I won't be gone long."

"Wait." Bly was moving now, tossing the sleeping bag back. "I'm coming." She grabbed her shoes. "Hang on. You're not supposed to do heavy exercise after a concussion."

"I don't have a concussion."

"How are you feeling?"

"Like running." And he really had to pee.

They went to the same gas station they'd visited the night before. There they used the facilities and bought water and bananas and protein bars. After they'd eaten while they walked a few blocks, Nils set them on a slow jog through town.

Bly matched Nils' stride, moving easily beside him.

His muscles began to warm and he stretched his legs and let his body naturally pick up the pace. Bly seemed to loosen and warm at the same rate as Nils, and she continued to run easily beside him.

They came to the water and Nils turned north. His speed was creeping up. If Bly noticed the faster pace, she didn't show it.

A boat horn sounded in the distance. Bly looked that way. Nils pulled a step ahead. Bly stepped up to match him.

Nils looked over his elbow.

Bly grinned. "You should see me going up a mountain."

"I have."

She inched forward. "You trying to lose me?"

"Where would I go?"

Bly pointed ahead. "You see the road?" It was a spur or a driveway. "First one there?"

"It's not a race."

"You bet." And she was off.

Bly beat him by a thumb. They both breathed hard and walked off the run. Bly put her hands on her hips. "I think you won."

Nils raised an eyebrow. That was generous.

She circled around next to Nils. "Ready to go back?"

"Yeah. I'm still hungry."

"Me too."

"Place back in town looked good."

"It did."

"We could indulge."

"We don't know when we'll have another chance."

"Then it's only the right thing to do."

They jogged back to town at a gentle pace. There they got breakfast, paid cash, and went back to the gas station for more supplies, cash again, each of them tossing in some money. Some sandwiches. An insulated lunch sack. More water and some snacks. Sunscreen. Nils wanted extra clean clothes, but Bly wanted to keep things light. They bought a roll of paper towels for cleaning up.

Then they were back in the SUV, and ten minutes later they were down at Fort Casey waiting for the ferry to Port Townsend.

They boarded without notice or incident and got out of the car. As they leaned against the ferry rail, Nils felt oddly relaxed, though he knew he shouldn't be. He couldn't explain it. Maybe the endorphins from the run.

Bly looked up at the sunlight. "You know, right now, this seems so…like the past couple of days weren't real. Like we just met on the ferry and…"

"And were not running from anything?"

"Or to something. This feels less complicated than what things really are."

"I was just thinking that. It'd be nice if we could walk away from this whole thing. If we could be just riding on a boat and that's all."

Bly leaned back. "That sounds nice. But I'm afraid things aren't going to stay that simple."

Nils had the same feeling. He desperately wanted it not to be true.

10

THEY DISEMBARKED AT PORT TOWNSEND. Directly across from the exit of the ferry terminal was a high, sheer bluff. Bly stopped at the light and looked up at the rock. "What's up there?"

"Town, I guess."

She turned right.

"Uh…"

"I know. It's the other way. I want to see it."

Nils did too. He had a dim recollection that he'd been there before, but he couldn't recall details.

The bluff gave way to storefronts, and after a few blocks more the incline began to play out and a side street let them ascend to the road above. That had a few more shops and a skinny park with a fountain and steps up to a higher road.

Bly looked at the steps. "What's up there?"

Nils couldn't see much through the park trees. "Houses, I guess. And maybe a better view."

Bly drove them up there, and it was sparse but there were houses and a nice view of the water. She circled around back the way they'd come. "Okay, nice. I get the idea. Now tell me about Sequim."

"Back down the hill." Nils pointed. "Take the road toward Port Angeles."

They cleared Port Townsend and moved down onto the Olympic Peninsula. The sun climbed and Bly put her window down and let some air in. It was sweet and crisp and smelled of juniper and evergreen. The wind competed with the radio, which wasn't picking up much anyway, and they opted for the wind and fresh air and turned the radio off.

Nils' thoughts went again to how he'd gone from alone to here with Bly. How he'd gone from unknown to wanted. He figured they wouldn't find anything in his storage unit, and he wondered what would happen then.

It was about an hour to Sequim. When they got there, Nils directed Bly through town and to a turnoff that led to some squat buildings with a storage sign. He pointed. "There."

The buildings were industrial, but it was a nice view beyond that, the peaks of Hurricane Ridge rising in the distance.

The area was empty except for Nils and Bly. He took them to his unit. Bly watched as he pulled the door open. "Tiny."

"Smallest they have." He heaved the door up.

Even so, the unit was half empty. There was enough room for the two of them to get in and move a bit without knocking elbows too much. Nils' gear from the trail was there. His larger backpack, sleeping bag, tent, camp stove and cook pot, first aid kit, boots. Jacket, raincoat, gloves, folding fire grill, binoculars. Snacks. A box of work clothes. A bicycle, helmet, biking clothes. A smaller box full of books.

Bly looked around. "This is everything?"

"Everything."

She picked up the sleeping bag and looked at it. "Enough room left over you could sleep here if you wanted."

More than there'd been in the back of the SUV. "What are we looking for?"

Bly handed him the sleeping bag. "Anything you don't recognize."

"Like a flash drive?"

"That would be nice. Or something it could be tucked into. A box. An envelope, a tin."

"Tin? Like for Altoids?"

Bly wrinkled her nose. "If there was an Altoids tin here, I'd smell it." She ran her hands along the seams of the pack. "A key, a note. Anything. Feel around."

Nils did. He spread the bag out, and Bly started into his pack. Nils took his shoes off and poked his toe around gingerly over the bag. "Does it seem odd that Jimmy would put the files on a flash drive? Do people really use those anymore?"

"Can't be hacked from the cloud."

"I guess so."

Bly was giving the pack a good workover. Taking everything out, reaching into pockets, pushing her fingers into the corners.

Nils moved from the sleeping bag to other items. The camp stove. He took off the grill and burners, looked around inside, turned the stove over and shook it.

Bly had the pack subdued and was moving on to the gear she'd pulled from it.

Nils sighed. He knew his gear intimately, like a good pair of socks or his favorite pair of underwear. "We're not going to find anything."

"Don't give up yet."

Nils dutifully inspected other items. Bly pulled the plastic caps off the ends of the aluminum backpack supports and peered into the narrow tubes.

Nils half-heartedly peered into the box of books. "Real cloak and dagger stuff."

Bly set the pack down. "I'm sorry, Nils. I know it's not exciting. If you have a better idea…"

He toed the sleeping bag again. "No."

"If we don't find anything, we're going to have to go retrace your trip and look."

Nils stopped toeing. "The whole trip? Is that even possible?"

"I don't know. We have to make some sort of effort."

Nils peered into a box of clothes.

"Nils?"

"Yeah?"

"I really do appreciate this. I just need…something. Anything. Some thing that can make me feel like I have a little control over the situation."

"I haven't felt that way for some time."

Bly felt the seams of a jacket. "I know. Me either."

Nils didn't say it, but he wondered how Jimmy would have been able to unstitch a sleeping bag or jacket or anything else, stuff a flash drive inside, and stitch that back up on the trail. It was possible, sure, but the odds seemed long at best.

They searched for longer than Nils was interested. He started packing things back away, putting clothes into the box, stuffing gear back into his pack. He watched Bly searching for something else to look through. "What is it you'd like to do?"

"Keep looking, I guess. We can go back through it again."

"No. I mean instead of the family business."

"The what?"

"You said your father wants you to take over the family business. You don't want that. Something about all of this is supposed to be your way out. Well, where do you want to go?"

"Go?"

"If you get out. What do you want to do? Instead of the family business."

Bly blinked. "I don't know."

"No idea?"

Blink.

"All this, and you have no idea…?"

"Give me a minute."

"I mean—"

"Nils. A minute."

"You just…" He saw her eyes go down. He gave her a minute.

Finally, Bly raised her head. "Nobody's asked me that before."

Nils was sorry for that.

"It's like this. *Not being in the family business* is what I want to do. That's not me. Never will be. Daddy tried, but it's not me. I don't feel like I have to know beyond that right now."

"You don't."

"Thank you."

Bly stood and scanned the contents of the little storage unit. "What I'm noticing is that there's not much here."

Nils glanced around. "All the trail stuff."

"No. I mean not much personal. *Your* things. Laptop. No TV, blender, coffee maker. The things people own."

"Nope."

"No personal items."

Nils hefted the box of books. Toed the stack of clothes.

Bly shook her head. "No, personal items."

"Personal?"

"Pictures, keepsakes. Yearbooks. Something from your childhood."

"No, not much of that."

Bly looked at the box of books. "You keep it light."

"I have been."

One of her hands rested on a hip. "You're a real enigma."

"Not really."

"And it had to be you. Of all people, Jimmy had to find you. No house, no home, no car. Nowhere else to look. Just all that trail out there where you walked. If he hid the flash drive, it could be anywhere."

"I know."

"How'd you get here, Nils?"

He looked her a question.

"Here. Floating around. Just this little storage unit which you just filled."

He shrugged.

"No. Tell me."

"Not much to tell."

Her eyes said she doubted that. So he told her a little. About his family. That he'd wandered. And he didn't know how to stop wandering. He was okay with that.

Bly listened to all of it. Then she asked Nils his own question. "And what do you want to do?"

"What do you mean?"

"There's no family business to run away from. What is it that you'd like to do?"

He thought a moment. "Maybe this is it. Work a few gigs, wander, keep things free and open."

"Maybe."

"I've never been asked that before either."

"Have you thought about it?"

"Not seriously." Or had he? "I guess I always thought it might be nice to have a little place somewhere. Out of the way. Back in the woods. Remote."

She was listening.

"A little cabin. Something simple. Maybe in the hills. Or near the water. Some place to fix up, make it my own. Plant a garden. See how much food for the year I could grow." It sounded nice when he heard himself say it.

"Can you see it?"

Nils shrugged.

"When you close your eyes. Can you see it?"

"I don't know."

"Try."

He closed his eyes. Imagined the garden. A little shed. Beans growing on a tripod. Compost pile. A shimmery, blurry house with a big window and porch on the front and nothing further he could call into view.

"Can you see it?"

"A little."

"Then you're ahead of me. All I have is, maybe if I could find this thing that Jimmy took that's probably lost forever, then I could start to imagine. But all I can see now if I don't find a way out is being under daddy's thumb forever."

Nils wasn't sure of that, but there was no way he was going to argue.

"What we need is—maybe it's not a thing that Jimmy left with you. Maybe it's something he said. Or something he did."

Nils' vision of the garden and house evaporated. "Could be, I guess."

"What do you remember about him?"

"Not much. Like I said, he was real quiet."

"Did he know anyone else on the trip?"

"No. I'm pretty sure on that. Someone dropped out of the trip late, and Jimmy picked up that spot just before we left. I hardly remember him even talking to anybody out there."

"Think."

Nils did.

"How long was the trip?"

"Six days. Supposed to be."

Bly rolled her hand for an explanation.

"Jimmy disappeared at the beginning of the third day. We cut it short then. They pulled us out."

"Pulled you out?"

"It's remote, but you're never more than a day from a road or some place where they can bring a van and come get you. Usually it's not even that far. They drop food for the night and extra gear or clothes if we need it."

"So you have cell phone reception."

He nodded. "Some of the time. Goes in and out. We encourage everyone to leave their phones off, but the guide has one on all the time. And a little GPS transmitter."

"Doesn't sound so remote."

"You still have to walk it. Even if they know where you are, that doesn't mean they can get to you quickly if something happens."

"Okay." Bly nodded her head as if that meant something. "You didn't go look for Jimmy when he disappeared?"

"Sure we did. And I hiked up the hillside to get a signal and called it in. They pulled us out and sent rangers and the locals in to search."

"You didn't stay to help look?"

"No. They didn't want any more trouble. I took the others out. They picked us up at an old logging road. Everyone except Jimmy."

"Okay." Again, like it meant something.

"So you made three days of hiking. That's a lot of trail."

"Not as much as you'd think. It was more like a little more than two days. And these weren't all seasoned hikers. That's why they went with a guide. And some of them weren't in great shape. We took it slow. Not that many miles a day. You and I could have covered the whole thing, all six days, in two if we'd wanted."

Maybe one, the way Bly moved.

"Okay. So I know that Jimmy was in better shape than that. How'd he do on the trail?"

Nils tried to remember. Jimmy really had been a ghost. He kept to the back of the pack like an old horse, ate by himself, slept away from the others. Didn't say much. Nils had thought Jimmy was bored, but now he guessed it might have been something else.

"There is one thing I remember."

Bly tilted her head.

"He didn't bring his shovel."

"Shovel?"

Nils held his hands out to demonstrate. "Little orange shovel. Like a gardening shovel. About this big." He indicated something a little longer than his hand.

"You were planting something out there?"

Nils smirked. "In a manner of speaking."

Bly looked confused.

"There aren't always bathrooms. You need the shovel to—"

"I get it."

"There were a lot of things Jimmy didn't bring that you're supposed to, but one thing I remember is he didn't bring his little orange shovel."

"Why orange?"

"So you don't lose it."

"And Jimmy lost his?"

Nils shook his head. "I don't think so. I think he never brought one." Now Nils was thinking about it. "Jimmy wanted to borrow mine."

"Is that unusual?"

"It can get kind of personal. Most folks bring their own."

"And Jimmy borrowed yours."

Now Nils remembered. "Not until the last day."

Bly made a face. "What did he use before that?"

"No idea. Maybe he didn't. Went au naturel. But on the day he disappeared, Jimmy wanted really bad to borrow mine."

"And you gave it to him?"

"It was weird. It was the first he'd really interacted much with anybody. Jimmy kept going up and down the line, asking everyone. Begging them to borrow their shovel. It made people uncomfortable. That's why I gave him mine."

"And then he disappeared."

"Right. And here's the other thing. Jimmy never gave me my shovel back."

"I'm listening."

"I figured he was just being a jerk, you know. Or he was going to keep it for the rest of the trip. But now I'm wondering…"

"It's orange so you won't lose it."

"When you set it down."

"Or if you want to mark a spot so you can come back later and find it."

"Maybe. It's just a little shovel."

"But it would stand out."

"If you put it in the right place. If you knew where to look. Maybe."

"Nils, do you remember where you were when you gave Jimmy your shovel?"

"Generally. I could get pretty close.

"You could find it again?"

"I could get near the place he borrowed it. It'd be really hard to find a little shovel out there. Even an orange one."

"Unless you knew where to look."

"We don't, exactly."

"I don't. But you might. If we go back, you might remember something. Maybe we could find it."

"If Jimmy even left it there."

"And if it means anything."

Nils frowned. "Lot of ifs."

"You said the two of us could cover the whole way in two days."

"We wouldn't have to. I've already narrowed it down. Still really hard to find a little shovel out there. Jimmy wouldn't have had to wander too far off the trail to get fairly deep into the woods."

"But he might not have, if he wanted to find that shovel again."

"Good point. But it's still a lot of ifs."

Bly looked out the storage unit door to the hills in the distance. "We have to look. If we don't, someone else is going to ask you these same questions, and—"

"I follow you. Look what happened to Jimmy."

"Sorry to say that."

"You have to. It's why this whole thing…" He twirled a finger.

"Makes sense?"

"As much as it can."

Bly nodded. "Still a bit like trying to find a needle in a haystack."

"More like trying to find a shit shovel in the redwood forest."

"Thanks for expressing it so clearly."

Nils closed the top on the box of books. "There's one thing though. I'm not getting back in the kayak. Not while it's on top of the car."

Bly laughed. "Let's get going. I think Jimmy may have buried something on the trail other than his business."

11

THEY CLEANED UP the storage unit a little. It only took a minute. Then Bly went to the SUV with the kayak still on top. "We need to switch vehicles."

"What's wrong with this one?"

"I made a mistake at Deception Pass. We shouldn't have gone down. If a local had seen the car parked where it wasn't supposed to be and called it in, or if a county car had driven past."

"We could have gotten a ticket?"

"They would have run the plates. And then we could have had trouble."

Nils considered that. "It's a rental. On a fake I.D."

"Caution, Nils. That's what keeps me from getting nervous."

"You don't look like you've been nervous a day in your life."

"Like I said: caution. I don't want any more digital trail. Not even to extend the rental."

"When is this one due?"

"Two days. Seattle airport."

"Two days won't be enough time."

Bly pointed at Nils. "Bingo."

"So what then? Buy an old car?" He thought how much cash he had, how Bly might be fixed for resources.

"We'd need license, registration, plates. That doesn't work."

"We could go rogue. Find a private sale. Get a title notarized.

Forget the rest of it."

She raised an eyebrow. "Now you're thinking like a criminal. Why even get it notarized? Why not just steal a car?"

"Is that an option?" It didn't sound like a good idea as soon as he said it.

"Stolen cars get reported. We want to stay off the radar." Pause. "And it's a stereotype to think the mob boss's daughter should know how to steal a car."

"Sorry."

"So no, we're not going to steal a car."

"I said sorry."

Bly crossed her arms. "And by the way, I *do* know how to steal a car. And that's one of the worst ways to keep your head down. A stolen car is good for a quick, one-time thing. Not for what we need."

"That's actually more than I wanted to know."

"We need something that won't get reported missing. As long as we don't get stopped, or drive over a road or a bridge where a camera takes a picture of the license plate for the toll, the rest of it could be okay."

"Doesn't leave many options."

Bly leaned against the SUV. "It doesn't."

"Bus ticket? Train?"

"Need an I.D."

"Flight?"

Bly rolled her eyes.

"Bicycles?"

She ran a hand over her chin, thinking. "You and I could do it. Not ideal. Slow going, not much mobility. No shelter." The hand came away from her chin. "We'd have to travel light. Doable, but there might be better options."

"Like what?"

"We could pay someone to buy bus tickets. Two someones. Then we get on the bus instead of them. If they don't check I.D. when you board."

"Do they?"

Bly shrugged. "Could be worth a try, maybe."

"So how do you travel off the radar?"

"Well, there are the classics."

"Hitchhike?"

Bly nodded. "Or walk."

They needed something like Nils had found getting up there to Sequim. He leaned against the door frame of the storage unit and casually reached a hand up. "I might know a guy."

Bly watched Nils. "You've been holding out?"

"No. But I'm thinking about the guy I rode up with. The one I dropped at the garage. Might be worth going over there to talk with them."

"Them?"

"The guy and his brother-in-law."

"You think they'd be friendly?"

"I think they might be flexible."

"Sell us a car?"

Nils stepped from the unit. "Or maybe let us drive one."

"Like a rental?"

"If that kind of thing can be done."

Bly opened the SUV door. "That's here in Sequim?"

Nils closed the storage unit. "It is."

On the drive over, Nils started thinking it through. "I could ask them if—"

"Hold on."

"If they would—"

"They'll recognize you."

"Of course they will. I drove the guy all the way from California, then the brother-in-law's kid took me to Anacortes."

"From the news."

"Uhm?"

"When you jumped in the roof of that car. There were pictures. Not a lot of good shots, but enough if you look closely. There's some video."

"That was up at Orcas."

"We're not far from there. And like I said, you'd have to look close. But you know—cautious."

"I wonder if those guys at the garage watch the news."

"Everyone sees social media. It's better not to risk it. I'll do the talking."

"But they know me."

"That's the point."

Nils looked out the window. "How are you going to do it? Convince them to let you use the truck?"

"Doesn't have to be that truck. It could be any vehicle."

"Okay." Nils gave some directions, heading Bly toward the garage. "Guy I drove up with, who owns the truck, is named Mike. He's recently paroled. He won't want trouble."

"Paroled?"

"Just got out. He's trying to make a fresh start."

"By crossing state lines?"

"I'd thought of that. It didn't come up in conversation."

"That might give me an opening."

Wow. Mob boss's daughter knew how to steal a car and how to leverage a parolee. "Mike seemed like he was really trying to go straight. I don't want to make trouble for him if we don't have to."

Bly stopped at a sign. "If we don't have to." She looked ahead. "How far?"

"Just after the light. On the left. I think you can see the sign for the garage."

"I see it." Bly made a right and pulled to the curb in front of a small, empty brick building that looked like it might have once been a donut shop. "Out."

"Here?"

Bly sat, engine running, her hands on the wheel.

Nils unbuckled and opened his door.

"And keep out of sight."

He went to the corner of the building and found an angle with just enough sliver of a view that he could see the SUV when Bly pulled into the garage lot. The kid who'd driven him to the ferry at Anacortes came out and seemed real interested in the kayak, until he saw Bly. Then he seemed real interested in Bly.

Nils watched and saw some back-and-forth, the kid's lips moving and then the kid cocking his ear as he listened to Bly. After a minute or so, the kid turned and appeared to call something back toward the shop, which was out of Nils' view. Then the kid windmilled an arm as if to bring someone else out.

The SUV nosed forward a bit, and a figure Nils thought might be the garage owner appeared at the edge of Nils' angle of view, and then everyone moved and Nils couldn't see any of them.

He waited. He got bored. He wanted the donut shop to be open so he could get a Boston cream.

Then he wondered how suspicious he looked leaning against the dirty brick wall of a dead donut shop. Maybe he'd leave a clean spot where he'd leaned. A clean spot here would look suspicious. Nils started walking.

He walked down the block away from the direction of the garage, past modest homes whose greatest asset was the promise of scenic peaks rising in the distance.

He turned at the corner, walked, turned again, and again, and came to a view of the garage from farther away. He saw neither the SUV, nor anyone at the garage, nor any sign of activity in that direction. And Nils got a familiar but strange feeling that he'd been abandoned, left alone again, as if recent events had never been real and he was just Nils, wandering again and left to his own devices. It wasn't an altogether unpleasant sensation.

He started back toward the one-time donut shop, considering walking a second loop, or a reverse loop, see if that undid anything. Then a pickup truck backed slowly from the garage lot. It was an old truck, and Nils was pretty sure it was the one he'd driven up from California.

Nils stopped and waited and the truck came straight at him, through the light, and passed by on the opposite side of the street. Bly was at the wheel. She pointed to Nils and made a circle with her finger to indicate that she was coming around.

Nils waited and Bly did the U-turn and stopped to pick him up. "You were supposed to wait where you were."

"They didn't have any donuts."

"What?"

"Never mind." He got in.

Bly took them into the driving lane. "And you were supposed to stay out of sight."

"You think they saw me?"

"No."

"Then I stayed out of sight."

"I found you."

"But you were looking for me."

Bly let it go. "I got the truck."

"I see that."

"This is the one you drove?"

Nils looked, sniffed, tested a radio dial. "Sure is."

"Was there a doubt?"

"No."

"Then why did you need to sniff and check the radio?"

"Just getting the ambiance."

"Have I told you you're a little odd?"

"It's been implied."

Bly made a left. "We're going to wait about ten minutes, then I'm going to walk back and get the SUV."

"What's the deal? How'd you get the truck?"

"I rented it from him, sort of, for the kayak and some cash. The kid really liked the kayak."

Nils thought that wasn't all the kid had seemed to like.

Bly parked at the curb in front of a house. "We'll wait here." She turned off the engine and leaned back in the seat.

"So? That doesn't really explain it."

"It's a little gray."

"Try."

"I'm not sure if they want the truck back?"

Nils frowned. "How does that work?"

"It's legal. Plates, registration, insurance—all in place. It turns out that in Washington you can make a private arrangement to lease your vehicle to another party. There are even templates online. You get one, download it, fill it out. They'd done it before."

"These guys did that?"

"Yeah, the shop owner. He knew how."

"And it looks legit?"

"Seems to be. We don't want to get stopped. But if we drive careful and nothing happens, we won't."

"That's it?"

"They gave us a lot of time."

"How much?"

"Lease runs for a month. I told him if we weren't back by then we'd ditch the truck and they can call it in stolen."

Nils leaned forward. "You what? Why'd you do that?"

"Not stolen by us. He'd report that we reported it was stolen."

Nils tried to keep up. "Is that better?"

Bly shrugged. "We have a month. If we don't have it back by then, we'll have to ditch the truck or it'll look like us who stole it."

That didn't sound great. "Whose name is on the agreement you signed?"

"Nobody you know. Matches the name on the SUV rental."

"So fake."

"And if we get this back in less than a month, even that name won't come up."

Nils was thinking about it, the whole deal.

"Any other questions?"

"Why a month?"

"We're going to need cash for other things. A month should be long enough. I mostly traded for the kayak."

"That wasn't a rental?"

"Not exactly."

Nils tried to decide if he wanted to know more.

"This thing might not last a month anyway." Bly moved the shifter through the gears. "Rattle in the gearbox, clutch is getting soft."

"It's an old truck."

"Tires are almost gone."

"It did fine getting up here."

"And it'll have to do fine getting us down to California." She slipped her seatbelt off. "Now I'm going back to get the SUV."

"Okay. But just explain that part to me first. For my edification."

A slick grin crept onto Bly's mouth. "Edification?"

"I've been to college."

"I bet you made a good frat boy."

"I was never a—stop that."

"Stop what?"

Good question. Was this teasing? "Never mind. Just go."

Bly lingered in the door. "I told them I have a shy friend."

"Great. That's supposed to be me?"

"Sit tight, college boy. I'll be right back." And she slipped away.

Five minutes later the SUV pulled up behind the truck. Nils had moved to the driver's seat. Bly got out of the SUV and came up to the truck.

Nils rolled the window down. "I assume I'm driving this?"

"You're driving the truck. Keys are still in it."

"I noticed."

"We'll go down to Seattle and I'll return the car at the airport, then we'll head to California."

"Just like that?"

"We need to work out some logistics. Without phones we won't want to get separated. Follow me and we'll find some place to stop and hash out details. We'll have to drive down around Tacoma or take the ferry." She turned to go.

"Hang on."

"What?"

Nils didn't know what. His stuff was still in the SUV. Should he move it to the truck? He couldn't shake the feeling that this was too easy, that they just trusted each other now. That they wouldn't get separated and he would never see Bly again.

"Nils?"

"Yeah."

"You okay?"

"Sure."

"Then let's go."

They stopped to gas up and use the restroom. When they came out, Nils moved his things from the SUV to the truck. Then he came back to the SUV and reached in for the sleeping bag and Bly's backpack. She put an arm out to stop him. "We can do that later."

"We'll be at the airport later. It'll be harder to stop."

"We can find a lot."

"Be easier now."

Bly's arm stayed suspended between them. "I…"

Here it was. Nils stepped back. "Show of faith."

Bly's eyes roamed over Nils once, twice. "I thought we'd been through that."

"We have. I'm with you. You're with me."

Bly crossed her arms, seemed to notice that she'd done it, and uncrossed them. "Everything but the backpack."

Her backpack with the pistol in it.

Nils carried Bly's things to the truck. Then they plotted a route. Neither of them wanted to drive all the way down around the Sound and through Tacoma, so they opted for the ferry.

That took them across the floating bridge. They might not have even noticed that the bridge was floating, if they'd missed the sign, but for the luck that landed them there when the middle of the bridge was opened for water vessel traffic.

Traffic was stopped on the bridge, and Nils and Bly exited their vehicles while they waited. Two sections of bridge on either side of the center had been raised on pneumatic jacks, then slid backward over the span behind. It left a large gap for ships to pass through.

Nils leaned out over the rail to see. "I didn't know it could do that."

Bly leaned beside him. "I didn't know a bridge could float."

They watched a ship navigate slowly into the breach. After a few minutes, Bly pointed down at the water. "Guillemot."

Nils looked. He didn't know what for.

"The birds."

He looked again. Black birds floated on the water below. "I thought those were cormorants."

Bly shook her head. "Guillemot. You don't see those too often."

"Hardly ever." Like he knew.

They watched the birds float and dive, then Nils said, "How do you know what bird that is? I've never heard of a guillemot before."

"I read a lot when I was a kid. I had a lot of time alone."

So they had that in common. Time alone. But had Bly also liked it, or was it just something she'd had to endure? Either way, it wasn't how Nils would have pictured Bly as a kid. Reading. So how would he have pictured her? Riding in a big gangster car, her father sitting in back with her behind bullet-proof glass? Suckled by a long-suffering mother who wanted nothing more than to free her daughter from a woe-begotten life? Out at the shooting range, learning to aim a pistol under the guidance of her father? Ninja training? How did this sit with the image of her alone in a corner reading a book? About guillemots?

Nils' reverie was interrupted by the grind of the bridge moving back into place. All that engineering and construction and waiting, just for a single ship to pass. He guessed if you were on the ship, that made it worthwhile.

Nils' musing was broken again by Bly calling out. "Nils. Get in. We're going to move."

Her optimism was a bit premature. They sat in the vehicles for several more minutes while the bridge reassembled and secured itself. Then they completed the crossing, and the Kingston ferry terminal was only about fifteen minutes away.

The ferry lot was nearly empty when they pulled in. The previous ship had just left. They purchased fare and lined up at the front of the queue, Bly in front in the SUV and Nils behind in the truck. Then they locked the vehicles and walked across the lot to a small business district by the water.

Bly did not carry her backpack. Feeling confident, Nils guessed.

On the corner across the street from the ferry lot was a coffee shop. Bly headed for it. "J'aime les crepês."

Nils followed her. "That's kind of random, but I like them too."

"No." Bly pointed.

Nils' eyes caught the sign. *J'aime les Crêpes*. Crêperie and espresso. Excellent.

The place was tiny, but the weather was good and they waited for crêpes and coffee and carried them to a little patio outside and settled into chairs at a table under a bright red umbrella.

There were trees and shade and plants. It was very nice. Then Nils bit into his food. Steam rose from the chicken and spinach and almonds inside. Nice wasn't the word for it. He tried another. "Galette. Jackpot."

Bly looked up. "You all right?"

Nils held up his crêpe as an answer. "Galette."

"Galette to you too. I don't know what you're saying. Is that French?"

"The French make a savory crêpe from buckwheat. It's called a galette. This is it. You hardly ever find these." He took another bite. Superb.

"How do you even know that?"

Nils chewed around his words. "French cooking school."

Bly gawked. "Really?"

Nils grinned and took another bite.

Bly waved him off. "Nah."

Nils swallowed. "There. Now we know something about each other. You know what a guillemot is, and I know galette."

"Well, it looks like we have the Gs covered."

The time passed gently and so did the galettes and coffee. The ferry lot had filled while they were away, and now people moved to their vehicles in anticipation of the next ship's arrival. Bly headed for the SUV. "Don't lose me."

Nils turned for the truck and gave a thumb's up. He didn't plan to.

12

THEY TOOK THE I-5, Bly in front and Nils behind hugging the SUV's bumper. Traffic was steady, but not so thick that Bly wasn't good at picking a center lane where they could cruise near the speed limit and not get separated. The truck rattled a bit but did okay.

An hour later they exited the highway for the airport and Bly pulled into a gas station near the vehicle rental return. She gassed up the SUV and Nils gassed up the truck. Then Bly drove off to return the rental and Nils pulled around beside the station and waited.

Fifteen minutes later, Nils drove slowly in the direction Bly had gone. He caught sight of her skirting a low retaining wall at the facility perimeter. Nils slowed, put on his flashers, and stopped at the curb. Traffic flowed around him like wind over an airplane wing. Bly cut through the shrubs and landscaping and jumped into the truck.

Nils was already zippering back into traffic. Bly slipped her backpack off. "I don't think they're used to seeing someone walk out of the lot instead of into the airport."

"You get some funny looks?"

"A few." She snapped her seat belt into place, opened a pocket on her backpack, and took out a pair of sunglasses and put them on. "They looked at me like I was some hippie girl walking out into the big world for an adventure."

Nils didn't think so. A hippie girl? That's what Bly thought of herself? Not a chance. With the sunglasses and dark flowing hair and her runner's body she looked more like a movie star. Out promoting her latest movie, maybe. A blockbuster. *Bly Something and the...*

"What?"

Nils glanced over and back.

"You were giving me a funny look."

"Sorry."

"What's so funny?"

"Nothing."

Bly tilted her head, and sunlight glinted off the movie star glasses. "If you must know."

"I must."

"I was thinking about your last name."

The sunglasses leveled on Nils. "You don't know my last name."

"That's why I was thinking about it."

Bly held her pose, a movie star smiling for a still. "That's what you want to know?"

"Yeah."

"I tell you I'm a free-spirited hippie girl out looking for an adventure, and what you want to know is my last name?"

"You didn't say free-spirited."

"Well, if I had."

"That might have made a difference."

Bly apparently wasn't ready to let it go. "What kind of difference?"

"I probably would have asked what's your sign."

Bly snickered. "Isn't it implied that all California hippie girls are free-spirited?"

"I wouldn't know. And we're not in California yet." But that was interesting. Bly thought of herself as a free spirit out for an adventure in Cali?

"Aquarius."

"Huh?"

"My sign would be Aquarius."

"Oh." Right. "Is it?"

"No, Nils. This is the hippie girl scenario."

Aquarius. Nils shook his head. "Nope. Doesn't work."

Bly frowned. "You don't like the hippie girl thing?"

"The name. Bly Aquarius."

"My name's not Aquarius."

"I know. Aquarius Bly. Warbly Aquarius."

"What are you doing?"

"Aquarius Warbly. Nope. Doesn't work. Your name can't be Aquarius."

"It isn't."

"I know." Nils wondered just how odd Bly might be beginning to suspect he was. "Okay, I was thinking you look more like a movie star and—"

"You think I look like a movie star?"

He nodded.

"Why?"

Nils looked over. "It's the sunglasses."

Bly pushed them up on her forehead. "These little 'ol things?"

"And the hair. And…"

"And what?"

Everything. "What I was thinking was what would be a good title for your new action movie. Bly *something* and the… That's why I wanted to know your last name."

"All right. If you knew my last name. Bly *something* and the…"

"Couldn't get there. Stuck on the name."

"Try."

"*Aquarius Bly and the missing flash drive.*"

"Sounds like a kids' book."

"Maybe I'm not so good at this."

Bly put a finger to her lip, then an eyebrow went up and the finger rose. "*Warbly Sapphire and the missing flash drive.*"

"Eponymous."

"What?"

"Too geeky?"

"By far."

"Too descriptive. Title describes the plot."

"You could have just said that."

"I did. That's what eponymy means."

Bly pushed the sunglasses back down over her eyes. "Moving on."

Nils shook her off. "Nope. Not ready."

"Not ready?"

"Aquarius Warbly's big California adventure."

"Better. But it sounds like a sixties beach movie."

"You could do worse." Nils navigated through merging traffic. They were making good time.

"Nils?"

"Yeah."

"This is more fun than listening to the radio."

He laughed. "It'll wear thin."

Bly pushed some hair behind an ear. "Why don't I just tell you my last name?"

"Good idea."

"Milkov."

He turned that over.

"M-I-L-K-O-V."

"I figured. So Bly Milkov?"

"Warbly."

"So Warbly Milkov. Very distinctive."

"Does that still work for your movie title?"

"Assuming we can forget that the character's name would be different from your own?"

"Assuming."

"I'm thinking."

She thought quicker. *"Warbly Milkov and the enigmatic stranger."*

"Enigmatic? That's what you think of me?" It didn't quite sound the way he'd intended it. "Besides, that's not much of an action adventure title."

"You didn't say it had to be an action adventure."

"I thought it was implied."

"Like California girls are free-spirited?"

"If that's the way you want to think of it."

Bly smoothed some more hair behind an ear. "You were elusive. I thought you were shy. That was enigmatic to me."

"Elusive?"

"You ran away."

"I was being chased."

"Before that. On the mountain. When it was only me chasing you."

Nils thought back. "I just wanted to be alone."

"See? Enigmatic."

"Because I wanted to be alone?"

"You ran away after you jumped into the car with that woman and child. Most people might have stuck around for the hero worship."

"I wasn't sure it was going to go that way."

"Or at least for the police report."

"Attention is not really my thing."

Bly held her palms up as if to say *see?*

Nils did. "Fair enough. Enigmatic stranger."

Bly snickered again. "We'll see how the plot evolves."

Nils jockeyed again for a slower lane. The truck was a bit bumpy at higher speeds. "*Bly Milkov and the local yocal?*"

She laughed. "Not an adventure title. And yocal?"

"Rhymes with vocal."

"You have not been particularly vocal. And you are anything but a yocal."

"I can be a yocal." Nils cleared his throat. ""Yocal-alul-aluleelu."

"What was that?"

"A yodel."

Bly did not try to hide her grin. "Yocal and yodel are not the same thing."

"Local yocal yodels."

"Stop."

"Stop what?"

"Making me laugh. This is supposed to be serious."

It was serious. Everything about meeting Bly had been serious, even if Nils wasn't sure yet that she was telling the whole, exact truth. But some part of him was enjoying this.

"Why are you in such a good mood anyway?"

"I have no idea." That wasn't entirely true, and Nils suspected that Bly knew it.

He changed lanes again. Traffic had picked up. There was no single fast lane now. Every lane was a fast lane.

The truck rattled more, an unevenness opening up in the ride.

"Nils?"

"Yeah."

"You think it would be better if we got off the highway?"

"I was hoping we could maybe make it past Tacoma." He found a stretch where he could slow down a little and the truck smoothed some.

"It did okay before this? On the way up?"

"It was back roads. Slower. Might need to check the air in the tires."

"How far to Tacoma?"

"Almost there. It'll take longer if we get on the back roads. You're okay with that?"

"I am." Bly looked out the window. "In fact…"

"In fact?"

"We could drive down the coast?"

It was a question. "We can."

"There's a scenic route?"

"The one-oh-one. Yeah."

Nils exited the highway after Tacoma and they found a gas station with an air pump. Nils put dollars into the machine and pumped air into the tires while Bly rearranged some things in the truck cab. It was tight. They could carry gear in the back if they wanted, at the risk of rain or items falling through the rusty holes in the bottom of the bed. They'd taken a tent, Bly's sleeping bag and one of Nils', some trail food and a tiny camp stove made of a grill that snapped over a miniature gas tank, jackets, and a change of clothes and boots for Nils. Bly had no extra clothes or shoes, and she didn't seem worried about it.

Nils finished with the tires and peered into the cab. Bly had mashed some more things behind the bench seat. The cab was a little roomier.

They didn't need gas. Bly came around to where Nils was wrapping the air hose back on the hook. "You want me to drive?"

Nils really didn't. It felt good to be driving, for Bly to be in the passenger seat for a while. He didn't know why exactly. He held the keys out anyway. "If you want. Can you drive a stick?"

"I can build a manual shift transmission."

Nils didn't doubt it, cloudy images of a dirty chop shop run by Bly's father's men forming in his thoughts. "Then by all means."

But Bly didn't take the keys.

Nils jangled them.

"Unless you want to keep driving."

"I could."

"Good. Then I'll sight-see." And she opened the passenger door and got in.

The roads were smaller and more rural and with less traffic. The truck did better with air in the tires. It was a nice drive, but it was a while before they approached the coast.

When they got their first look at the big water, Bly sat up in her seat. "Is the drive as pretty as they say?"

"You wouldn't believe it. Even in an old truck." What he'd meant to say was especially in an old truck.

They drove for a long time, Bly watching out the window at the trees and hills and at the ocean when they had a view of it. They crossed from Washington into Oregon and snacked. Bly asked a couple of times to stop at scenic views where they pulled off the road and looked down at the Pacific and the waves and rocks.

They passed through small towns and got off the route at Cannon Beach to go past the water. Nils pulled into the lot at the beach and a cool mist rolled in through the window. Haystack rocks rose from the water in the distance and waves broke against the sand.

Nils found a spot and parked. "We should get out."

"It's getting late."

"We came all the way here. It's the scenic route. This is scenic."

Bly had her window down. The cool salt air rushed in. "I guess we could indulge."

"There's not really a rush. We have the truck for a month."

Bly got out.

They walked the beach, holding their shoes and getting sand between their toes. Other people walked, a few jogged, and several sat in low foldable chairs or watched kids play in the sand. It was populated but not crowded.

They'd left their jackets in the truck. Wind and mist blew, and Bly hugged her arms to her ribs. "Is it always this cold?"

"No."

"California beaches are warm?"

"I've never been to southern California. I guess the beaches are warm there. Northern beaches can be warm. It varies a lot. You want to turn back?"

"No, but we probably should."

They did. As they walked, seagulls hovered and dove, piercing the wind with the sound of their calls. Nils looked up to track them. "Vocal locals."

"What?"

"Nothing."

They continued toward the parking lot. Nils watched Bly shiver but put her toes in the water anyway. "Where did you grow up? No beaches?"

"New Jersey."

"There are beaches in New Jersey."

Bly followed the line of a retreating wave. "We never went." She left it at that.

They got back to the truck and Nils stayed behind the wheel and they made more miles.

The day grew long, as they did near the solstice. They passed through Depoe Bay late in the day and stopped to look for whales. Nils took them to the low stone wall at the lookout point and they scanned the water. Someone near them pointed and traced a line with a finger. They followed the direction, and a minute or so later a spout of water broke the surface out in the bay.

A moment later, the spout rose again farther away. Nils got the feeling that Bly could have stayed all night watching for more spouts, but it was near dark and after their lone traveler out in the water drifted away they didn't see more spouts.

They reluctantly got back in the truck, and Nils drove them south as the sun dipped a toe, then a leg and a hip, into the Pacific before it disappeared.

Bly had been quiet and Nils drove on in the dark, fatigue from the long days and from sitting in the truck setting up in his muscles. Bly appeared to be asleep or dozing.

Nils grew more tired and concentrated on the little slice of road illuminated by the arc of the headlights. The trees beside them grew larger and taller as they burrowed into the redwoods.

There was a long stretch with dark curves and giant trees and not many places to stop. Nils grew more tired and began to think about a place to sleep. Bly had already found one in the passenger seat.

Finally when Nils thought he could drive no farther, they came to a small roadside motel. He pulled into the lot. "Bly."

"I'm awake."

"I need to stop."

"Huh?" She blinked and rubbed her eyes. "It looks like we have."

"I can't drive anymore."

She straightened. "Where are we?"

"Redwoods somewhere."

She mustered a lazy yawn.

"Can you drive?"

"No. Sleepy."

"We'll have to find someplace."

Bly's mouth opened in an *O*.

Nils set the parking brake. "We have the tent."

"Campground?"

"Haven't seen one. Would they ask for I.D.?"

Bly blinked. "I don't know."

"There's the back of the truck. If we can find a place to park."

"We can't sleep in the back. It's rusty. Big, sharp holes."

"We could look for a place to set up the tent."

Bly looked out at the motel and the dark redwoods beyond. "You see anywhere?"

"No. It's dark."

Bly yawned again, bigger this time. "We should have thought of this sooner."

"Yes."

She looked out the window again. "I'm sleepy. We could try the motel."

Nils was sleepy too. "Your call. They'll want I.D."

"We can use the fake I.D. It's just this one night. I have enough cash so we won't have to use the credit card."

"If you use the I.D., why not just put the room on the card?"

Bly blinked in the dark. "I can't think anymore. Maybe they'll take cash for the room."

Nils imagined a bed and a hot shower. "I have cash."

"No. I'll pay." She opened the door and walked toward the motel office. Nils shut off the engine and followed.

The price of the room was good. The place was good. They wanted a credit card for the room and deposit. Bly turned to go.

They reached the truck and Bly touched the handle before she stopped. "Let's just do it."

Nils shrugged and followed her again.

Bly checked them in and got a key, then they carried a few things to the room. Their day packs, with water and granola bars and toothbrushes.

It was separate beds and they didn't even discuss it. Bly took squatter's rights on the bed nearest the bathroom, and Nils took the bed by the door.

Bly showered first, and while she did Nils noticed her backpack on the floor beside her bed, the top zippered open for access. Nils wondered if her gun was in there. He stopped himself from looking.

Then Bly came out and got into her bed and muttered something about wishing she could wash her clothes. She turned off the light on her nightstand.

Nils opened one end of a curtain a couple of inches to let in some light from the parking lot, then he turned off the lamp by his bed too. He went to shower and found Bly's shirt and socks airing on a bathroom hook.

When he came out, Bly was asleep. It was a soft sleep, quiet and with very little rise and fall from her breath.

Nils got into the other bed and thought about how this night felt new and odd and awkward but entirely different from the night before when he'd been squeezed and contorted around Bly in the back of the SUV. Last night Nils had been crowded tight with a stranger. Tonight he felt he knew Bly a little better, but the space between them had opened like an endless, dark ocean. If he hadn't been able to hear her breathing, Nils might not have known that Bly was there beside him at all.

He wondered if those thoughts spinning in his head would keep him awake.

They didn't.

13

DAYLIGHT TICKLED NILS' EYES and he woke. Bly was looking out the window and had pulled the corner of the curtain farther open so that sunlight canted in around her. It was early but not the break of day.

Nils got up quietly, went to the bathroom, and ran some wet fingers through his hair. He came out and found Bly still at the window. What view of the redwoods he could see through the little space where the curtain was open was spectacular. It would have been even more spectacular if he hadn't been so hungry. They'd snacked last night as he drove but had not eaten a real meal since the galettes in Kingston. That seemed a million miles away now.

Nils rounded the bed and came beside Bly at the window. "Pull it. I'm up."

She rattled the curtain wide and the view opened to giant redwoods blooming like sentinels up a mountain slope. Across the street at the base of the slope was another larger parking lot and a building and signs for an attraction.

Bly spread her arms as if to absorb the view. "Where are we?" It was the same question she'd asked the night before. This morning she amended it. "California?"

"Yeah. Near the top."

"Hmm." It was a pensive *hmm*.

"You've never been to California before?"

"No. Is this what it looks like?"

"It's what it looks like here."

Bly scanned the view across the road. "I like it." She pointed out the window. "What's that?"

"Roadside attraction."

"I didn't notice it last night."

Nils hadn't either.

"And what's that?" She pointed again.

"Tree?"

Bly pointed with more emphasis. "The big guy."

"Paul?" There was a giant statue of Paul Bunyan across the road, towering maybe fifty feet over the lot and the entrance, Paul with one big boot forward, resting a hand on an enormous axe.

Bly raised an eyebrow.

Nils filled in his answer. "Bunyan?"

"Vaguely rings a bell. The logger?"

"Lumberjack."

"Same thing."

"Not if you're a lumberjack."

Bly didn't argue. "He's big."

"That's part of the story."

She pointed again. "And the big blue bull?"

"Ox. Paul's big blue ox. Babe."

"I thought Babe was the pig."

"You spent your childhood reading, and you don't know who Paul Bunyan and his big blue ox are?"

"I've heard of them. I guess I was more into guillemots."

Nils thought it was a joke. He laughed a little. Bly seemed pleased. Good. "This might be your lucky day. Great big slice of Americana right there across the street waiting for you, if you want it."

"Looks roadsidey."

"You say that like it's a bad thing. It is roadside. It's literally on the side of the road."

"You read me wrong, Nils. I like roadsidey."

"That's not even a word."

"But you know what I mean."

"I do."

"Americana, here I come."

"Unless we're in a hurry?"

"Not that much of a hurry." Bly was still taking in the scene. "Paul looks interesting and everything, but those trees might be the real attraction."

"Definitely."

"So what are we waiting for?"

Nils picked up his wallet. "Breakfast. And lots of coffee."

They walked to the café attached to the motel. Bly had her jacket but took it off. "Warmer here."

"Cooler by the water. And gets really hot if you go inland down toward the valleys."

"You know your way around this part of the country."

Nils shrugged. "A little."

Bly opened the door to the café. "Talk to me when we get to a beach."

They ordered breakfast and coffee. Nils casually asked the woman working there about the attraction across the street. She winked. "Redwoods, rope walk up in the trees, gondola ride. What's not to like?"

Bly mouthed *better than roadsidey*. Nils replied with a grin.

When they had finished eating, Nils laid down cash for both meals. Bly watched and didn't say a word.

Then they carried the few things they'd taken to the room back to the truck, and Nils waited while Bly went back to check them out.

That done, Nils started the truck, drove straight out of the motel lot, straight across the street, and straight into a spot in the lot across the street. "We're here."

Bly opened her door. "What a trip."

When they approached Paul, the big statue spoke. The words were apparently aimed at a young boy who had wandered under Babe the big blue ox and was gazing up at the animal's underside. Maybe wondering at Babe's anatomical integrity. Nils knew if it was truly an ox, there would be something missing.

Paul said to the boy, "Are you having a good time today?"

The boy leaned out from under Babe and looked up at Paul with a thumb up.

Paul said, "Groovy."

Nils leaned to Bly's ear. "That's lumberjack talk. Part of the folklore."
She smiled. "Groovy."

Nils paid cash for tickets and they went in. Bly stopped for everything. She ran a hand over the redwood carvings of people and animals,
touching fingers into the gouges made by the big saw blades and chisels.
She read the placards and looked at the various formations and arrangements of trees indicated by them.

When they came to a very large tree in the path, Bly stepped onto
a root and stretched her arms onto the trunk. "How many of us do you
think it would take to reach around and touch hands?"

Nils stepped up next to her. "You think they're big around, look up."

Bly did. "I ain't in New Jersey no more." She leaned into Nils. "And
that's not lumberjack talk."

The intensity Nils had seen in Bly seemed to have melted away. She
was relaxed and fun. He remembered the feeling when he'd first encountered her, on the mountain on Orcas Island, when she'd touched him and
the world had seemed to tilt and skew with a wild intoxication. It was an
effort for him to remember now that he was not with her for fun. They
had business to attend to.

"Nils?"

"Yeah."

"Where are you?"

He was on the root. "Just thinking."

"You seem lost."

"Nope."

"Then come on. There's stuff to see."

He imagined for a moment that Bly would take his hand, but instead she shuttled off through the redwoods. The strangeness for Nils
was still that a few days ago all he'd wanted was to be alone. Now solitude was a distant stranger. But what of Bly? Was she as she seemed?
And what of the trouble that still faced them? How had it slipped so
easily from his thoughts?

Nils left those thoughts behind when they entered the canopy walk.
It was wondrous, but if there was one thing Nils feared, it was heights.

Bly showed no such fear. She clambered up the wooden steps to the platforms and swinging rope bridges.

Nils moved slower and was swallowed up by others on the ropewalk trail. When he finally descended again to solid ground, Bly was waiting for him. "Again?"

"I'll wait."

Her look was quizzical.

"You seem to enjoy it so much."

"Don't you?"

He twirled a finger upward. "Heights aren't my favorite thing."

"You came down off the bluff on Orcas all right."

"I didn't have to look down. It was just rock in front of me."

"All right. We don't have to do it again."

"Yes, we do."

"I could go alone."

He pointed. "Go."

Bly did, running off like a kid in a—well, in the redwoods.

And as he watched her go, Nils felt again that tiny little twinge of something in his body that wondered if Bly would come back, or if she would disappear and all of the past few days would evaporate as if they hadn't been real.

He took a deep breath and centered himself. *Nils, what are you doing?*

Bly returned from her second trip in the canopy walk, and they moved to the gondola. Bly pointed to the gondola basket. "Enclosed."

Nils had noticed. "I'll be fine."

They queued up. It was still fairly early in the day, and the line was short. Bly got the attention of a guy working the rig and pointed to a sign in the trees. "Is that a trail entry?"

The guy shook his head. "Not an entry. Exit only."

Bly cocked her head. "Where's the entry?"

He pointed up. "Top. You can only walk down."

"But not up?"

His head shook no.

"Why's that?"

"Well I guess you could if you really wanted. But people don't do it. Too steep."

"Oh."

"A lot of people can't even make it down."

The line moved and Nils' and Bly's gondola came and they stepped into it. The door slid closed and Nils sat. The thing swung a bit when they moved, but it was steady and slow and he could look out and up and not down and be fine. Bly could look anywhere she liked.

The ride to the top wasn't long, and they exited onto decks that offered views over the redwood hills. They spent some time gawking with the others at the top.

Eventually Bly got antsy and turned back toward the landing. "Let's go see what that trail is all about."

They went over and read the caution sign. It didn't look too bad. The gist was that it was steep and slippery and for prepared hikers only. Not for the faint of heart or weak of knee. Reasonable footwear, please.

They descended.

A few other hikers were walking down. They passed them and encountered a couple more who had turned around and warned Nils and Bly to do the same. The two who'd given up had bare feet in sandals, one of them in flip-flops. Nils didn't take that as a warning they needed to heed.

The entered a stretch where it was just Nils and Bly. The trail grew steeper. The ground was dry and the little rocks and dirt were slippery on the slopes. They came to a long, thick rope tied to the side of the trail and used that to control their descent.

Nils thought it really wasn't for the faint of heart or feeble of footwear, but it wasn't overly challenging for him and Bly. Much easier than climbing down the bluff on Mount Constitution.

Bly reached the bottom of the rope hold and let go. She picked up the pace to a jog on a less steep stretch. Nils stayed right with her.

They came to a washed-out slope with a deep rut in the trail. It was steep enough for a rope, but there wasn't one here. It was clear that when the rain came it ran right down the rut in the center of the trail.

Bly slowed but kept a steady pace down. The trail made a turn and there was another long rope down a steep, slippery grade. They navigated that and still hadn't seen any other hikers since they'd been near the top.

Nils had caught a few glimpses of gondolas slipping by high overhead in the trees. Now one slid by lower than the others. He figured that meant they were nearing the bottom of the trail and the tram station.

The trail dipped steeper again and was peppered with rocks and roots. Bly slowed. Nils watched his feet. Then there was a sharp turn in the thick trees and Bly stopped cold. Nils high-stepped and kicked to avoid running into her from behind.

His mind said *snake*, but Bly's posture said something else. She stood akimbo on the trail, hands on her hips and elbows jutting out, staring down at a large shape below.

The shape lumbered and moved and took the shape of a man. A very large man. Bly called down the slope. "Zeke?"

The Zeke-shape looked up. He'd been moving slowly, holding onto branches and limbs and looking down at his feet. Far enough not to be too near them, but close enough that Nils could tell the man was probably sweating.

"Warbly, honey. I hoped we wouldn't find you."

Zeke wore a black New York Giants warm-up jacket and looked like he could play for the team if he was twenty years younger, thirty pounds lighter, and quicker on his feet.

Bly stood immutable, as if she was some solid thing that had sprouted from the ground or from the trees themselves. "I'm not coming home."

"Now, honey…"

"You can tell daddy—"

A big hand came up. "You know ain't nobody can tell Dommy a thing he don't want to hear."

Zeke had stopped ascending toward them. Nils could tell even from where they were above him on the trail that the man was working to level out his breath.

Bly hadn't moved. "What are you doing here?"

"Looking for you, sweetheart."

"The card. I shouldn't have used it."

"Honey…"

"You can tell daddy—"

"I told you." Zeke's words had hardness now, no longer placating. "I'm real tired. We been all night coming here to look for you, and I ain't in the mood for a lot of games." He straightened, and Nils saw it, the shape of the old linebacker stretching up to intimidate the opponent. "Already games enough, out here in this shit…"

Bly shifted her stance, hands coming off her hips but still tight at her sides. Nils wondered at the day pack on Bly's back, if the pistol was in it. Reality rushed back, Zeke, the linebacker, blocking the play from below. Bly was mystical, but she was a stranger to Nils, and he'd taken on faith what she'd told him was her role in these proceedings. Now he might find out how much truth was behind her story.

Nils backed a couple of steps up the trail behind Bly.

Zeke's eyes caught Nils moving. "This the guy?"

Bly stepped sideways to block what she could of Zeke's view of Nils. "What are you doing here, Zeke?"

"You know why we're here."

Nils caught it again. *We*.

"You was supposed to be on an island with a uh—boyfriend." He said it like it hurt his mouth to form the words. "But Dommy knew. He knew that wasn't where you were."

"You tracked the card. Daddy said he wouldn't do that."

"Your daddy's always watched over you. He knows. We all know. You two ain't getting along like you should."

A guttural sound crept from Bly.

Nils backed another step up the trail.

Zeke's hands were parked in his jacket pockets. "This thing with Jimmy. It's ain't a coincidence that you're smack in the same place as what all everyone is looking for the guy Jimmy was with."

The language was garbled, but Nils knew Zeke was talking about him.

Bly wasn't having it. "I saw what your fed guys did on Orcas."

Zeke's big head wagged. "That wasn't us. We weren't even on the island. Dommy wouldn't let us."

Bly glared.

Zeke took one big step up the trail, his foot rising and falling like Paul's giant foot on the statue out front. "Dommy don't like how that went down. Crazy shit. Too public. And they couldn't even get you." He reached for a trunk and pulled himself up. "It's just us here now. Just family."

Something in Bly's stance shifted. She spoke to Nils without turning to him. "Start back up."

He already had. And Nils wasn't sure if Zeke had heard what Bly had said, but the man's eyes went to Nils. "What all you want with this guy anyway?"

"Same as daddy does."

"Now you know that ain't gonna work. We just need to talk to your friend. Ask a few questions. Be real nice."

"I know what happened to Jimmy."

"Jimmy weren't family no more. He turned. You're still family. You'll always be family. You got to come home."

"Nils." Bly still didn't turn. "Why aren't you going?"

It was a good question. Stay with Bly, or run away to—what?

Zeke sweated another step up the trail. "You know this can't play out like you want it. Dommy won't let you go. And he won't let—" he gestured now at Nils— "this guy—"

"You can't have him."

"That ain't all up to you."

Bly eyed Zeke. "This has been coming between me and daddy for a long time."

"Aw, honey. Now don't say that."

"I've always liked you, Zeke."

"And I've always liked you, Warbly. You was like a daughter to me."

"Who else is here?"

"Aww."

"Who else?"

Zeke didn't say, but one hand moved inside a big jacket pocket.

"You can't shoot him. You need him."

"Dommy don't want him dead. He don't need to get banged up if we don't have to."

"You won't catch us."

"Petey's here."

Bly twitched. "That city boy wouldn't come here. He can't stand the dirt."

Zeke took another ragged step up. "Petey does what he has to."

Bly backed up a step.

Zeke looked up the slope to Bly. "We don't have to do this. Dommy just wants you to come home. And he wants this guy. We can do it all real friendly."

Bly took another step back and she had retreated nearly to Nils.

Zeke called louder. "Warbly."

Bly grabbed Nils, spun him and pushed. "Go."

They ran up the mountain. Bly moved like she was trying to win a medal. Nils worked to stay with her, nerves and adrenaline making the effort easier.

"Dommy is my father."

"I figured."

"Dominykas."

He hadn't figured it was short for Domino.

"And Zeke…" Bly breathed, scrabbled on the grade. "Zeke is Zeke. He's known me since I was a kid. Zeke could be a real nice guy if he had the chance."

"And if he doesn't have that chance?"

"You saw Zeke."

A freight train.

"It's Petey that scares me."

"Who's Petey?"

They reached one of the long ropes. This time they used it to pull themselves up instead of steadying themselves down, Bly going first and using her arms to gain thrust and balance.

"Petey taught me to fight."

Nils had seen some of Bly's moves. He wondered what else she'd learned to do.

"But Petey liked it too much. He likes hurting people." Bly high-stepped and pulled herself over slippery grade. "He liked hurting me."

There it was. Nils heard a hurt in Bly's voice. A darkness at what she remembered.

"Petey has a…loose switch. He thinks he's a berserker."

An image formed in Nils' head. "The Viking thing?"

"It's my fault. Petey was always crazy. Then I told him about the berserkers. You remember I said I used to read a lot?"

Nils remembered.

"I told Petey the berserkers were crazy and did drugs to fight better and thought they could change into animals and—"

"Heeyyaaah!"

"Oh, shit." Bly climbed faster and reached the top of the rope. She looked back for Nils.

Nils cleared the rope. "He can't catch us."

Bly was already running again. "Maybe."

Nils ran at Bly's heels. "What do we do when we get to the top?"

"If it's just Zeke and Petey…"

That wasn't an answer.

"We might have to go off trail."

They'd done it before. And Nils would follow Bly again if that's what she did.

The high, keening yell came up the mountain again. "Heeyyaaah!"

Nils didn't have to ask if it was Petey. The way Bly ran told him it was. Petey, the berserker. Berserking up the mountain after them.

"Woooormbleee-eeeyyy."

"Aw, fuck. I'd forgotten about that."

"Wormbleeeey. The wolf is here!"

"Don't call me that, shithead!"

"Worm-bly!"

"Wolf-head!"

They reached another rope and Bly started up. "Nils, stay with me."

"I'm right here."

"Awoooo-ooooo."

"He thinks he's a wolf."

"I got that."

"Wooo-oo-ooohooo."

"It's his berserker animal shape."

The rope ended at a sharp rise and a hairpin turn. Bly grabbed limbs and trunk to pull herself up. Nils came close behind her, almost tucking himself under her elbow as they rose.

Then Bly stopped short. Nils shot past. He slowed and looked back. Bly had stepped back around the turn. She had a hold of the top of the rope and was trying to swing and slap it against the ground. "Petey!"

"Aaa-rooooo!"

The rope was long and heavy, but Bly's efforts had some effect. At the bottom of the rope, trying to take hold, was a thin man with wide shoulders and kinky black hair. He wore a shiny and rumpled gray business suit jacket. Beneath it was a t-shirt with something printed on it.

Bly yanked and slapped the rope again. "Petey. You whore."

In a different situation, Nils might have blanched at the language. "Wormbly!"

Petey gripped the rope and tried to steady it.

Nils stepped down and touched Bly's shoulder. "Let's go." He could see now the wolf printed on the front of Petey's t-shirt, a big, ugly thing with horns and a long snout and fangs that bugged out and bobbed with Petey's arms as they worked the rope. That made it look like the wolf on the shirt was laughing.

"Petey, you shit."

"Wormbly!"

The wolf continued to rise.

Nils touched Bly's shoulder again. "He's coming. Let's go."

Bly held.

Nils tightened his touch on her arm. "Let's go."

Bly twitched, turned to Nils, then back to the rope and Petey.

"We need to go."

The rope fell from Bly's hands. She turned with Nils and he ran back up the mountain. But Bly was not with him. She'd folded herself into the trees and shadows at the turn and rise in the trail.

Nils saw a head of kinky hair emerge at the steep turn. A jacketed arm swung up to seek a hold and climb. The wolf rose.

Bly glided from the trees. A sylph stalking the wolf.

Petey pulled himself up, the wolf on his shirt grinning with the wolf on his face.

Bly turned in a graceful arc.

Petey's eyes caught sight of the movement.

Bly spun through that graceful arc, swift and sure, her foot rising to connect with the side of Petey's head with a sound like wet mulch dropped onto concrete.

The wolf's grin froze, sagged, and fell.

Bly spun for another kick.

Petey tucked a shoulder and got under the foot, twisted and flipped both him and Bly into the dirt. "Ah-roooo!"

Bly and the wolf toppled and disappeared down the rope.

"Ah-roooo!"

Nils ran back down to the turn. Below him was a tangle of arms, legs, and wolf parts, the grinning image on Petey's shirt flashing beneath the shiny suit jacket.

Bly's knee emerged from the tangle and connected with a sharp thud into Petey's jaw. The wolf flopped and rolled but didn't stay down. Petey and Bly slipped down the slope. The wolf broke from Bly's grip and raised haltingly to his feet, bent at the waist and arms scrambling, trying to stop his downward slide.

Petey looked insane. Nils wondered what substances might be coursing through his brain.

Then the wolf lunged, a move that looked practiced and true, a dip and roll that swept a leg out and tilted Bly off her feet. "Rooo-ooo!"

Bly was already spinning through the fall, fighting Petey's leg off, coming to her feet. She spun and kicked again.

Petey's hands waved and parried in front of him. The kick landed but glanced. "Ah-r—"

Bly's next kick landed with authority.

Petey tried to recover and block.

Bly stepped back and gave him room. Petey took the bait and stepped into the space she'd opened, and Bly spun fast, backward, and dug an elbow deep into Petey's neck.

The wolf whimpered. "Ooooh."

Bly slapped at Petey and swept a foot from under him. Petey fell, scrambled, rolled, and slipped, and grabbed wildly for the rope. He got a hold with one hand and steadied.

When his gaze came up, Bly's foot pressed into Petey's forehead. Bly pushed.

The wolf tumbled, ass over shiny city-boy suit coat and shoes. "Ah-ah-rooo!"

Bly jumped down after him. "Nils! Let's go!"

Nils did. He said he would, and he did, taking the rope behind Bly and going down fast after Petey.

Petey came to rest on his hands and knees, banged up and facing up the steep slope toward Bly, who clung to the rope.

Petey reached and grabbed for Bly. She planted a foot on the ground and pushed, swinging on the rope in an arc around the wolf. Nils tumbled and slipped, keeping hold of the jangly line.

The wolf's paw grabbed nothing but air. "Roooooo."

Bly slid to the end of the rope, let go, and ran, Nils right behind her. He sweated and watched his steps. "What now?"

"Go. He'll be packing."

"That doesn't answer—"

"Zeke."

The big man stood in the path like an iron gate.

Bly didn't slow or break stride. She ran harder, straight at Zeke.

Zeke's eyes widened and his hands came up.

Bly jumped, lifted, used the slope to gain altitude against the big man. Zeke ducked.

Bly jumped nearly over him, shins and feet catching Zeke's shoulder. She windmilled her arms and landed, feet scrambling and slipping.

Speed, gravity, and the angle had worked for Bly. Zeke was slow. He bobbled for a moment, tottering like the seven pin on a seven-ten split. Then he toppled and sat down backward hard.

Nils zoomed by like a colt with a horsefly on its ass.

Then Nils was streaming through the giant trees with Bly, past the gondola station and under the ropewalk trail. Down through the entry building and out into the parking lot and the sun.

Bly pulled Nils and they veered into the trees bordering the lot. There they slowed, and Bly kept them hidden in the trees and took them in an arc around the lot and out to the road.

They emerged at a curve that gave them line of sight to the parking lot and the building if they stepped from the trees. Bly bent at the waist and—giggled?

Nils frowned, confused.

Bly stopped the laugh. "Sorry. It's just that—I've been waiting my whole life to kick Petey's ass."

Nils didn't know what came over him. Something sudden. He leaned his head back and opened his mouth. "Ah-rooooo."

14

NILS WIPED A PALM across his brow. "It's not funny."

"I know."

"We shouldn't be laughing."

"I know. But Nils?" Bly tilted her head back. "Aah-roooo."

He worked hard not to grin.

"Sorry. I just, you know…" She composed herself now and the giggles went away.

"It's a release."

Bly eyed him. "Of a sort. Getting the best of Petey. After all these years." A bird called. A tiny breeze found its way through the redwood trees. "This is going to sound awful."

Nils waited.

"I wish I hadn't been born into my family."

The birds quieted and the breeze calmed, as if the redwoods had stopped to listen. "It's not so awful."

"You know how Petey treated me when I was little? He's only seven years older than me, but he treated me like—you know what kind of thing he used to call me?"

"Wormbly."

Bly rolled her eyes. "Twerp. Egghead. Dunce—mental midget."

"Ouch."

"He made fun of my books. That was the only thing—my only way out. I didn't go to school. I had tutors, lots of them. Old women who home-schooled me. It was just a job to them, nothing personal. No connection. They were the only women in my life and they were just—distant. I didn't have friends, I didn't play sports, I didn't go to sleepovers. There was no one to go to a sleepover with."

Nils listened. Birds chirped, and Nils listened.

"It was just me. Alone. I was *dying* for friends. They came in the books, and Petey..."

A strand of Bly's hair raised on an unimaginably fleeting breeze.

"Petey stole them. He threw away my books. It was like he was throwing away my friends."

Double ouch.

"There were no school dances."

Nils could relate.

"No graduation party. No college. I took online courses. Business. Accounting. Things that could help daddy." Bly found the dancing hair and brushed it away from her face. "He never took me anywhere. We never went to the beach. I can't remember seeing the ocean as a kid, and it was *right there*."

"That one we can fix."

Bly sighed. "Daddy was busy with *the business*. Mother was gone. It wasn't until I was an adult that I spent much time around anybody except just a few people. And then it was *family*. Introducing me to the people who did things. Things I needed to know about, for the business. People who did things I would never do." A big sigh leaked out. "It felt like I went from being a kid to being an adult in one step. And now daddy wants me locked into that life. Forever."

It was a lot to take in. Nils tried.

"I don't have the stomach for it. I never did. Jimmy Cheek knew it. Petey knows it. Zeke has always known. Everyone knows. I can't do it. It's not me."

And for that, Nils was glad.

"Daddy won't let me go. If I do, he'll make them come get me. And they'll do whatever daddy says. They have to. And now this FBI thing. I thought..."

It hung in the air for a while, twisting. Nils tried to finish it. "You thought you could use it to blackmail your father and get away from him."

The look on Bly's face told Nils she didn't like the way that sounded. He tried again. "How would you put it?"

"Well, there's no other way to say it. I guess it's like that."

"And you can't just walk away?"

Bly's head shook no. "I've explained that."

Had she?

"I have to see this through. One way or another. Daddy has to see that..."

Nils didn't want to fill this one in for her. But there was a niggling thought. "You might show him that you're serious about not wanting the family business, but this could do something else instead."

Bly was listening.

"If you find the files Jimmy took, or if you show that they can't be found, if you put this to rest one way or another, it could show that you're capable. You've already found me, and your father's men and the FBI agents couldn't."

"You mean...?"

"You're capable. You said they don't think you are, but look..." Nils spread his arms. She'd gotten him.

"It might show that I have some skills. But what I have in mind won't show that I'm loyal."

That seemed fair.

"And I could never do the other stuff."

The things the wolf would do.

"They'll keep looking for me." Bly shifted, antsy now, breaking the spell. "Sorry. I don't know where all that came from. Something broke loose."

Nils resisted the urge to let rip another howl.

Bly glanced around the trees and the road as if she'd just realized where they were. "Look, if you want to quit now, I'm okay with that. Just tell me where to look. I know the shovel might not be there, and I know it might not lead to anything and I might never find those files Jimmy took. But I have to try this. I have to look until there's nothing else to look for. And if I never find anything, if all this just disappears, I'll look for another way out from daddy. Just tell me where to go."

The redwoods were quiet.

"I said I was with you."

"I'm giving you an out if you want."

"Bly." Nils reached a hand out.

She looked at the hand.

"I'll go with you." Nils' hand stayed out palm up, waiting. "I have some things to settle here too."

Now Bly reached for Nils' hand. She took hold of it and shook once, firmly, and let go.

Nils looked at his hand then put it back at his side. It wasn't a shake that he'd wanted. Still, her touch was bewitching. Interesting—Bly had been alone and wanted people. Nils had been around people and wanted to be alone. What would this mixing of matter and antimatter between them result in?

Bly was thinking now, getting focus. "They want you because you were with Jimmy. If I can find what Jimmy took, they'll forget about you. Or if we can show that there's nothing to be found, maybe they'll let you go. That's what you get out of this."

"All right. We need the truck. Why did you take us here?"

"Caution. The truck is clean. I didn't want them to see us in it."

"So we wait?"

A sound carried through the trees and broke their conversation. "*Warbly…*"

They stood in the shadow of the trees where they couldn't be seen and looked back at the parking lot and listened.

"*Warbleey…*"

It wasn't big Paul calling. They could see Paul but not Zeke. Zeke they had to imagine, standing out by the trees with Paul, lowing like Babe the big blue ox for his little lost bird, Warbly.

"I hated to do that to Zeke."

"I know."

"I had to."

"I know that too."

"Warbleey?"

Did it seem fainter now?

Bly took her backpack from her shoulders. "I have an idea." She extracted a bottle and drank.

Nils hoped that wasn't the idea. He floated his own. "They probably know we'll be headed south. And the general area, whatever Jimmy could tell them." Nils got a bad feeling. "I hope they didn't do anything to the business I worked for."

Bly picked up on that. "What they'd probably do is pay them off. See what they could learn."

"If they were lucky. It sounds like your father's men might do more than that. Or the FBI."

Bly pulled her phone from a pocket in the pack. "What's the name of the place you worked for?"

Nils gave it to her. Bly held the phone out, got a signal, and swiped. When she found something, she pushed the phone toward Nils. "Is this it?"

He looked. It was. The website said they were temporarily on hiatus and to check back later for details.

"That make sense to you?"

Nils shook his head. "No. They were booked out for the summer."

Bly scrolled down. "Notice here about saving your credit or getting a refund."

"That's not good."

"Sounds like somebody knows about where we're headed."

"We already kind of knew that. Jimmy would have told them."

Bly lowered the phone. "I don't know if that makes it harder or…"

"Or something. Why do you still have your phone?"

She stared at him. "It's a burner."

"Mine was a burner. You made me get rid of it."

"You called the FBI on yours."

Right.

"I didn't." Her phone went back into the pack. "We're going to need to get rid of the credit card. And the I.D. Avoid temptation."

"Uh-huh."

"And we're going to need some cash."

"I have cash."

Bly grunted. It wasn't lady-like. "We've talked about this."

"We have."

She stared again. "Can you get to it?"

"I already have."

Her look said *what does that mean?* and *how'd you get cash?* What she asked was "How long?"

"We can go for a while."

"Okay." Bly swung her pack back on. "We're going to need a place to hole up and figure out what to do next. How to do it."

"First we're going to need the truck."

"Like I said, I have an idea. If that kid is still by the restrooms smoking and looking at his phone."

Nils hadn't noticed a kid.

Bly backtracked them through the trees around the perimeter of the lot the way they'd come. When they were behind the restrooms, out of view of the lot and the building, she stopped.

The kid was standing ten feet away, a thin teenaged boy in pants that were too tight for anything practical and a black concert t-shirt for a band Nils didn't know. The kid hugged the shrubs behind the restroom wall. His hair fell over his face but didn't quite hide the look of tranquility there. The tranquility didn't come from the nicotine. It came from the phone the kid's face was buried in.

Bly tapped Nils' shoulder and whispered. "The key."

Nils gave her the truck key. Bly stepped from the trees and walked quickly but casually to the kid. The kid didn't look up until Bly was close enough to touch him.

Then he jumped.

"My friend and I need a favor."

The kid's eyes roamed over Bly.

"It'll be easy for you. You can make some money."

The kid stopped looking at Bly the way a teenaged boy would and scanned around the restrooms.

Bly stepped closer to keep his attention. "There's no trouble in it.

We just need somebody to go get our truck. Can you drive a stick?" She reached to her pocket, pulled out a bill and held it up.

"A stick?"

"Stick shift. Manual transmission." Bly made motions with her hand.

The kid's eyes shifted, still checking for other people. There weren't any. He looked at Bly, looked at the money. "Can't be that hard."

"I asked if you've ever done it."

"I've driven an ATV." Now he made motions with his hands. "It shifts. Same thing." He shrugged. "I know how it works."

"You have a few minutes? Anyone looking for you?"

The kid gave a short, staccato laugh. "My mom and sister could probably look at stuff in the gift shop all day."

"Good." Bly held out the money and the key.

"Why do you need somebody to get the truck? Are you stealing it?"

"Does it matter?" Bly pulled the money and the keys back. "Maybe I asked the wrong person."

"Wait."

She reached to her pocket and added another bill to what she'd been holding out. "You don't know anything. These are my keys. You're just doing a favor. I asked you to bring the truck around for me. You're a nice guy, so you did. You didn't even take this money I'm holding out for you." Bly winked.

That did it. It was a bigger adventure than smoking an illicit cigarette behind the bathrooms. Bly described the truck and where she would be, and the kid was off.

Then Bly was back with Nils and they were re-tracing their way through the trees again. Bly took them out of the foliage near where they had emerged the first time.

The truck was there, down the road a bit, moving slowly away from them. Bly ran to the shoulder and waved her arms over her head.

The truck's brake lights flashed. The kid pulled over and let a couple of cars go by, then executed a beautiful three-point turn and drove to where Bly was standing. He executed another perfect three-point turn, this time weaving around a camper van, and pulled to the shoulder where Nils and Bly waited.

The sound of the parking brake clicked, and the driver's door opened. Bly reached for the passenger door, and Nils came around the front of the truck.

The kid jumped out. "Cool."

Nils held out a hand. "Thanks."

The kid looked at the hand.

"Shake. It's what people do."

The kid shook. "Cool."

"You want a ride back?"

"Naw. Walking will give me something to do." Then he sauntered down the side of the road with his head back in his phone.

Nils got in and pulled into the lane. "Nice kid."

"You think so?"

"You don't?"

"I wonder what his mother thinks."

Nils accelerated. "She'll appreciate him one day."

The road stretched out behind them and the kid faded in the mirror. Petey and big Zeke and whoever else might be looking for them were gone. Only Paul lumbered above them in the skyline, until he, too, slipped from view.

15

NILS DROVE down the one-oh-one. The plan was as clear as—what he was doing with this woman beside him. "So…?"

Bly pointed forward. "Let's put some distance."

That made enough sense. Nils kept driving.

Bly watched the road go by. "We need a little town somewhere. Some place to stop. You can show me where we're going to look on that trail. We can figure how to get there without…"

Nils looked over. "Without Petey showing up?"

She nodded. "That would be nice."

Okay. There was some inertia now. Find a town, stay away from Petey, figure out how to get out on the trail where Jimmy had disappeared. He could do that.

The drive was as scenic as advertised. A redwood canopy swept the slopes and disappeared up into the sky. Scents of juniper and musk washed in through the vents. Nils tried to think ahead. "Maybe we could pitch a tent on a beach somewhere?"

"We can do that?"

"People do." Nils held out a hand and tipped it slightly back and forth.

Bly watched Nils' hand tip. "*Comme-çi, comme-ça.*"

Nils chuckled.

"What?"

"I don't think they say that anymore."

"Who?"

He shrugged. "People who speak French."

"They don't?"

"No."

A beat passed. "What do they say instead?"

"For what?"

Now Bly put her hand out and tipped it. "Like this, like that. *Comme-çi, comme-ça.*"

"Maybe that's what it means *literally*. But that's not what people use it for—used it for."

"Well I read it in a book."

"Maybe a textbook."

"Don't make fun of me. Maybe I saw it in a movie. Maybe that's where I saw the hand thing." She did the movement again.

"I'm not making fun of you. You know French?"

"No."

"Watch French movies?"

"No."

"Maybe you did read it in a book."

"Well I picked it up somewhere." Bly grinned. "Nils?"

"Yeah."

"This is kind of fun."

"What is?"

"Just…" She shrugged.

"I was just thinking the same thing."

"I don't usually, you know, just—riff?'"

"I know. You didn't have anyone to play with when you were a kid." What he didn't say was that maybe Bly hadn't had anyone to play with as an adult either.

After a moment, Bly said, "So what do they say?"

"What does who say?"

"People who speak French."

"For what?"

"Instead of *comme-çi, comme-ça.*"

"Oh. If someone asks how you're doing, you say something like *Bof.* Or *on fait aller.*"

"And what do those mean?"

Nils held a hand out flat and tipped it slightly back and forth.

Bly laughed. "So you know some French."

"No."

She tilted an eyebrow.

"I worked with some people came down from Canada. I speak about enough French to order coffee and a crêpe and find the bathroom. You saw me do those things."

"I can do that, and I don't know any French."

"You've never been up to Quebec? A Jersey girl like you?"

"Never."

"Trip to Toronto?"

"No."

"Across the border into Ontario? Or New Brunswick?"

"Why would I go to New Brunswick?"

Nils smiled. "People do."

"I haven't even been to the beach."

Nils called up an image. "We walked on the sand in Oregon yesterday."

"I don't think it counts until I've been in the water."

"You should have mentioned that yesterday."

"I didn't think of it until today."

"Well that's bad timing. The water can be cold up here."

"At least my feet then."

Nils nodded. "Sounds sensible."

They rode for a few minutes. Bly was looking out the window. "Tell me more about the tent thing."

"What about it?"

"You've done it?"

"Slept in a tent on a beach?"

"Yes."

"I've seen it."

"Not the same thing."

It wasn't.

"Is it legal?"

"Depends where you do it."

"Where would we do it?"

Nils thought about it. "Not in a state park. That'd be the same problem we've been running into. Have to be some place without much chance of getting caught. There are some remote beaches. Not easy to get to. I think people camp because there's no one there to tell them not to."

"Probably more trouble than it'd be worth if we got caught."

"Maybe. We'll have to sleep somewhere. Pitch a tent in the redwoods. Probably hippies still up here from the sixties doing that."

Bly turned one eye to Nils. "Is that a hippie girl reference? Because of what I said earlier?"

"Earlier?"

"At the airport."

He called up the memory. "Oh. The movie star thing."

"*Warbly Milkov and the big redwoods adventure.*"

Nils didn't say anything.

"Well?"

Nils held out a hand, palm down, and tipped it back and forth. "Keep working on it."

They rounded Big Lagoon and passed a sign that said *Redwood Highway*. Then another announced simply *Camping Lodging*, and another proclaimed the *Trinidad Recreation Area*. There were few other cars on the road and it seemed like the middle of nowhere. That seemed like what they were looking for, and Nils took the exit for Sue-meg State Park.

The road was narrow and tight with trees. After a bit it opened to a view of the Pacific down the bluffs. Bly oohed out the window. "You know where we are?"

"Been here once before. The state park was called something else then."

"Uh."

"Little town down here I remember."

And a few minutes later, that little town appeared. It was a handful of blocks with some places to eat, a little grocery, a shop or two, and some houses stretching farther out. There were walkers about, but not a lot of people.

Bly put her window all the way down. Sea air wafted in. "Where is everybody?"

"I think people come here mostly to be out in the redwoods. Or at the beaches."

Nils drove them to a pull-off beside the road where they got out and looked down a steep slope to an empty beach below. Rocks jutted from the sand and from the water beyond. A rounded peninsula humped to the West. The beach was small. To the south and east it dissolved into rocks and bluffs and grasses. The sand was dark and wet.

Bly leaned into the sound of the waves rolling up from below. "I see what you mean."

"About remote places?"

"Yeah. I don't think there's even a way to get down there."

They lingered. Finally, Bly said, "This is the place."

"For?"

"Where we should hole up for a bit."

"I didn't know it was still a question."

Bly sighed. "It's nice here, but we can't get too distracted."

"Who's distracted? You haven't even been to the beach yet."

"I need to do more than see it. We've done that."

"You have to get your feet wet."

"At least."

The place put them in such good spirits that they splurged on lunch. There was a little café with coffee and a good vibe that called to them. They ate and rested and lingered. Bly seemed relaxed and she leaned back in her seat.

Nils worked on the dregs of his coffee. "Work first, or should we see about getting your toes in the ocean?"

A guy working the place walked by and seemed to have picked up on the gist of their conversation. Bly caught his eye and the guy stopped.

She said, "Favorite beach around here?"

"Any of them. All of them."

She gave him a smile of encouragement. "Any in particular?"

"You walking or driving?"

"Walking?"

He described a route to a beach north of town. "Way down is a little tricky. You'll do fine."

"Thanks."

"Another one the other way. A little farther, but some people walk it." The guy winked at Nils. "Fewer people there. Kind of remote. I think you'd like it."

They finished up and left the café. Bly looked back as they exited. "Friendly here."

"You're not in Jersey anymore."

"What do you think?"

"Dealer's choice. It's your feet that need to get wet."

"Second one sounds interesting."

It did.

They went to the truck, made sure they had sunblock and water, and Bly very coyly tucked her pistol into the springs under the seat and insisted that Nils make sure the doors were locked and the windows rolled all the way up.

They found a trashcan in the little clutch of shops and Bly took out the fake credit card and bent it back and forth until it creased and broke. She did the same again with the smaller pieces, then deposited them in the can. She did the same with the fake I.D.

Nils watched. "Now it's just the real you."

Bly gave the movie-star grin and pushed the sunglasses up on her nose. "Just me."

It was mid-afternoon and the sun was high and the air was warm. They were getting a late start, but the light would last. Nils suggested a run. Bly suggested they walk and enjoy the views. They did that.

When they reached the trailhead down the bluff to the beach, it was in deep shade at a gravel pull-off big enough to hold only a few cars. None were parked there. The trail was sandy and narrow and crowded by tall plants and small trees and vines. Signs at the top indicated that camping and fires were prohibited. No problem. There were no facilities, just beach. No problem. It was maintained and protected by community stewardship, and please do your part to keep the beach pristine. Great. Clothing was optional. It was?

Nils read it again. "What do you think?"

"Good thing we used the facilities at lunch. And you were right about the camping."

Nils cut his eyes to the sign.

"I saw it." Bly looked down toward the Pacific. "Seems like nobody's there."

Nils couldn't see the beach below.

Bly clarified. "Based on there being no cars."

"Okay."

She nosed toward the trail. "We can have a look. We walked all this way."

"And your toes aren't wet."

"Not yet."

They went down. The trail bottomed with a steep ladder built from driftwood logs and cables. There was no one in sight, and they had seen no one as they descended the trail.

They removed their shoes and socks, bundled them, and hung the shoes by their knotted laces from their day packs.

It was then that Nils saw they weren't alone. Farther down the beach up at the treeline were a couple of low chairs, with two people of indeterminate age sitting in them. They were nearly but not quite shadowed by the foliage.

Nils could see from where he was the pale line of naked thigh and the outline of a wayward breast, and nothing more.

Bly followed Nils' gaze. "Ever been to a nude beach before?"

"Nope."

"What's the etiquette?"

Nils looked away from the couple. "I can only guess."

There was no one else, and the couple in the chairs seemed unconcerned with Nils' and Bly's presence.

Bly faced the Pacific. "Let's go down to the water."

They did, and the couple disappeared behind them. Bly put her toes in the water, and Nils trailed the edge of the tideline with her. "Now up there behind us in the chair is your free-spirited California hippie girl."

"And a guy with her."

"Far as I could tell."

"Good for them." Bly rolled her pant cuffs up and waded farther into the water.

They aimed for a large rock formation and tidal pools maybe forty feet away. Nils had rolled up his pant cuffs too and now both of them were dipping their toes into the Pacific. The water was cold.

They came out of the water to walk around the rock and heard a yip.

A fortyish woman emerged from behind the formation. She had dark hair cropped at her shoulders and a long, pale body with a few healthy and noticeable curves. She wore nothing and carried a small dog that was draped over one arm. The dog was interested in Nils and Bly and yipped again.

The woman walked toward them and raised the hand without the dog in a brief and silent greeting.

Nils raised a hand back. He wondered where her clothes were. She carried no bag or pack and had nothing with her except the dog and a large sun hat. Maybe her clothes were tucked away somewhere on the beach, or maybe she'd walked here nude?

The woman passed them and smiled. The dog yapped and seemed happy to be carried.

Bly scanned the beach.

Nils scanned too. "Anyone else?"

"Could be." She took the pack from her shoulders and set it on the sand. "I've heard that on a nude beach people might sometimes expect you to be nude."

"You're serious?"

She tugged her shirt up and off to reveal a sports bra. "I seem to be."

"You read that in a book?"

Bly's eyes danced and Nils caught that intoxicating look she possessed. The mysterious but come-hither. The look that said anything was possible, but nothing was a given.

Bly angled from Nils and the bra came off and a hand reached back. "Sunscreen, please."

Nils was with the program. He got the tube and handed it to Bly.

She began to rub lotion over her shoulders and arms. "It's about the freedom. It's not about…"

She turned to him now and Nils saw that Bly's hands had ranged to more delicate places to apply lotion. She seemed at ease and as if she was doing something that was just part of a normal day for her. She handed the sunscreen back to Nils. "You don't have to…be in Rome, if you don't want to." She unzipped her pants and slowly pulled them off. "You can wait here. Or at the top."

Like hell. Nils got his shirt off. "But etiquette."

Bly handed the sunscreen back to Nils and rolled up her pants and stuck them in the pack.

It was slow and excruciating and wild and free and Nils didn't know what they were doing and he didn't care. They lotioned and screened and Bly was naked and then so was Nils and they had their things in the packs and they held them and walked.

Nils kept his eyes mostly on the sand and the water and the rocks, but those eyes were acutely aware of the naked woman beside him. He felt pale next to the subtle hint of color in Bly's skin, like a surfer dude next to the island goddess with the long black hair. He wondered what Bly's eyes were aware of.

They stayed at the waterline and passed by the couple in the chairs up at the treeline. Definitely naked. The woman raised a hand when she saw Nils look in her direction, and Nils raised one back. "Probably less awkward when there's more people. You don't stand out as much."

Bly splashed water with her feet. "You think this is awkward?"

"No. I was thinking of you."

"Sure you were."

Bly separated from Nils and put her toes farther into the water. She danced. "Cold, but it totally counts now."

"It didn't count before when you had your clothes on?"

She pirouetted. "Extra points."

The extra points were spectacular. Nils tried not to keep his eyes on Bly.

"It's a nude beach, Nils." She dropped her pack and ran into the water. Nils followed.

It didn't last long. The rocks were rough and the water was cold. They got out far enough to go under. Then they came back in carefully over the jagged rocks.

Nils tried to be a gentleman. Did he look? He wouldn't tell.

Bly shivered. "You know what's good at a beach?"

"A towel?"

She squeegeed water from her arms with her hands. "Worth it."

For Nils too.

They squeegeed and flicked water from their bodies and Nils was glad for the sun. They carried their packs and walked to dry more and warm.

The woman and her dog were not in sight. Down the beach where they'd come in, Nils could see shapes moving down the trail. The shapes were people. He couldn't tell much more, except that none of them were big enough to be Zeke.

Bly seemed unconcerned, and Nils figured their trail was about as buried as a trail could be. They drifted down the sand, looking at the water and the rocks, looking or not looking at one another and not giving anything away.

They neared the driftwood ladder and found that the beach-goers they'd seen arriving were three young guys who were now undressing on the sand.

Bly casually stopped, opened her pack, and extracted her rolled-up clothes and began to put them on.

Nils did the same.

By the time the men were near, Nils and Bly were fully clothed. As the three passed, one of the men glanced to Bly and gave a quick and snappy salute.

She rewarded him with a smile.

They reached the ladder and Bly went up first. She called back over her shoulder. "Nils?"

"Yeah."

"This doesn't change anything."

He was silent. They both knew it had.

16

THEY WALKED BACK to town. Nils still wanted to run, but Bly favored not getting so gritty without a place to wash up. "In fact, I may want to look for a laundromat."

"You don't seem to have brought much with you in the way of things to wear."

Bly agreed. "This whole thing is taking longer than I expected. And I left some stuff behind on Orcas when…it got dicey."

"Dicey?"

"There wasn't much time to come get you."

When he was in the van. When Bly stopped the crooked feds and took him away from them at gunpoint. Nils had to remind himself that this was the woman Bly was. The kind of woman who could do that sort of thing, and also this other one who walked with him now. Bly was dangerous and complex.

That made him remember the blow to his head and the wound there. He reached up to touch it.

Bly saw the movement. "Almost healed. You'd have to know to look for it."

"Seems like a long time ago."

"It was some time ago. So you understand about the need to do laundry."

Nils looked at what Bly was wearing. T-shirt, pants. He thought she still had the stretchy running pants with her. There was a jacket in the truck. He hadn't seen her wear anything else since they'd been on Mount Constitution.

"And I don't really have anything to wear while I'd do the wash."

"Might be able to get something in town."

"Sure. Probably find a shirt. Pants. Maybe even socks. Might be harder to find personals."

"Personals?"

"What my daddy called them. After mama left us. Everything having to do with women's things became *personal*."

"I see." They walked some more. "To be clear, you're talking about underwear?"

"In this case, yes. You're already more mature about it than my father."

Nils didn't ask if that was a compliment.

The sun was falling and they briefly debated the merits of sleeping on the beach or in the redwood forest. Nils was a woodlands guy and thought that's where they'd be least likely to run into trouble, but he'd seen Bly's penchant for the beach. When they got back to town it was still an open question.

There were places open to eat, but they opted for the grocery and bought fresh fruit, cheese, and bagels. They carried those to the bus shelter at the road and sat on the bench there. Nils took nuts from his pack and they shared some of those.

Bly was making good headway on the berries. "One question though. What do we do if a bus comes? Should we get on it?"

Nils got up and looked at the map on the side of the shelter. "Probably not. We're headed someplace very specific." He ran a finger down the arrival times. "And we went to all that trouble to get the truck."

Bly slid her eyes to Nils. "Joke."

"Oh, sorry."

She laughed. "You are...*something*."

He didn't know what something was, and it didn't sound so bad so he didn't ask. He sat down again and they ate some more.

When they'd finished, Bly passed Nils a napkin they'd taken from the store's deli. "Satisfied?"

He wiped his fingers. "Late lunch helped. Kind of wish that café was still open though."

"Little late for coffee, isn't it?"

"I was thinking I should go back and give that guy a bigger tip." He tried to read her reaction. She looked down, up, then away. "Sorry. Joke."

The corners of her eyes crinkled. "That's one attempt each."

"Touché." Nils got up from the bench. "We probably could have found a better place for a picnic."

"Definitely. Let's walk."

Nils held a hand out. "First, your phone."

Bly looked at his hand.

"Can you get a signal here?"

"Probably."

"Can it be tracked on that phone?"

"Probably not."

Nils' hand was still out, and it was still empty. "And you have some credit left on it?"

"Some."

"You want me to show you where we're going?"

"Oh." Now Bly's phone came out and she handed it to Nils. He pulled up a map of the area where he'd led the hike that Jimmy Cheek had been on. Bly looked over his arm. "So a few hours south of here?"

"Roughly."

"And you have a good idea where we should start looking?"

"I remember where on the trail Jimmy borrowed the shovel. Yeah."

"And you think if he left something out on the trail, that's where it would be?"

"If it's not, we'll probably never find it." What he thought was no, they weren't going to find it. But if he wanted this to end, this seemed the path to take through. "That's where we should look, anyway."

Nils zoomed in and maneuvered around on the map. "I can get us real close. It's going to be around here."

He pointed and they both looked. There was wilderness and the Noyo River and some roads and state forest. There were no street views.

Nils looked closer and tried to remember and pinpoint. They'd been near the river and the old railroad track. What would be a good route if someone was watching the trailhead he'd used for the trip?

Bly was still zooming in and out on the map, looking for details. "Where'd your trip start?"

Nils indicated the area. "It's very near here."

"Long walk."

"It was a nature hike."

Bly frowned and worked the map. "Any other way in? Something quicker?"

"That's what I was just thinking about." He showed her the old train track and the river. "There are paths and trails down here. Lot of the old track is still there. We could walk that."

She tracked it on the map. "Uh-huh. Uh-huh."

"We'll want to pack a few things, travel light. You and I will be able to move quickly. Looking for the shovel when we get there could take a lot longer."

"How long?"

Nils lingered over his answer. "We should set a limit."

Bly looked up from the map. "What do you mean?"

"How long do we look?"

"Like, in days?"

He nodded. "Days."

"Until we find it."

"Is *it* the shovel?"

"Or whatever Jimmy buried with it."

"What if it's hard to find? What if we can't find it? When will we know we're done looking?"

Bly let out a long stream of air and rubbed a palm over her eyes. "Are you trying to make this harder than it already is?"

"I'll need some idea what to pack. How much food."

The palm stopped rubbing. "Let's say three days. Once we get there. Can you look with me for three days?"

It was better than he expected. A shorter time. "That sounds about right." He felt now that there was a potential end in sight, at least to this part of what they were doing.

Bly was done looking at the map and put the phone back in her pocket. "So? First thing in the morning?"

Nils gave a tiny salute, remembered that's what he'd seen the man at the beach do, and killed the gesture. "We leave at dawn."

Bly packed up what was left of the fruit and cheese. "That's just an expression, right?"

"Could be. But we'll leave first thing." If he had to. He liked the feel here.

"Leave from where?"

Nils' brow folded.

"We need digs for tonight."

Right. That hadn't been settled. And it would be dark soon.

Bly lifted her pack. "Reckless of us not to decide where to bivouac sooner."

It was. "Two nights in a row."

"Don't remind me. Redwoods or beach?"

"Redwoods."

"Okay."

"Beach seems more risky. People go there."

"I said okay."

She did. Nils started out of the bus shelter. "I have a place in mind."

"To the redwood forest." Bly didn't seem too sore about not sleeping on a beach.

They went to the truck and got the sleeping bags, tent, and jackets. Nils thought he was happy to see that Bly left the pistol tucked under the seat in the springs. He would be happier to not see the gun at all, but something about knowing it was there stayed with him.

They walked out of town as inconspicuously as possible carrying the gear, Nils with most of it. He took them down the road to a break in the treeline. In the almost faded light, he stepped from the road into the woods.

It was darker under the canopy. The undergrowth was sparse, and Nils took them in far enough to be discreet and where the ground had a soft covering of leaves and needles. He laid the tent down. "We're not supposed to do this."

"Just this one time, boy scout. We'll carry our trash out."

"There won't be any."

"Then we should be okay unless bigfoot finds us."

"I'm more worried about somebody's dog."

Bly looked around. "Really?"

"Probably be okay if you don't smell like bacon."

Bly raised a hand and drew two fingers down through the air. "Failed attempt at a joke number two for you."

"I'll keep trying."

It was an easy-up hiking tent made for one but big enough for two if you didn't have much gear and didn't mind being friendly. Nils figured they were good on both counts, so long as Bly really didn't smell like bacon.

He got the tent up and tossed the sleeping bags in. It was nearly flat-out dark now, and Nils took a small keychain light from his pocket and held it out. "Last chance for a trip into the woods before bed if you need it."

Bly took the light and crunched away through the ferns and duff.

When she came back, Nils had the sleeping bags unrolled in the tent. Bly handed the little light back. "Your turn."

"Already did."

"You *are* a boy scout."

Nils got in the tent first, then Bly. She reached for the tent's zipper. "Leave the backpacks outside?"

Nils pulled his pack in. "Not if you don't want some critter to chew through and eat whatever you've got inside."

Bly pulled her pack in too, and to make more room they tucked them under their heads for pillows.

Bly tried to arrange her head on the backpack. "You really know how to treat a girl."

"You ain't seen nothing yet." It didn't quite feel like a joke to Nils.

"Won't matter. I'll be asleep in a minute."

"No way."

But she was, breathing quietly right next to Nils.

He tried to get comfortable. He tried to do that without moving.

It seemed impossible. He thought about dragging his bag out and sleeping on the ground where he could stretch and roll over. Take his chance with the critters of the woods. Then just when he'd decided that was what he was going to do, he fell asleep.

His dreams were bizarre, though he couldn't remember them. Almost equally bizarre was that he woke with this mysterious woman still curled next to him.

Nils extricated himself from his sleeping bag, unzipped the tent screen, and crawled out. The light was almost there, the forest canopy harboring the illusion of an orange-red glow, if not the reality of it.

He took his jacket from where it hung on the tent pole and walked off to water the redwoods. When he came back he was wide awake and itchy for something. A little run, some push-ups, some kind of distraction that would burn energy.

Instead he sat outside the tent and waited.

A few minutes later the tent flap fluttered. "What are you doing?"

"I didn't want to wake you."

"You did that when you got up to pee."

"Sorry."

"Don't be sorry. Just tell me if you're getting back in here or not."

"Not."

Now there was more movement from inside the tent. "Then I guess I'm getting up too."

Bly came out, huddled, and grabbed her jacket. She started off into the woods.

Nils held up a hand. "Other way."

Bly looked confused. "It's a big forest."

"Light." Nils pointed. "We're closer to a house than I thought."

Bly saw the light and went the other way. A few minutes later she was back and reached down to pull her backpack from the tent. "Should we go?"

"It's dawn. We said we would."

They de-bivouaced quickly, and Nils wondered if that was a word. When they reached the road and headed toward town, Bly watched him closely. "Something on your mind?"

"Is de-bivouac a word?"

She laughed. "You can be so odd." They walked. "Anyway, I know what you mean."

They came to town and Bly went right.

Nils didn't. "Where are you going?"

"Truck."

"Coffee."

Bly held out a hand. "Give me the keys. And your things. I'll meet you there."

It seemed sensible, so he went back to the café where they'd gone the day before and hoped that's what she'd meant. The guy who'd been working the day before wasn't there, so Nils couldn't thank him for the tip about the beach.

No matter. He bought coffees and two breakfast sandwiches to go and had those in hand when Bly found him. She scanned the little town as they walked back to the truck. "I kind of hate to go. Maybe we'll come back here some day."

Nils wondered if Bly had noticed she'd said we.

They left Trinidad and got south of Humboldt Bay and found a dollar store in a little town. Bly went in to look for clothes and personals. Nils walked across the street to a little park to stretch his legs.

The park had swings and a climbing gym, a picnic table, some grass. One area was mostly taken up by a baseball diamond. It looked exactly like a small park in a small town would, except this one was smack in the middle of the redwood forest that Woody Guthrie had sung about.

Nils rounded the bases once as he always did when he came across an empty baseball diamond, then went back to the truck and found Bly waiting there.

"Where'd you go?"

"Home run." He made a swinging motion as if he was holding a bat. Bly obviously didn't know what he meant.

"Baseball field." Still nothing. "Never went to a Yankees game?"

"Huh?"

"Doesn't matter."

Nils backed out and Bly pulled some things from a dollar store bag and tucked them into her backpack. "If my daddy knew I was buying personals at the dollar store…"

"Your father will never know."

"I'll know."

"You'll be all right."

Bly took out a shirt and held it as if trying to decide where to put it.

"You want to change?"

"I want a shower first."

"That's going to be a little harder."

"I bought a swimsuit. We can wash off in the ocean."

They could. "Better than nothing. But I don't have a swimsuit."

She reached into the bag. "I noticed that yesterday. I bought one for you too." She held up a baggy blue thing printed with little suns wearing giant sunglasses.

"Great." Nils didn't think of the swimsuit as a step up from what he'd worn the day before.

They'd planned to drive straight through and get on the trail. Nils wanted to get the three days done. Then they could think about what came next, if there was a next.

But the route put them going down the Avenue of the Giants. It was the most scenic pass through the redwoods, right in the heart of the Humboldt Redwoods State Park. Even for Bly and her quest, it was too much to pass up.

They easily burned through the morning and a good part of the afternoon just on the short walks and attractions near the road. Lunch was the rest of the fruit and cheese and what they had in their packs. They climbed to the top of an enormous felled redwood stump to eat. The food was unremarkable, but the views made it spectacular.

After lunch they burned through the afternoon at a roadside walk through the redwoods. Streams, bridges, fallen trees big enough to build a one-lane road on. Bly finally looked at the time. "Here we go again. How far to Fort Bragg?"

"Couple of hours."

"And how much more to see on the way?"

"Lots."

"And we haven't eaten or got cleaned up or figured a place to sleep tonight."

"That seems to be our way."

Bly turned her face up to the sunlight that filtered through the trees. "Sure is pretty here though."

They reluctantly started south again and got down to Legget. Nils planned to take them from the one-oh-one to the one and toward the coast. But there were signs for the drive-through tree, and they debated.

Nils looked at the sign. "It's still open."

"It's getting late."

"Doesn't look too far."

"And how many times do you get to drive through a tree?"

"Not many."

Bly checked the time. "Seems unkind to the tree."

Nils hadn't thought of it that way. "Can't be helped now."

That convinced them. They drove the old truck through the tree.

Then they headed to the coast road and it didn't take long to find a beach. They stopped and changed into their swim suits in the beach vault toilets. Nils wasn't sure that was better than changing in the privacy of brush and weeds. He came out in the dollar store swim suit feeling dressed like a salesman at a convention searching for the hotel hot tub.

Bly came out wearing a dark blue two-piece that seemed to be hugging her in the right places. Nils looked her over. "Well, yours looks good."

"Thank you. And yours looks…"

"Dollar store-y?"

"For lack of a better word."

"So, one question."

"Uh-huh."

"Did you buy any towels?"

Bly grinned. "Oops."

Nils turned to the beach. "All right. Let's do this. It's going to be cold. And I'm getting really hungry."

They managed to get over the rocks and through the waves and into the water. It was cold. They came out chilled and salted and cleansed of sweat and grit.

Bly put on new clothes, and Nils changed his shirt. He spread the shirt he'd worn over the truck seat to let it air out some.

When they had their feet cleaned of sand and it appeared they were ready to go, Nils looked back at the beach. It was almost empty of people.

Bly looked with him. "I was thinking it too."

"We're close to Fort Bragg. We could stay here. Wait until dark and pitch the tent."

"Love to. But it's too exposed. Too close to the road."

She was right, and Nils drove them away.

At Fort Bragg instead of a place to sleep they found a place called Glass Beach. They weren't going to stop. Both of them said no. It was almost dark. But how many glass beaches were there? Then they found the smaller and even more secluded Secret Glass Beach, and neither of them said no when they got out.

It was a small stretch of sand in a tiny cove that had once been used to dump trash. What resulted over the years was brightly colored bits of broken glass washed clean and smoothed by ocean waves.

They walked the little stretch of sparkly beach. When they walked back to the truck, Bly was quiet. When they got in, she didn't say a word. Nils didn't start the engine. "Something wrong?"

"This has been fun."

That didn't sound wrong.

"But I'm ready."

"Ready for what? To eat?" He was starved.

"No, I've been sight-seeing like I'm on vacation, and I appreciate that. But I don't want to sleep on a beach or in a field. I don't want to see more sights right now. I want to do what we came here to do."

"First thing in the morning."

"Now."

"It's almost dark."

"Nils, I'm ready."

"That's fine, but—"

"We get on the trail now. Pitch the tent. I don't care if it's dark. We've done that in the dark. We sleep in the woods, get up first thing, and go."

"Okay."

"Like we said we were going to do today."

"Okay." Nils started the truck. "I thought you wanted to do all those things today."

"I did. And now I'm ready for what comes next. We can't keep putting this off."

"I'm not putting this off."

Bly clicked her seatbelt. "Sorry, I just…things are a bit mixed up."

"And we're hungry."

"What does that have to do with it?"

"You can't think straight when you're hungry."

"I can."

"Well, I can't." He backed the truck from the parking space. "We'll get some food and supplies and we'll go."

They found a little grocery. They went in and bought food and water, choosing sparingly so they could travel light and move fast.

Less than an hour later, Nils had them inching along an abandoned logging road, searching in the arc of white from the headlights for a break in the growth.

He found one and pulled off the road. The opening broke left through smaller trees and scrub. Nils inched forward and put the truck under a pocket of low-hanging limbs where it was mostly hidden.

They got out and Nils flipped the bench seat forward, pulled out the larger frame backpack, and began to quickly sort the gear and food he wanted. Bly stuffed granola bars and water bottles into the pocket of her backpack.

Nils paused. "Both sleeping bags?"

Bly raised an eyebrow in the dome light.

"I can do it with two. It'll just take up more room. We can go faster with only one."

"Okay."

Nils finished packing and he hoisted the frame onto his back. Bly shouldered her smaller day pack. They tied their jackets around their waists and locked up the truck. Then they walked cautiously out under the moonlight.

Nils took them across the abandoned road. "We're just going to get down the slope some. Toward the river. Find a place to pitch the tent and sleep and then we'll cut a path in the daylight down to the rail line. That will take us far enough we can bushwhack over to the trail where I led the group with Jimmy in it."

Bly let him lead. They went slow in the dark, off trail, downslope, watching their feet and searching for a place to sleep, as the giant redwoods swallowed them up.

17

MORNING BIRDSONG FLITTED through the big trees. Nils and Bly had made it down the slope the night before in the dark—not a good idea, but they'd done it, and camped on a flat spot in the redwoods near the Noyo River. Behind the birdsong, if he listened, Nils could hear water percolating over rocks on the river.

What he couldn't hear was Bly. She'd gone off to do morning things while Nils heated water on the tiny camp stove to make coffee. The stove was fragile, made only of a wire frame that screwed onto a miniature canister of gas. Nils could get the little pot to balance on the stove if he dug the bottom of the canister into the dirt to keep it from tipping over.

That would heat enough water for two small cups of coffee, but they only had one cup. He compensated by putting extra grounds into the pot to make the coffee strong. It was cowboy coffee, grounds boiled in water. You waited a few minutes for most of the grit to settle, poured off the top of the pot into the cup, and didn't worry too much if things got a little thick toward the bottom as you drank.

He and Bly could share the one cup, or he could let her drink one and then boil another for himself. They were getting friendlier, and he wondered how this would go. The gas in the canister wouldn't last long if they got in the habit of double-boils. Worst case, they could switch to cold brew. Dump some grounds into a water bottle and wait for it to darken. It would be air temp brew, not cold brew. Not as good, but it was what they could do.

There was no cream and nothing that should be kept cold except sandwiches they'd bought at the grocery and would eat for breakfast and lunch today before they could spoil. Then it would be cold food and no cooking for the rest of the trip. Nuts, turkey jerky, tuna in sealed pouches, raisins and seeds, granola, enough bagels for the first day or two. Chocolate that he'd bought without letting Bly know. Nils would save that for later.

It would be lean and fast and hard going. He knew Bly could do it, maybe better than he could, for the three days they'd allotted. But this morning there would be coffee, and more coffee as they wanted it, at least while the gas for the stove held out.

It was just Nils, the stove, the pot of water, the tent, sleeping bag, and packs. Birds, trees, river. This was the first he'd felt alone and quiet since Orcas Island. Since he'd sat in the dark on the little strip of beach in Eastsound and listened to the orcas sing, since the solitude of paddling the channel and the night on Clark Island. The most still he'd felt since the solstice parade.

Nils watched a fat, lazy banana slug on a downed redwood limb. The slug neither watched Nils nor knew he was there. Alone on a different plane. The water boiled and Nils let the brew steep, then swirled the pot to help the grounds fall to the bottom. The coffee hissed when he poured it into the cup.

Then Nils sensed a subtle change in the sound of the birdsong, an imagined shift in the quality of the particles of air around him. There was the snap of a twig. The arrival of another human being.

Bly entered the arc of Nils' peripheral sight and moved to where he hunched over the camp stove. She knelt beside him. "Coffee."

Nils offered the cup. Bly took that and drew it to her lips.

"It's going to be—"

"Hot!" The cup came away and Bly sucked air around the hot liquid in her mouth. She swallowed and wiped a finger over her lip. "And grounds."

"Wait a minute. It'll be better."

Bly blew over the rim of the cup. "River's over there." She pointed. "You know that. Train tracks run along the far side. Looks like they may cross. Must be a bridge somewhere."

"Several bridges. Tracks go back and forth across the river."

"Uh." Bly drank again, tentatively, a little sip. "Train still run on them?"

"Just a tourist train."

Bly held the cup, thought. "We'll have to cross the river?"

"We will."

"You know when the train runs?"

"Not exactly. You can hear it."

She sipped again. Made the face. Hot again. "How far off?"

"Hmm?"

"How far off can you hear the train? Say if you were on a bridge?"

"Yeah. Train doesn't come very often. Our chances would be good."

Another sip. More confident now, the coffee cooling. "And if they weren't?"

Nils made motions with his fingers as if they were running.

"Nice." Bly got into the coffee now, drinking it down. "Strong."

"We can share that."

"Okay. Tell me again why we came in this way. Where we'll have to cross the river to get where you took Jimmy."

Nils gestured around the big forest. "Not a lot of options. This is remote. No trailhead. No parking area. No access roads. No place for anyone watching."

"Like Zeke and Petey."

"Had them in mind."

"Nils? I've been thinking."

"Yeah?"

"I don't think they'd come onto the trail after us."

"They did at the last place."

"That was different. One way in, one way out. They knew where we were, knew where to look. Here is…enormous. They'd be insane to try to find us here."

"Depends on what Jimmy told them. How much about where that hike went."

Bly drank more of the coffee. "What would he tell them?"

"Where we started, the name of the company, where we came out. Whatever else he could remember."

"Looks like they knew the company. It's shut down. What else?"

Nils shrugged. "Not sure what else he'd know. Where on the trail he borrowed the shovel from me?"

"Would Jimmy know that?"

Nils tried to remember. "Jimmy seemed…disengaged. Right up until he wanted the shovel. Maybe he wasn't. Maybe he paid attention all along and I didn't notice it. Then as soon as he got the shovel he disappeared. I assume he walked out. Somehow."

"You're trying to think like Jimmy."

"Much as it pains me."

"You remember the spot? Where he disappeared?"

"I do. Like I told you. We can find it again."

"It was near the tracks?"

Nils thought back. He had a clear memory of where they'd been when Jimmy had become vocal about the shovel. He wasn't sure exactly where that was in relation to where he and Bly were now, or exactly how far, but he could take them in the right direction. Once they got close, he figured he would recognize the landmarks. The river and the train tracks were the key.

"Nils?"

"Thinking."

"You think Jimmy could have walked out on the tracks?"

"Exactly what I was thinking."

"And if he did…"

"If he did, Jimmy would have been smart to leave the flash drive somewhere near the tracks."

"Out of sight, but put the shovel down as a marker."

Nils got up. "It's what I'd do." He stretched. "We'll start where Jimmy left the group, then make our way to the tracks." This was actually beginning to sound almost plausible, assuming Jimmy had acted as they were guessing. And it gave Nils an itch. He wanted to go. He pictured the tracks and the river and bridges. Where they were and where they had to go.

Bly tipped the cup back and finished the coffee. She spat some grounds. "This what you give them on your hikes?"

"No. They get the good stuff."

"Little barista station on the trail?"

She was apparently in a good mood. Making a joke. "They drop stuff off. Designated camp sites. There's a stove and plates and a couple of tables. Food locked up."

"Locked up?"

Nils made his hand into a claw. "Bears."

"There are bears out here?"

"Don't worry. They aren't any more interested in you than you are in bumping into one of them."

"You ever see them on a hike?"

"Heard them at night a couple of times. Trying to get into the food."

"Hence the food locked up."

Nils nodded.

Bly watched him. "What?"

"Hence."

"I told you I was a reader." She handed the coffee cup back to Nils. "You already have one?"

He took the cup. "I'll make another."

He did, leaving the grounds still in the pot and adding only a little more to make his cup. That would stretch the coffee farther. Now that they had a plan, one that made a little sense and was maybe even worth pursuing, he might want to make a little more coffee, stay alert and see if this turned into anything.

Bly pulled her backpack and the sleeping bag from the tent. She rolled the bag and laid that at the base of a tree where Nils' frame pack leaned. "We left our food in the tent last night—we don't have anything to lock it in."

"Probably won't see a bear. Only three days."

"*My* pack was in the tent. I have food in there."

"We'll string them up tonight." He pointed up. "From a limb."

"Why didn't we do that last night?"

Because he'd been tired. Because it was late and they'd just done a thing more precarious than worrying about bears when they'd come down the slope through the woods in the dark. He shrugged. "Living on the edge."

Bly turned away and struck the tent.

The water boiled again and Nils made more coffee. He drank that and let the stove cool while they strapped the sleeping bag and tent to his pack. He had expected it to be tighter in the tent with just the one bag than the night before that with two, but it had actually worked out better with just the one. He'd kicked leaves under the tent for warmth and to soften the ground. The single bag stretched over them had surprisingly offered less restriction and more room to move than Nils had felt when he and Bly were zipped into their own bags.

He didn't know how Bly felt about the sleeping situation. She hadn't commented on it. Things had remained gentlemanly and ladylike, even after their interlude on the beach the day before. He wasn't going to push it. There was no telling what would come between them when the three days were up.

When his coffee was gone, Nils tucked the cup and stove into his pack. Bly reached over and hefted the rig to test the weight. "Want me to carry this one?"

"I've got it."

"I can do it."

"I know you can. I'll want you to take it later when I get tired."

Bly picked up her own smaller backpack instead. "So gentlemanly."

That's what Nils had been thinking.

They ate one each of the sandwiches as they navigated the rough forest floor. Nils took them to the water. "We'll follow the river and look for a place to cross."

They picked through the trees and rocks near the water, going upstream, away from the coast and into the valley. The tracks came in and out of view across the river. Nothing moved on them, and they heard no train whistle. It was mostly slow and mostly careful work.

"Nils?"

"Yeah."

"They'd wait for us."

Nils was listening.

Bly picked up the thread. "To come out. Zeke and Petey. Or daddy, or whoever else daddy might send."

"The FBI guys on your father's payroll."

"They wouldn't chase us through the woods. I don't think I'd thought this all the way through. Daddy was just looking for you. Then he put together that I was doing the same thing."

"Well, he knows for sure now."

"And he can just wait for us to surface."

Nils looked upstream. The shadow of a structure emerged. "Surface?"

"If I find what Jimmy took, I'll only be able to use that if I…"

"If you contact your father. Make a deal."

"Yes."

"And he'd just wait for you to do that."

"Daddy's smart."

Nils didn't want to think about a really smart mobster looking for him, or for Bly. "And if you don't find anything?"

"He'll still wait for me to surface. And for you. To make sure. We'll have to turn up somewhere some time."

Nils had thought about that, for himself, if not so much for Bly. "And will we? Surface?"

"Be hard not to eventually."

It would.

The thing Nils thought he saw ahead turned out to be a train bridge, as he'd hoped. They emerged from the trees and the river's edge and climbed the embankment to the crossing.

Nils started onto the train bridge, matching the length of his stride to the distance between the ties.

Bly did not. "We going to look?"

Nils stopped. "We can. Place Jimmy ditched is farther off." He pointed downriver. "Across the river, up the hill. Jimmy probably would have walked out that way too, toward town."

"He would have known which way?"

"Everyone had maps."

Bly looked downriver and over the terrain Nils had indicated. "Then why'd we come all the way up here?"

"I didn't want to miss anything important. We can come at it the way the group did."

"Look where Jimmy first left."

"Then down the tracks toward Fort Bragg."

"High value locations. Search the bridges."

"It's what we were thinking."

Bly looked down through the ties, down at the water maybe twenty feet below, the stretch of river beneath them. "So should we look here?"

It was all speculation. Hard to say. "Your call."

Bly called for looking, but only medium-hard looking. The sun was already high and the day was getting warm. They had a lot more territory to cover.

It turned out that medium-hard looking for Bly meant about half an hour. Then she climbed up from under the tracks where she'd been looking up at the structure. "Lunch time?"

"Always."

"Those sandwiches still good?"

"We'll find out."

They ate and sipped from their water bottles and wiped sweat and grit. The terrain had grown hot and dusty.

Then Nils took them off trail in the redwoods again, striking a path north, intending to bisect the east-west trail he'd led Jimmy's group on.

It grew hotter. The forest grew thicker. The slope was steep and slippery and the trees closed in on them.

There was some risk. People got lost in these woods. Most found their way out. Nils had his compass and had hiked the area before. Bly still had the phone and a chance that she might get a signal somewhere.

"Bly?"

"Yeah."

"If anything goes wrong, head downslope."

She didn't answer.

"Look for the river and the train tracks. You can follow those out if you have to."

Bly climbed behind Nils. "Nothing's gonna happen."

They climbed some more, high-stepped over ferns, limbs, and roots. Bly said, "So is this what those hikes you lead are like?"

Nils laughed. "Exactly."

They reached the high rim above the river and had heard no train and seen or heard no other people. Nils took them farther north, and they came to a narrow trail.

They paused to drink water sparingly, and Nils turned them west on the trail. Not long later he pointed out a blaze painted onto a tree trunk. "Okay, we're on the right track."

"Good. How far?"

"Not long if we're where I think we are."

"You think we'll see any other hikers?"

"Who knows? My group isn't out here. They shut down." He wiped sweat from his chin. "And it's hot."

They walked. Bly got ahead and looked back at Nils. "Can you pick up the pace?"

Nils could, but it was tough in the heat with the big backpack on. Which he didn't ask Bly to carry.

Roughly a mile and a half later by Nils' calculations the trail widened and a short spur of about thirty feet jutted onto a rock ledge that opened to a view over the redwoods. Nils stopped and dropped his pack. Bly walked to the ledge and looked over. "Nice view."

"It is. This is where we stopped when Jimmy borrowed my shovel. Then we never saw him again."

They stood on the ledge and looked out at the redwoods and into the distance where the valley twisted and Nils knew the river ran. It was hot. He felt heat around him, entering and leaving his body. He felt Bly's presence, warm. He felt as if the air breathed them in.

Bly reached for her water. "So we look here."

"We do."

"For the little orange shovel."

"And the treasure buried beneath it."

She gave him the stink eye. "That supposed to be some kind of joke?"

"Doesn't sound like it."

"That's what I thought. Let's get to it."

They searched, for a long time. Much longer than they had when they crossed the bridge. They toed aside ferns and looked behind trees and limbs on the ground. They looked over the rock ledge and felt around. They walked into the redwood trees and toed the ground, toed the duff, toed everything.

They searched for much longer than kept Nils' interest. After what felt like an hour but may have been half, Nils wandered back to the rock ledge and looked out.

After what felt like another twenty minutes but might have been five or ten, Bly came to the ledge beside him. "No luck?"

Nils didn't need to answer.

"Maybe Jimmy didn't leave it here."

"Yeah."

"Or someone else saw the shovel and picked it up."

"Yeah."

"Or maybe this whole thing is futile."

"We knew that coming in."

Bly rubbed a toe of her shoe in the dirt. "How long do we look here before we move on?"

"Your call."

The toe went through some more dirt. "Now, I guess."

They thought about what Jimmy would have done. Look for a way down. To the river, to the railroad tracks.

They searched and found that in a natural seam where water would run down during the rain. Now it was dry and dusty. Bly moved off the trail toward the run-off.

"Wait." Nils took out the compass and plotted a course south, marking a tall sentinel tree that topped the others. Then he and Bly went down the seam in the slope and kept their aim at that sentinel whenever it rose into view.

Eventually glimpses of the river became visible, winding like an errant string through the valley below. They abandoned the marker tree and went for the water, as they figured Jimmy might have done.

It took them some time to reach the railroad tracks. There they drank more water sparingly, though they had sweated a lot. Bly said, "How is it this hot? It was cold at the coast."

"Gets hot quick as you move into the valleys. The rail line goes to Willits. Probably a hundred there today. Maybe more."

"Willits?"

"Maybe thirty miles by crow." He pointed east.

"Good that we're going the other way."

"For now."

They walked down the tracks, beside them when they could, in the shade of the big trees. Occasionally the trees crowded in and they had to walk the sloped gravel bed or stride the ties. That was sunnier, hotter, and more work. They saw or heard no train as they walked, and they encountered no other people.

It was late in the afternoon when they reached a bridge. They searched there, the trestles, the understructure, any area beneath that they could get to. Any part that they thought Jimmy may have reasonably, or even fairly reasonably, considered for a hidey hole.

And as before, they searched until Bly made the call to give up.

Then they walked again, going slower and snacking, preserving water and energy.

They'd been quiet for a while and Nils was thinking how sweaty and dusty he was, and Bly must have been thinking the same thing, because out of nowhere, she said, "What kind of shape was Jimmy in?"

"He'd be dead by now."

It was a joke, but Nils could see that Bly was thinking about it. They kept walking.

They made it to another bridge before the sunlight faded. It was a short set of track that curved over an expanse of maybe fifty yards, maybe twenty feet above the water. They searched.

Nils was hungry and tired. They had eaten jerky and dried fruit as they could in the heat, and drank water but wanted more than they consumed, saving what they could before they had to resort to river water and purification tablets.

Bly lasted longer at the search than Nils expected. Gray twilight hovered over the redwoods before she gave up and they made camp.

They ate bagels with dried fruit, and Nils removed a small can of beans from the backpack and pulled the top off. He located a fork and handed that and the can to Bly.

She took a sizable bite. "How many of these have we got?"

"Two. That one's for sharing tonight."

She took another bite. "I'll eat a little less than half."

"You should eat half."

Bly did, then rinsed the fork with a bit of water, wiped it, and handed that and the half can of beans to Nils.

Nils finished the beans and washed the can out with as little water as he could. He set it into the top of the backpack with the stove.

"What's the can for?"

"Second cup for coffee."

Bly raised a weary grin.

They finished eating and Bly packed away the remaining food.

Nils reached into the pack and found the chocolate bar. He offered it to Bly.

She laughed. "You brought chocolate."

"For sharing."

Bly reached into her pack and came out with another chocolate bar. Hers was very melted. She laughed when the bar wiggled and sagged.

Nils held his chocolate bar out and it stayed straight.

"How'd you do that?"

"Trail guide secret."

"Really?"

The bar sagged. "No."

And they ate one of the messy chocolate bars.

Then Nils tied a thin rope to his pack, and then the Bly's. He walked a short distance from the tent and tossed the rope over a branch above his head. He felt in the dark for the end of the rope that had come down and pulled that to raise both packs into the air, and tied off the rope to a tree.

Then he did what he needed to before sleeping and went into the tent with Bly.

She rolled over. "Bears?"

"Just a precaution."

"If I wasn't so tired, I'd be more worried about that."

"Probably no need."

She yawned. "Worth it if it saves my chocolate."

Then she slept and Nils figured he was acting as gentlemanly as possible again. He had to be if he was sound asleep.

18

THE MORNING WAS COLD. Nils woke with Bly more entwined than tucked with him in the little tent.

They separated themselves and got up and put on jackets and went out to do morning things. Nils returned to the campsite first and poured water into the pot and set that on top of the stove. The burner lit with a pop, and the flame tickled the bottom of the pot.

Bly came back and watched Nils trying to adjust the flame. "Coffee ready?"

"Working on it." Nils shut the flame off, then blew across the holes of the burner to try to clear them out.

"Something wrong?"

"Might be a little dirty. Maybe some lint in there." He used a corner of his shirt to rub the burner clean, then re-lit the stove. The flame sputtered and popped, then dwindled. "Unless…"

"Don't tell me."

Nils removed the pot, unscrewed the burner, and shook the canister. "I thought I brought a full one."

"Nils…"

He shook the canister again.

"Empty?"

"Feels like there's some left. We'll see." He screwed the burner back on, set the pot on top, and lit the stove once again. The flame sputtered and faded to a tiny blue ring. "Guess we won't need the bean can."

He managed one cup of lukewarm coffee. That, he offered to Bly. She took a few graceful swallows and passed what remained to Nils.

He had already poured grounds into a water bottle, shaken that, and tucked it into a pocket on his pack.

Bly stretched her arms over her head. "Doesn't matter. We'll have good coffee soon. Today is the day." She leaned sideways and stretched some space between her shoulders. "The day we find the little orange shovel."

They ate jerky and dried fruit and shared a bagel. Nils was still hungry, but Bly was ready to go. They struck camp and walked.

Nils warmed as they traveled down the tracks again, searching for that elusive bridge and hiding spot that they hoped existed. He stopped to take his jacket off and stuff it into his pack.

Bly did the same. "How many more bridges do you think between here and Fort Bragg?"

Gravel from the railroad bed crunched under their feet. "No idea."

"Guess."

"Between zero and four?"

"Based on...?"

"Based on you made me guess. I've never been down this way before."

More gravel crunched. The sun rose.

Bly drifted from the hot gravel bed to the shade beside it. "Was this a bad idea?"

Nils shrugged. Bly probably didn't see it.

"To come look here? Do you think we'll find anything?"

Nils wanted very much to not answer.

"Nils?"

"Okay. One—no, I don't think it was a bad idea. If you hadn't, it would have eaten at you. You have to get past this, no matter what it leads to."

"And number two?"

"I don't mean to be a party pooper. But I'm starting to think there's not much chance we're going to find anything."

Bly didn't push back. Nils drifted toward the shade with her. They walked, getting hot and dusty, down the side of the railroad tracks toward Fort Bragg and the ocean.

At mid-morning they encountered another bridge. It was a short stretch not high above the water. The Noyo River here was wide and shallower, moving steadily but without hurry toward the Pacific.

They searched as before, Nils dutifully looking, Bly dutifully in charge of how long it made sense to keep doing that.

Not long into what was becoming a practiced ordeal, a new sound began quietly in the distance, drifting to them from downriver.

Bly had been walking the bridge slowly, stretching her steps tie to tie as she scanned down through the gaps. Now she stopped. "Nils?"

Nils was at the abutment, where he would have chosen to hide something if had to. Easily accessible, out of sight from above, high enough from the water to be safe from washing away. "I hear it."

"Train?"

He turned an ear down the tracks. "Doesn't sound like it. Better get off the tracks anyway."

Bly was already moving. Running the ties, feet thumping on the big wooden supports.

Nils rounded the abutment and came up to the tracks, stretching a hand out to her for encouragement.

The rail didn't hum. No engine sounded. No whistle blew. There was a soft—squeak or hum?

Bly reached Nils. He took her hand and they scrambled under the bridge where they pressed against a wooden pier.

There was quiet for a moment. Nils looked up between ties, in the slits of sunlight, for anything that might pass above. Nothing did, but a steady whirr grew more insistent and close. He tapped Bly's shoulder and whispered. "Do you think we'd be better in the trees?"

"I don't think there's—"

A voice drifted down. "—Flo and Eddie would love this. Here, get a picture."

"Was that a—"

"Shh." Bly put a finger to her lips.

Nils mouthed *what?*

Bly mouthed *no idea.*

The whirr slowed some. "Lean in. Smile."

Then above them shapes ticked by, a metal cart frame, feet turning, big wheels spinning along the rails. Two riders pedaling, their forms flickering in the spaces between the ties like the frames of an old movie.

Nils' eye followed the form as it moved away. "Huh."

"What was that?"

"I've heard of those."

"What was it?"

"Railbike."

Bly tracked the cart as it passed over the far end of the bridge. "You hear anything else?"

"No."

"Odd that there was only one?"

There wasn't. A steady stream of railbikers pedaled by, Nils and Bly attempting to come out from under the bridge to restart their search when the first couple passed, then retreating like trolls to wait for the parade to end.

After some time when no more riders had come, Bly crawled up the embankment slope and looked down the tracks. "How long do you think until it's over?"

"I don't know."

"You think it's over now?"

"I don't know."

They waited some more. When after another time no more riders had come, Bly called for them to resume their search. Some of the steam seemed to have gone out of her. Much of the steam had gone out of Nils. He took from his pack the water bottle with the coffee grounds in it, shook that, and waited for the cloudiness to settle. Then he sipped.

Bly approached. "Let me try that."

She sipped. Swallowed. Wrinkled her nose. Sipped again and swallowed. Handed the bottle back. "Not desperate enough yet."

"Wait until we have to make it with purified river water."

Her nose wrinkled more aggressively.

After some more time searching, Bly called for lunch. There were no more sandwiches. They sat in the shade by the tracks, under the giant trees, and ate bagels with turkey jerky. Bly sipped water. Nils sipped the warm brew coffee.

Bly was quiet while she ate, until she set down a bag of raisins. "Bagel, raisins, nuts, jerky."

Nils looked up. "What?"

Bly tapped out a beat on her leg with one hand. "Bagel, raisins, nuts, jerky."

"I'm saving the tuna."

She tapped the rhythm faster now, with both hands. "Bagel, raisins, nuts, jerky. Bagel, raisins, nuts, jerky."

Nils took out a bag from his pack and held that out to Bly.

She tapped again. "Bagel, raisins, nuts, jerky." A fast pause and one hard slap. "Granola. Bagel, raisins, nuts, jerky—granola!"

Nils watched her. "How you doing?"

"I could be getting tired of this. Wish we'd find something."

Nils did too.

Bly put a hand out. "Keep the granola. Give me that coffee."

Nils did.

Bly tried another swallow. "Tastes like you already drank it."

"You're in a good mood."

"Getting there." She gave the coffee back. "Let's just go."

They packed up and walked the tracks again. After a few minutes, Bly stopped. "Wait!"

"What?" Hope sprung.

"We forgot the chocolate."

"Oh. You already ate yours."

"Yes. But I didn't eat ours."

"Oh." Nils took his pack off and searched for what was left of the chocolate and handed that to Bly.

She ate a bite. "How much more?"

"That's the last of it."

"You want some?"

He did. What he said was "No."

They walked some more, neither of them asking if there would be another bridge or how many more. After a long stretch of nothing but gravel ballast crunching beneath them, Bly began to sing.

"Bagel, raisins, nuts, jerky. Bagel, raisins, nuts, jerky."

A moment of quiet.

"Bagel, raisins, nuts, jerky—granola! Bagel, raisins, nuts, jerky—granola!"

More gravel crunched under their feet.

"Bagel, raisins, nuts, jerky—granola! Bagel, raisins, nuts, jerky—granola!"

"You've got to stop that."

"I know."

Bly hummed instead, but by now Nils knew the tune. He didn't mention that there was still tuna in sealed pouches in his pack. The trip and the heat were enough already. He didn't need anything else getting into his head.

They walked, Bly's tune eventually subsided, and Nils didn't think he was imagining that the forest grew a little cooler as they traveled down-river toward the coast.

At mid-afternoon the old rail line dipped slowly into a valley that deepened and narrowed to a gorge. The air grew noticeably cooler now, not just Nils' imagination. The gorge grew deeper and the sides drew closer and finally there was another bridge.

Across the bridge was a large rock face. In the rock face was a tunnel. And stretched across the front of the tunnel opening was a high and wide chain-link fence.

They both saw it. They crossed the trestles, careful to step tie-to-tie and aware of the precipitous drop. Nils pointed to the bolts and lock securing the fencing. "Last bridge."

They reached the far side and hard ground. Bly shook the fence. It rattled and held. "What now?"

Nils took his pack off and relished the air that moved across his back. "So far it's been a guessing game. What did Jimmy do? We don't even know if he came here."

Bly didn't look happy about his assessment. Nils amended. "Your call. We should at least look here."

Bly scanned up the steep ridge. "Could Jimmy have gone up there?"

"I suppose."

"Anything up there?"

"No idea. Probably a road, if you go far enough."

Bly looked at the bridge, down to the river below, upriver and down. "What do you think?"

"Water and snacks. Then we search here. It's what we came for. After that, we'll decide what's next."

Bly agreed. She took water and nuts and raisins and granola, but the song didn't return. One thing to be grateful for.

They couldn't search as hard. Not even medium-hard. There was no easy way to get under the bridge. Or even a hard way. Bly couldn't reason out that Jimmy would have tried to get down under the thing, or that it would be safe to even try. It was too steep to get down to the river, and there wasn't much ground on either side of the tracks to hide the shovel in.

After a time, Bly sat down on a rail near the fenced-off tunnel.

Nils came and stood next to her.

Bly looked at her hands. "We could go up."

"Or back."

"Back?"

"More bridges. The other way."

"I don't think Jimmy went there."

Neither did Nils.

Bly turned her hands over, examining something. "You know what I think?"

He didn't want to guess.

"I think Jimmy didn't bury anything out here. I think he borrowed your shovel because he needed to take a shit. A big, long dump before he walked out of here with that thumb drive still with him."

Nils raised an eyebrow. Language. Then, "Why would Jimmy borrow my shovel to bury his business if he was going to run off anyway? Why not just do like a bear?"

That got him a dirty look. "I think you're missing the point."

Nils wasn't sure he was.

"This is stupid. All this." She waved both hands in the air. "Jimmy didn't leave anything out here."

Well, maybe one thing. What the bear would. But Nils didn't say that.

"I wanted to believe it." Her head went down. "I needed to."

Nils waited. This was Bly's gig. He would let her play it out.

"And even if Jimmy did leave something, there's no way we'd ever find it. It's like—trying to find a…"

"Little orange shovel in the great big redwood forest."

She didn't look up at him. No laugh, no acknowledgement. Nothing.

Nils sat beside Bly on the rail. "We tried."

"We did."

She held her palms out. "Look at my hands."

Nils did. They were dirty.

Bly turned her hands over. "What I'd really like is to wash them. Eat my nuts and raisins with relatively clean fingers. But I don't want to waste water washing. We need that to drink."

"We're going to need more water. We'll have to get it from the river and use the purification tablets."

"I don't really want to drink river water."

"Bears do it all the time."

Bly's look was not a pleased one.

"You might as well use some water to clean your hands."

Bly pointed down. "It's going to be a while before we can get to the river again. I should just wait and clean my hands then."

Nils didn't know where to take that conversation, so he didn't.

Bly stood and wiped her hands on her pants. "How do you think Jimmy got out?"

Nils pointed a thumb to the fenced tunnel. "He didn't walk the tracks." He turned the thumb down to the water. "And I don't think he swam to Fort Bragg."

"Climbed out somewhere?"

"Maybe?"

"Or walked back the way your hike came in? Found his way back from there."

Nils shrugged. Could be.

"We said we'd go three days."

Nils knew. It had been two.

"I just really wanted this to work. Somehow I thought, if you came along. The two of us together…"

It was the most vulnerable Nils had ever seen Bly. The first vulnerable.

She lowered her head. "I need a shower."

"Me too."

"I want clean hands."

Nils didn't mind dirty hands, but he said, "Me too."

"Clothes." Bly pulled out the bottom of the new dollar store shirt to show grit.

"Me too."

"Food."

"Yeah."

"Real coffee."

You said it.

"Nils? Are we done?"

"Your call." It had always been her call.

"We've looked everywhere. We searched your things, the storage unit, I even looked through your backpack."

"My backpack?"

"Not that one. The one you had on Orcas."

Wen she'd taken his paperback novel.

"The smaller one."

"Bly."

"I wasn't trying to be a snoop. I—"

"Bly."

"What?"

He didn't know how to say it. He'd made a mistake.

"Nils?"

He rubbed his palms together. Now his hands felt dirty too. "That's not the pack I carried on the trip with Jimmy."

"What do you mean that's not the pack? Which one?"

"Neither of them. Not this one." He pointed to the one he'd been carrying. "Or the littler one I had when you found me on Orcas."

"So which pack was it? Where is that one?"

"Orcas."

"On the island?"

"Yes."

Her eyes narrowed and she pinched her nose. "I don't understand."

Nils remembered details. "When Jimmy borrowed my shovel, it was in my backpack. I told him to just go get it."

"You didn't see him?"

"No."

"So Jimmy could have left something in your pack then? The thumb drive?"

"He could have."

"You didn't look?"

"Not thoroughly."

"Not thoroughly, or not at all?"

Nils held out a hand and tipped it back and forth.

"Oh, that's not funny now. Where's that pack?"

He told her about the ride in the sunroof of the Civic, losing the pack.

Bly nodded, nodded again, looked down.

Nils looked to the river and trees. "We probably should have started there." Not that he held any real hope that Jimmy had told the truth when Bly's father's men had interrogated him, when Jimmy had said that Nils held the key. But if he was going to hold out hope for finding anything, he would put it in that backpack if it wasn't with Jimmy. And Jimmy had given up the ghost.

Nils turned back to Bly. "What do you want to do?"

"What do you think?"

"I think this should be your call."

19

BLY BLAZED BACK through the redwoods. Nils neither asked her to slow nor to carry the pack, his whole attention on keeping up, staying hydrated, and trying not to show weakness. Though he wanted to.

The heat clung to them like a glass jar over a bug. They ran alongside the uneven ground next to the railroad tracks when they could, on the gravel ballast when they had to. Nils had the big backpack cinched tight so it wouldn't slop and bang when he ran. That just made it hotter against his back, raising a big slick of sweat that dripped down into his waistband. The one saving grace was that they'd drunk most of the water, so the pack was a little lighter.

He didn't know if Bly pushed because she had renewed hope for finding his backpack lost on Orcas, or if the motivation ran more to the line of creature comforts. Whatever it was that motivated Bly, man, she had grit. She *moved* through that redwood forest.

Shower, water, food, coffee, clean clothes—all that sounded good, but what Nils really wanted right then was just to stop.

Bly finally pulled up at a tiny glade made by a fallen tree at the edge of the railbed. She drank some water, then handed the bottle to Nils.

"I thought you said you couldn't run with that thing on."

He loosened the shoulder straps and leaned back, allowing the pack to rest on the hip belt and open some space between the frame and his back. "It's not a good idea."

"You look hot."

"Thanks."

She wiped sweat. "Not what I meant."

"I'll take what I can get."

"Actually, you look like you might fall down."

That thought had occurred to him. He sat down and let the pack fall free. "We're not going to be able to go much farther without more water."

Bly watched him. "You don't look so good."

"I'm fine. Just need to cool down for a few minutes." What he needed was electrolytes, but he hadn't packed any. Instead he took out the peanuts and sucked salt from them.

Bly reached a hand out and Nils put nuts into it.

He sucked more salt from the peanuts. "How long have we been going?"

"Long time. I kept waiting for you to ask to rest, but you never did."

"If I had known."

"Can you keep going? I can carry the pack for a while."

Nils tried to get his bearings. "How many bridges have we crossed?"

Bly counted in her head, and on her fingers. "Should be one more?"

"That's the way I make it too." He stood and walked to the tracks and looked up the river. Then he pointed.

Bly came out and looked with him. "I think you're right. That's it."

Nils went back to the shade. "That was an incredible run."

"Good for me too."

If he wasn't so tired and hot, he would have enjoyed that more. "Most people couldn't have done that."

She waved a hand. "Mere mortals. I didn't have to carry a backpack."

"So you noticed."

She looked closer at Nils now. "It only seemed fair."

"Fair?"

"I chased you. Now you had to chase me."

"Uuuhm…"

"Tell you what." She held the water bottle up. "Let's go for broke. Finish this. Get hydrated, get across that bridge, and get up out of these woods."

"We should slow things down."

"We'll walk. In the shade."

"Get to the truck, get to town and get more water, and get cleaned up."

"A big meal."

"You make it sound so easy."

Bly stood. "I'll even carry the pack."

Nils moved to his backpack. He slid his sweaty body into the sweat-soaked straps. "I got it."

They slowed it down. Nils managed. It was easier out of the sun and at the slower pace. He sucked on some more peanuts and ate a bite of jerky.

They talked a little, but mostly Nils focused only on putting one foot in front of the other and keeping his temperature regulated. They came to the bridge and crossed it.

They were both looking into the woods, searching, when Nils recognized something. Some flat ground, a slope beyond, a subtle seam farther out that ran down through slump rocks and growth. "That might be it." He pointed.

Bly looked. "Any way to tell for sure?"

Nils realized then that he should have marked their descent location. A rock pile, twigs woven into a cross, fabric tied to a limb, something. Rookie mistake.

But it had been dark and late when they came down, and he'd been tired. Rookie excuse.

He took out the compass, read some bearings, and thought about how far they'd come the first day before they'd encountered a bridge. "If we get up the ridge and keep going north, we'll hit the road. Worst case is we don't know which way to go on the road to find the truck."

"But we'll be on the road?"

Nils looked at the compass again. "Should be."

They moved into the woods, the walk changing from the hard and open ground of the rail bed back to the roots and ferns and tangle of the soft redwood floor. Nils looked for a flat square of ground where they'd pitched the tent, an indent from the stove canister, or some sign that they'd camped there. He found none of those. Either they'd been good little scouts, or this wasn't where they'd come down.

But they were moving up, and up was the right direction. They passed slump rocks and climbed up a little seam that formed a now-dry gully. Then the slope was steeper, and they switched back along the silhouette of the land to cut a path to the top of the ridge.

Nils took the compass, adjusted for magnetic declination, and they followed the needle north. A few minutes later, the old logging road appeared from the shapes and umbrage of the trees. The sun was still up but low in the west. Nils looked left, then right.

Bly looked with him. "Right."

"So east?"

"We haven't come far enough."

Nils took that on faith. "At least that will put us walking away from the sun."

About half a mile later at a turn in the road, Nils pointed to a break in the treeline. "There."

They entered the break and followed that to the truck, nestled where they'd left it under the low branches that reached down and kissed the top and fenders. Nils patted his pockets for the keys.

Bly's face dropped.

Nils held the keys up. "Relax. Right here." He tossed the keys to Bly and dumped his pack into the bed of the truck.

When Nils looked back, Bly was looking at something on the ground.

"Uh-oh."

Bly bent, parted some weeds, and retrieved the keys. "Nils."

He knew. There was only the one set. "Sorry. Tired." He reached for the pack, pulled out granola bars, and tossed one to Bly. "I need to eat."

Bly caught the shiny foil package and opened it. "Me too."

Nils materialized a bottle that was still half full of water, drank some and recapped it, then tossed that to Bly too.

She caught the bottle. "Cheater. You held out."

He lowered the tailgate and sat. "Not my first rodeo."

When they were refreshed enough, Nils drove them to Fort Bragg. The daylight held until they got there, and they found a diner and ordered two of the specials, chicken breast with potatoes and green beans.

When that disappeared too quickly, Nils asked for another order to share. The waitress gave them a look but brought the third plate without further comment.

The diner had almost emptied out when they each had a slice of cherry pie. It was just Nils and Bly, one quiet gentleman at the counter reading something on his phone, and the waitress, and the pie. Nils eyed the pastry display and wondered if one slice each would be enough.

Bly licked red filling from her fork, then pushed her plate away. "I can't believe I ate all that."

"What I can't believe is that you ate as much as I did."

She set the fork down. "Never tell a girl that. Besides, you ate more from the extra plate than I did."

That was fair. He'd eaten most of it.

Bly wiped her fingers on her napkin. "And we did it again."

"It?"

She pointed to the big plate glass window at the front of the diner. "It's dark out, and we don't have a place to sleep."

"That seems to be our thing."

Now she rumpled her napkin. "I've been thinking."

"Uh-huh?"

"About that backpack you lost."

"Uh-huh."

"You think there's much chance of finding it?"

"Probably. If someone didn't pick it up. It's got to be somewhere."

Bly unrumpled, re-rumpled the napkin. "And the flash drive?"

"That, I have no idea."

"But what do you think?"

They'd covered this. "There's no way to know. We just have to go look."

"Best guess?"

"I don't have a best guess."

Rumple, unrumple. Rumple, unrumple.

"Stop torturing that napkin. What do you think?"

She stopped with the napkin. "I want it to be there."

"Sure."

"And I don't want to wait to find out." Hands rock steady now. No napkin rumpling.

"What does that mean?"

"My call?"

"Your call." He hoped he didn't regret saying it.

"I don't want to find a place to sleep. I don't want to stop. I want this to be over, one way or another. I'm ready for the good or the bad. I want to go. We can take shifts. Sleep in the passenger seat while the other drives."

Nils let an eyebrow drift up, then the other.

"I'll take the first shift."

He thought about it. "I'm probably tired enough I could sleep in the cab."

"We'll want coffee."

Nils wanted coffee just thinking about coffee. But he was going to sleep first. "Be nice if we could get cleaned up a little."

"We can clean up some in the restrooms. Better than nothing." She was already getting up. "Leave a good tip."

Nils asked the waitress if they could get coffee to go.

"Take a minute. I'll have to make a pot, this late in the day."

"I'll leave a good tip."

The waitress winked at him. "I heard."

When Bly came back Nils went to clean up a little, though they both had to stay in their dirty clothes.

The waitress brought coffee in big to-go cups, and Nils laid bills on the check.

They tossed most of the gear into the back now, not worrying much anymore about rain or the rusty holes in the bed. Nils did his best to bungee the packs over the worst of the holes to cover them, and he let the rest slide.

Then Bly settled behind the wheel and Nils did his best to curl and get suitably comfortable on the passenger side of the bench seat. He bunched his jacket for what it was worth into a make-shift pillow.

Bly took them out on the road and pointed the truck north.

Nils twisted on the seat. "I don't know if I can sleep."

That's the last he remembered clearly until he felt the truck come to a stop. He looked out at the lights of a gas station parking lot. "Where are we?"

"Oregon."

"You drove all the way to Oregon?"

"Yeah." Bly had her door open. The cab light flicked on. "Your turn to drive. I'll sleep now."

"What time is it?"

"Pretty much the exact center of the night."

Nils got out and walked with Bly to the station building. She peeled off for the restrooms. "We need gas. I'll meet you back at the truck."

A sign in the window said they were in Grants Pass. Nils used the facilities too, then browsed in the cooler and picked up egg sandwiches. He bought fresh coffee even though there was probably a cold cup in the cab. Then he prepaid for gas with cash at the counter and went out to the truck.

Bly was already curled on the seat. The key hung from the ignition switch. He gassed the truck and went in for his change from the fill. Bly hadn't moved when he had them back on the road.

Then Bly shifted, moved her feet around in the well, pushed the lock on the passenger door down, and leaned her head and shoulders against the window. "Guy said there are pay showers about an hour ahead."

"Guy?"

"When I came out."

"A guy just told you?"

"I asked him. He looked like a trucker." Sleepy talk. "Wake me when we get there."

The truck cab grew quiet. Bly slept, and Nils focused on the road and the white line going by.

When Nils saw the sign for hot showers, Bly was asleep. When he pulled into a spot at the twenty-four-hour truck stop, she moved. "We there?"

"If by there you mean the showers, then yes."

A yawn and a stretch. "I'm going in." She picked up her day pack and opened the door.

Nils followed and Bly seemed about half awake. He figured that was enough to shower and put on a clean shirt. They agreed to meet back at the truck and bought shower tickets.

Nils was waiting in the driver's seat when Bly opened the other door. The cab light blinked on and Nils saw that Bly hadn't put on a clean shirt. She was wearing a lightweight, white-and-yellow sundress with a subtle blue pattern interspersed.

"Nice dress."

"Don't start."

He recalibrated. "No. I mean that's a very nice dress."

"Thank you."

"Looks good on you."

Bly's eyes moved sleepily.

"You got that at the dollar store?"

"No." She tried some positions on the seat, trying to get comfortable. "There was a consignment shop a few doors down."

Nils tried to remember. "I didn't see that." He'd been in the little park across the street, rounding the bases after his imaginary home run.

"You wouldn't. Men don't see women's clothing stores. They're invisible to your gender."

That explained it.

Bly had her shoes off and her legs tucked up, testing how far the dress would come down to cover them.

"Are you going to be able to sleep in that?"

"It's the only really clean thing I have. And I just wanted to...feel clean for a little while."

"You want my jacket?"

"No." She turned again on the seat. "Yes."

Nils draped his jacket over Bly's legs and torso. She tucked into it.

He took them up the I-5, as Bly had done, hoping the traffic would stay light overnight and he wouldn't have to push the old truck too hard. He got into a groove in the right lane, the truck humming along comfortably right at sixty-five, the cab dark and cozy, Bly sleeping in the dim glow of the dash lights. Nils drinking his coffee.

"Nils?"

So not asleep.

"The reason I bought the dress—which, because it may seem a little impractical based on, you know, what we've been doing…"

"I didn't want to say."

"The reason I bought it—and I don't want to make more of this than what it is, is I've had some…."

The truck hummed. A Honda passed them on the left, the headlights sweeping into the sideview mirror, around, then past. Nils thought Bly might have fallen back asleep.

"Urges."

He glanced over.

"I'm—look, stop me if this isn't something you want to hear, I'm…"

He didn't stop her.

"I'm sleepy, and I want to tell you this before I wake up enough not to."

"I'm here."

"I know things are complicated. And I know we met because…that's not the thing. The thing is, I like you. I'm really getting to like you. And I thought we might…"

He waited in the darkened cab.

"But you've been a perfect gentleman."

"I know."

"And that's the thing. I thought you might be interested, but…"

Nils didn't say anything. He didn't know what to say, and he didn't want to break whatever spell had gotten Bly talking. But them when she didn't say anything more, he found his words. "I'm interested. I don't know exactly what you're suggesting, but that first time you touched me, up on the mountain? It was something."

"I remember."

"Your fingers touched my wrist." He placed his own fingers there now to recall, though he didn't know if Bly could see that. "I felt it all the way up to my brain."

Bly lay curled on the seat, covered by the sundress and Nils' jacket. "I think that's a nice thing to say."

Some moments passed. The road swept under them.

Bly sighed. "I thought you might...show me a sign."

Nils stared into the cone of the headlights in front of the truck. He could see only what the lights illuminated, nothing farther down the road except dim shapes and imagined objects. It was like that for him and Bly. He could see only Bly here, right now, on the seat beside him in the cab, nothing more, ahead. "It didn't seem fair."

"Fair."

"All that's going on. So many unknowns."

"Fair? Nils, everything is fair. We have so little time. But here's the thing—I also kind of *didn't* want you to be interested because...I'm not good at what comes after."

"After?"

"Sticking around for coffee."

"What does that mean?"

"Sometimes sex is just sex."

"Sure. You've had urges to have just sex with me?"

"No. Yes. I..."

"You want me to go away after?"

"That's the part I'm not good at."

"Going away?"

"Or not. What I mean is—I'm not explaining this well. Let's just stop talking about it."

"If you want to."

That cone of light. That's all Nils could see. Nothing farther.

Bly wasn't quite ready to let it go. "It's more than just coffee."

"Of course it is."

"If you stick around after. It's the other things I'm also not so good at."

Nils kept his eyes on that one little piece of road in front of him. "Well, we've already done that part. The coffee. The stick around after stuff."

"But we did it before, not after."

"And we seem to have been pretty good at the other stuff so far."

Bly made a tiny movement, a little sigh, a minute adjustment, something very small. "We seem to be doing it backward."

The cone of light seemed just a little brighter, the road a little more distinct. Nils reached a hand out and felt it gently touch Bly's cheek. "No. I think we're doing it right."

He left the one hand on Bly's cheek, steering with just the other. He felt her breathe in and out.

Bly's question came quietly. "How about I take you on a date?"

Nils let his hand drift from Bly's cheek and come back to the wheel. "Okay."

"Where would we go?"

"Anywhere. I'm a simple guy."

"You are, in some ways. But you're also an intricate and interesting individual."

Nils thought about that.

"What?"

"Intricate individual?"

"That's not what guys like to hear?"

"It is. It's just not exactly…"

"I told you I'm not good at this part."

He felt a grin tick onto his face. "Sure you are. You're plenty good at it."

Some road passed beneath them, the truck taking them on steady progress forward.

"Nils?"

"Yeah."

"Good talk."

Then they were quiet. Nils driving, Bly sleeping.

He drank coffee and the road swept by. He stopped to pee. Bly slept through that.

He ate an egg sandwich. The sun rose as he drove through the Willamette Valley. They traveled past Eugene and Corvallis. Bly slept.

The cab warmed in the sun and Bly turned and pushed the jacket away. Nils twirled the dash knobs and let some fresh air in from the road. Bly slept.

Nils kept them steady on the I-5 as traffic got heavier. He switched lanes as traffic entered and exited from the ramps, trying to keep an easy pace for the old truck.

Bly woke and sat up. "Where are we?"

"Bridgetown."

She mouthed it, as if trying to figure out what Nils had said.

"Portland."

"It's called Bridgetown?"

"Some people."

"Why is that?"

He made a wiggly motion with one hand. "Willamette River goes right through the middle. Lot of bridges."

"Makes sense."

"You hungry?"

"Yeah."

"Because if there's one thing Portland is known for besides the bridges, it's breakfast."

"Okay." She stretched. "Even if you just made that up."

He hadn't, and they had no trouble finding a breakfast place. They went in, and Bly swished the fabric of the dress as she slid into the booth.

Talk did not go to the conversation from the night before, though Nils suspected the memory of it showed in his eyes. They circled instead around deciding whether to find a place to nap—a quiet park or a pull-off, a parking lot—or keep going. They'd both ordered coffee, and when it arrived hot and steaming that decided things. Keep going. They felt fresh enough.

Bly drove them through the heavier traffic and mayhem of the I-5 through Tacoma and Seattle. They listened to the radio when they could get something they liked, Nils tilting more toward blues rock or classic country, Bly more of a nineties pop and grunge mix.

When there wasn't something they liked, they rode quietly or talked a little about getting to the ferry and the island and looking for the lost backpack. There wasn't much beyond that to plan.

Traffic thinned north of Seattle. They traced a line on the highway with the water to their left, winding up the Sound, across the neck of land between the bays, and reached Anacortes in the mid-afternoon.

There they got on waitlists for the remaining ferries that would leave the terminal for Orcas Island that day. Then they waited. A ferry came and went with no spots open for them.

They got sandwiches and ate at a table outside the terminal. They waited some more, sprawled for a while on the grass. There may have been some dozing for Nils. For Bly, he didn't know.

Then a spot on a ferry opened for them, and Nils drove the truck over the deck onto the ship and they traveled once more across the Sound.

They were back to Orcas Island before dark.

20

A MAN IN A YELLOW reflective jacket working the deck of the ferry caught Nils' attention as he crossed the ramp to the island landing. The man was pointing and appeared to be trying to tell Nils something.

Nils looked to Bly. "You get that?"

"I think he was telling you to keep going?"

"No problem. I'm going." Nils looked back, and the man was gone.

He drove them up Orcas Road and Bly watched beside the shoulder. "This the place?"

"Little farther."

A few minutes later Nils slowed at a curve where he recognized faint skid marks on the blacktop and a ragged scratch in the gravel beside the road. There was no other traffic. He stopped the truck on the gravel shoulder. "Here."

Nils took Bly across the road and down a bit. The daylight had almost faded.

Bly made a general motion with her hands indicating the near vicinity. "Somewhere in here?"

"I think so."

She scanned weeds, trees, and brush. "Kind of thick in there."

"Could be a little farther down."

She looked. "How much farther?"

"A hundred yards, maybe? Half a mile?"

"Okay."

"A little farther?"

"Okay." Quieter this time.

"It seemed more clear when it happened. I know the pack should be on this side."

"That helps. You want to look around a little?"

"Maybe. Is it more conspicuous to be out here in the dark with flash-lights, or tomorrow in the daylight?"

"We don't have flashlights."

"I have the little one."

Bly rubbed her temples. "Much as I want to get started now, I don't think that little light is going to do much. We'll look first thing in the morning."

They walked back to the truck. Nils opened his door and the over-head light illuminated the cab. "I hate to say this."

"I know. It's dark. We've done it again." Bly sighed and got in.

Nils found a remote little beach on some state land. They weren't supposed to camp there, but Nils figured it wasn't the worst of the rules they'd broken in the last few days.

The short stretch of rocks and sand was close enough to the road that they left the truck parked some distance away in a pull-off and walked in to sleep on the beach. The idea was that in the worst case if someone found them, a patrol car, maybe, or some interested local swinging by, they could walk or run away and leave everything behind. So they car-ried in only the tent and sleeping bag and their jackets and a few snacks.

Nils put up the tent in the moonlight and pushed the sleeping bag inside. Then the two of them sat on the rocks, looking out at the water.

Bly still wore the sundress. She tightened it around her legs.

Nils got up and went to the tent and came back with Bly's jacket. He held it out for her to slip into.

Bly snugged her arms into the sleeves. "Such a gentleman."

Again with the gentleman. He didn't exactly know what that meant.

"Nils?"

"Yeah."

"I really want to focus on finding that backpack."

"Me too."

"It'll be the last thing. If we don't find it, I won't keep looking."

He had expected that.

"But I'm really focused on that right now."

"I get that."

"I don't want to…"

"It's okay."

"After I said—"

"It's okay."

Water lapped the rocks at the shoreline.

"When this is over. When we know…"

"Bly?"

"Yeah."

"Your call."

He felt her relax next to him. Then they were both just sitting and looking out over the Salish Sea. The moon was a slice of white against the dark water. A glimmer in the distance marked where a freighter might be moving through a shipping lane.

Nils listened. He felt the tang of the salt air. He leaned to Bly. "Can you hear them?"

"Hear what?"

"The orcas."

Bly bent an ear toward the sea. "Can you?"

"I think so. I think I hear…something."

"What do they sound like?"

Nils didn't know. "Like they're calling?"

They listened for a spell. Then Bly broke the silence. "Can you still hear it?"

"I don't think so."

"I want to hear them."

"Me too."

They sat for some time longer. The air grew cooler. Bly got up. "Nils?"

He looked at her.

"This was nice." And she turned and went to the tent.

A few minutes later, Nils followed. They slept close to each other once more, sharing warmth.

Nils woke later from a strange dream. Something ethereal and slippery that he couldn't quite remember. He'd been swimming…

Bly shifted beside him. "What time is it?"

"Be light soon."

"We might as well get up."

They did, and broke camp and walked down the road to the truck. Nils held the keys up, a question in the gesture.

Bly shook him off. "You drive. You know where we're going."

"If I'm driving, I know a little café we're going to for coffee and breakfast first."

Bly got in the passenger door. Nils took that as a yes.

He drove them to Eastsound. They used the restrooms, and Bly changed out of the sundress back into clothes she'd worn in the redwoods.

They were at Olga Rising when the door opened and ate in the little garden again. Then Bly got them down to business. No more fooling around. They were going to find that backpack.

Nils took them back to the curve in the road. Their cover story, if they needed it, was that they'd been bicycling through the day before and a pannier had slipped loose without them noticing. They were hoping to recover it. That settled, they split up but stayed generally close enough to see or call out to each other.

The morning was cool but warming, the skies clear. Nils waded into the brush and a few minutes later he noticed a small brown spot on his pant leg. He called out to Bly. "Tick."

A moment later, Bly called back. "Tock."

What?

Bly called, "Marco."

"No, ticks."

"What? Your line is Polo."

Nils backed out to the road and brushed the dog tick from his pants. Finding no other little riders climbing on his legs, he tucked the bottom of his pants into his socks.

Bly had come to investigate. "What is it?"

"Ticks in the weeds. Tuck your pants into your socks so you can see them if they crawl up." He gestured to his own pant cuffs.

"You're kidding."

"Better than having them crawl up inside and find a soft spot to bite."

Bly's face twisted. "Jersey girls don't get ticks."

"Your call."

She tucked her cuffs in.

They searched for the backpack and watched for ticks. Some cars passed. Some bicycles passed. No one called out to or bothered Nils or Bly. If anyone even took notice of them, neither Nils nor Bly was aware of it.

About the time Nils started feeling sunlight warm the back of his neck, Bly called out. "Snake."

"Polo."

"That's not funny."

Nils laughed. "I'll keep trying."

"What do I do with this snake?"

"Well, nothing." It seemed like sound advice.

Nils searched more, leapfrogging around Bly to look farther down the road. Not long after, Bly called again. "Is the backpack brown?"

"Yes."

"Sleeping bag and tent strapped to the frame?"

"If there's a backpack there, that will be the one. And yes, sleeping bag and tent."

"Then I found it."

Nils came to where Bly stood looking down into a shallow ditch beside the road. The pack lay upside down at the bottom.

Nils stepped into the ditch and lifted the pack by its frame. A reddish-brown snake that had lay coiled beneath the pack slithered away.

Bly pointed. "Snake."

Nils stepped from the ditch and shook leaves and debris from the pack. "Polo." It still wasn't funny.

Bly wanted to search right there, but Nils convinced her to wait until they'd carried the pack to the truck. He lowered the tailgate and set the pack there. The fabric was damp. It seemed much longer to Nils than a week since he'd seen his belongings.

Bly dug in, reaching for a zipper.

Nils pointed to a different pocket. "This is where I kept the shovel."

She fished a hand greedily into the pocket. Her fingers dug into one corner, then the other, her expression indicating she hadn't found anything.

Her fingers dug some more. "There's another little pocket in here." Then her hand came out. Clutched in it was a stubby metallic key with a flat black grip. "What…?"

"Locker key."

"I see that. Is it yours?"

"Nope."

"And you didn't notice it before now?"

"Didn't look. Supposed to be just the shovel in there."

Bly held the key closer and squinted. "There are numbers, but it doesn't say where this fits." She turned the thing over. "No address or name or anything." She pulled at the plastic grip. "This doesn't come off. I don't see anything else…"

Nils didn't either.

Bly held the key up to the sunlight. "Jimmy."

"Nothing else makes sense."

"Like he said. You were the key."

"In a manner of speaking."

"You would be the one who could find the flash drive."

"Except…"

Bly's hand with the key came down. "Except you don't know where this fits."

"No idea."

"Jimmy didn't give you a clue?"

"Nothing." Nils had gone over this in his head. "I wonder if he meant to come back and find me later. Get the key back then?"

"That would be taking a chance."

"Everything here was chancy. It's a good bet that Jimmy left that key, but finding where it fits is another thing."

Bly entirely disassembled the backpack and opened every pocket, unzipped every zipper, felt every seam, and then searched again. She eventually pushed the pack away. "Just the key."

"Seems like it."

"No flash drive."

"No."

"No other clues, and nothing to tell where the key fits?"

Nils pulled the pack over. "You can keep looking."

"But why would he put the flash drive in the pack too, if he hid the key there? He wouldn't need the key if he had the flash drive."

Nils dropped the pack.

"Where does a key like this fit?"

He speculated. "Airport locker. Bus station." He tried to picture a bank of lockers. "Gym? Museum? Train station?"

Bly's face clouded. "Airport, bus station, train station where?"

Nils dropped his head.

"It could be anywhere." She tossed the key down onto the tailgate. "So that's it then. It's over."

"You could look for the locker."

"From here to New Jersey?"

"Here seems more likely."

Bly circled to the driver's door of the truck and pulled. The door didn't open. "Damn it. Give me the key. Not the stupid locker key. The truck key."

Nils came around and pressed the key into Bly's palm, then moved away. She was in and had the engine going before Nils could close the tailgate and get in the passenger side.

Bly drove fast. Nils clicked his seatbelt. "Remember we don't want to get stopped."

"Doesn't seem to matter much anymore."

It mattered some to Nils.

They neared some other cars ahead and Bly had to slow.

Nils put his window down and took some air. "Where are we headed?"

"I don't know. Does it matter?" She honked the horn, but there was nowhere for the other cars to go and she had to stay behind them.

They went slow for a while, Bly too close to the bumper of the car ahead of them. Then she flicked the wheel, took the truck onto the shoulder, and stopped and jerked the brake lever up. "Damn it." She banged the wheel with a palm. "I so wanted this to work."

Nils waited.

After a few minutes, Bly evened out. "I'll have to go back to daddy. Get you out of this."

"Get me out?"

"You're not going to be any more help to them. I'll have to convince daddy of that."

Nils didn't believe it would be that easy. He took the locker key from his pocket where he'd tucked it and held it out. "Take this."

She looked. "For what? A memento?" But Bly's hand came out and she took the key.

Then Nils remembered. "My phone."

"What about it?"

"In the pack. I thought I'd lost it."

"You did lose it. You'll have to get rid of that. Dump it."

"Probably won't matter now."

"Nils."

He exhaled. "Okay."

They sat in the truck a while longer. Vehicles went by. Nobody in any of them stopped to look at Nils and Bly.

The truck cab was warming, and now Bly rolled down her window. "Here's what we're going to do." Her voice was steady and clear. Assured. Decided. "We're going to get off the island. You'll drop me at the Seattle airport. I'll get a ticket home. It won't matter what license or credit card I use. Daddy will know, but by then I'll be on the plane. He'll have someone looking for me when I land, but that won't matter either—I'm going to him." She breathed. "We'll stop on the way to the airport to get you a burner phone. I can contact you on that."

"When will that be?"

"When will what be?" There was some heat in her words, but Nils didn't take it for him. "I don't know when. But there is no *if*. I *will* contact you, Nils. I'll find you. I owe you that."

It sounded good. Nils hoped it was more than just wishful thinking. He said, "What do I do? After you get on the plane?"

"What you were doing. Stay low if you can. This shouldn't take forever."

Lord, he hoped not.

"I can get you money. Since I'm blowing my cover anyway."

"I'm good on that."

Bly's eyes came to Nils. "You've been more than a good sport about all of this."

He thought she might offer to shake hands. He wouldn't have. "That's not what's been happening, and you know it."

Bly's shoulders rose, held for a moment, then released. "Okay. You're right. That wasn't fair. That's not what was happening with me either. This is just such a mess. It started out as one thing, and then…"

And then.

Bly twisted her hands on the wheel. "Here's what else I want. And this isn't just my call, okay? This is both of us, so you'll have to agree."

He didn't even nod. It was already a yes.

"I want that date. Today. Right now. While we can. In case…"

In case they didn't get another chance.

Bly had her phone out. She looked and swiped. "Spot open on a late ferry we can get."

"Okay."

"We'd have to drive in the dark after we get off. I can sleep at the airport. You can drive to—Sequim, I guess. Return the truck. You'd be driving in the middle of the night, or sleep somewhere if you want."

"All right."

"Unless you want to go down and wait for an earlier ferry."

"Not a chance." And there was no sense getting rested now.

She booked the late ferry. "I'm just going to go ahead and use my card. This thing is going to blow open anyway once I get home."

Then the phone went away. Bly turned to Nils. "That gives us the rest of the day. Noon to sundown for whatever we can fit in. Where do we start?"

Where indeed. But Nils knew. "Let's keep this simple. You seem to like the beach."

She grinned.

"And you bought those swimsuits."

The grin got bigger.

She drove them to Cascade Lake. They changed into the swimsuits, Bly in her slim two-piece, Nils in the baggy thing with the yellow suns wearing the sunglasses.

Not many people were in the water. A few dipped toes or waded in. Bly observed them. "Think it's going to be cold?"

Nils walked to the water. "One way to find out."

He was wrong. There were at least two ways to find out. Bly pushed him in and laughed, and Nils learned first-hand that the water there was refreshingly cool.

The beach area was small and roped with buoys. The boundary was shallow but deep enough to swim there. Bly cut a path from buoy to buoy, swimming through the water with clean, economical strokes. Nils swam behind her.

Bly picked up the pace. Nils picked up his pace to stay close.

Bly kicked harder, her body long and straight and her arms reaching forward. Nils struggled to keep up.

They came to the end of the buoys and Bly let up. "It's good to know you can swim."

"Why's that?"

"It's one of the few things we hadn't raced at yet."

Nils touched the buoy rope. "We haven't been racing."

"Then you haven't been paying attention." She splashed and turned. "Besides, I like you chasing me." She swam off again for the far side.

They stayed in the water a bit longer, and when they came out they were reminded again that towels would be nice in a situation like this. They walked in the sun to dry and warm.

Nils flicked water off. "That wasn't so bad."

Bly squeezed water from her hair. "Not like the Sound. Water there was freezing even from the kayak."

When they'd paddled out to Clark Island.

She smoothed her hair. "You'd freeze out there."

Nils supposed so, and he hoped never to find out.

When they felt dried enough, they went to the beach concession and

Nils bought sandwiches. They ate them leisurely without talking about what would come next on the date.

They cleaned up from lunch and Bly leaned toward Nils. "I'd like to get a little more mileage out of that dress if I can."

"I like that idea."

"But I'm conflicted. I also want to do something more active. Rent bikes. Ride up Mount Constitution."

"You wouldn't want to do those in the dress."

"Probably not."

Nils looked at the sun and thought about how much time they had left. "Your call."

Bly leaned back. "I want you to call this one."

Nils had no problem doing that. "Dress."

They changed clothes and the dress came out and Nils drove them to a pottery place on the north shore. There they climbed the treehouse that was on site and wandered the buildings and outdoor displays, picking up various pieces of pottery and admiring them.

Bly returned to a small coffee cup with an image of an orca and a ferry on it that she had picked up before, and Nils watched her look at it for a long time. He whispered over her shoulder. "Get it. You can take it home."

Bly set the cup back into its place on the table. "I'd like to, but I'm traveling kind of light."

"Get it."

She looked again at the cup. "I don't think I should take anything with me that I don't want to break."

So they went back to Eastsound and walked the little shops, lingering or not as they wanted, both of them knowing they were just window-shopping, not buying.

Dinner was a light meal they shared at a pub down by the water. Nils suggested a drink, but Bly looked out over the inlet bay and seemed distracted. "I'd like to. But we're going to have a long night."

It was sensible. They shared a slice of peach pie instead. After, they walked down to the little strip of rocky beach behind the restaurants and sat on driftwood. It was where Nils had been his first night on the island, after the ride in the sunroof. He looked up and remembered the moon shining down on him when he was here before. "This is the first place I heard them."

"Heard them?"

"The orcas. My first night on the island. After the woman and her daughter and the car. You were…"

"Before we met. When I was coming out to find you."

That about summed it up.

It was quiet and Nils sat with Bly and listened, but he didn't hear the orcas. Maybe they were farther out. Or maybe he'd imagined them. Could you really hear the orcas sing?

Bly set her head on Nils' shoulder. "I don't want to say this."

"Don't."

"But we'd better get to that ferry."

"Is there time for anything else?"

Her whole body sighed. "I don't think so."

21

BLY DROVE them down the island and put them in the queue for the ferry, lined up on the twisting little road with other cars and riders waiting for the ship to arrive. Darkness came while they waited. It was still warm and the truck windows were down and someone walked past carrying coffee in a paper cup.

Bly checked the time. "Seems late for the store to be open."

"It does."

"We have time to get a coffee."

They did.

Inside the store a man stood at the window with a paper cup in his hand, looking out where the ferry would arrive. Another man browsed through sandwiches in the cooler. A woman and young girl picked out fresh fruit and bottled beverages.

Nils and Bly splurged on lattes, Nils thinking this could be the last time he would buy anything for Bly. He hoped it wouldn't be.

As they walked back to the truck with their lattes, a subroutine started quietly playing in the back of Nils' head. He hadn't once worried since they'd been on the island that someone would recognize him. He hadn't kept his head down, worn the cap, or looked away. Things had felt normal.

Nils and Bly boarded the ferry, left the truck on the vehicle deck, and went up the stairs to stand outside and look over the water as Orcas Island disappeared behind them. The ship lights lit a pale yellow glow around Nils and Bly as they walked the deck. They rested on a rail very near the spot on another ferry, or maybe even this exact one, where Nils had been dangling when this adventure had started. When he'd seen the woman and child, and the man chasing them.

A breeze stirred the hem of Bly's dress and billowed the fabric around her legs. It recalled for Nils how the woman from that other ferry trip had tried to tuck her daughter under the folds of her skirt, holding the child there to protect her, the look on the woman's face telling Nils that she would have done anything to protect her daughter. Nils seeing that look and responding to it.

The ship's horn sounded, and Nils wondered what other souls out in the world beyond the ferry deck could hear it, who in the darkness knew they were approaching, what life lay beneath the dark waters where he couldn't see it.

They were maudlin thoughts, probably brought on by anticipation of soon not having Bly at his side. How different that was from the last time he'd stood at this spot on a Washington State ferry and wanted nothing more than to be alone. But Bly was still here now. He wasn't alone yet.

Nils turned from the rail and let an arm reach for Bly and wrap around her. She moved to accept the arm, her body nestling closer to his.

She felt warm against the chill that was settling into the air. Nils let the contours of their bodies find each other. "We'll have to get our jackets soon."

Bly didn't seem in a hurry to break away.

The ship's engines revved and the ferry slowed. In the gray near distance, the lights of the ferry dock at Anacortes cut across the water.

The ship slowed more, the deck vibrating with the strain of the change of speed.

A tone sounded, and an announcement came over the public address system. *All passengers please wait to depart. Please proceed immediately to the main passenger deck.*

Nils tensed. "I don't remember that announcement from before."

"That's because you didn't hear it before."

Bly broke from him and leaned over the rail with her nose in the wind looking left, right, down.

The rumbling in the engines and the deck floor faded. Nils leaned over the rail beside Bly. "I think we've stopped."

"We have. And you didn't see that before either." She pointed, and Nils followed the angle of her arm down to a shape sitting low on the water, up against the hull of the ferry. A small craft. Open at the back but with a cabin big enough to hold several people. The craft had no lights on. No white masthead or stern lights, no red and green port and starboard lights. Nothing to identify it at night on the water.

Dark shapes moved on the back of the craft.

"Bly..."

"I see them."

The message on the PA repeated. All persons to the passenger deck.

A few others on the upper level with Nils and Bly moved to the stairs. Nils turned to watch them.

Bly took his arm. "We're not going to the passenger deck."

"Where are we going?"

"Working on it." She pressed her hands onto Nils' shoulders. "Stay here. Promise me you'll stay here."

"What—"

"Just stay here. Until I get back."

"Where are you going?"

"Truck. To get my pistol."

Nils didn't like it. But he didn't have a better move. He heard Bly's footsteps ringing down the stairs, then he did not.

The PA message repeated, adding that the delay was unexpected and should be short. Please be patient.

The deck was empty now except for Nils. No one came to clear him out, move him down to the passenger deck.

There were footsteps on the stairs again. He hoped they were Bly's, and they were. She ran across the deck to him. "Daddy. And some men."

"Men you don't know?"

"Some. And Zeke and Petey."

"Who are—"

"Get ready."

"For what?"

"We're going to negotiate." She stepped beside Nils and checked the pistol. "This is happening a little sooner that I thought, but here we go."

Voices rose up the stairwell. Steady, deliberate footsteps plodded. Then, "Wormbleeey."

"Petey, you retard. Shut up!"

"Ah-roooo! You're not supposed to say retard anymore. It's not nice."

Bly stepped in front of Nils. "Stay behind me."

"I—"

"Get behind!"

He did.

Men appeared at the top of the stairs. Big Zeke, large and hunched in the Giants jacket. Petey, in a suit jacket with a t-shirt underneath, a watery look in his eyes.

A tall and wide-shouldered man with dark hair and a very serious jaw with a very serious set to it, standing between Zeke and Petey.

Three other men. Dark, nondescript clothing. Men who looked like those who had been drinking coffee at the window of the store on Orcas.

The man between Zeke and Petey stepped forward. "Warbly."

"Daddy."

"Girl, you wear a dress."

Bly stood unmoving, the hem of the sundress drifting gently at her legs.

"It wears well on you." Dommy slipped the heavy suit coat from his shoulders and held it out on a finger. "But you look cold."

"I'm not cold, daddy. I have a jacket."

His eyes ran over Bly. "You don't wear a jacket. You should put it on."

Bly stood as she was, the gun in her hand, hung down at her side.

Dommy handed his jacket to one of the men behind him, then adjusted the belt at his waist. No one else moved or spoke, only Dommy. He stood tall and squared to Nils and Bly.

Nils made the space between him and Bly and the others at about twenty-five feet. He tried to identify holsters or guns in the hands of the men, but he could see clearly only Dommy's hands, and those were empty.

Having removed his jacket and adjusted his belt, Dommy spoke. "This is the man?"

Bly was a statue in front of Nils. "He doesn't know anything."

"We will determine that." Dommy lifted a hand and wiggled two fat fingers in the air. He leaned to open a line of sight around Bly. "Come out so I can see you."

Nils stepped left and Bly let him.

"My daughter comes for you?"

"She…"

"She comes to this island looking for you, and she finds you?"

"Yes."

Dommy put a big hand to his chin and worked it around. "You are a lot of trouble, yes?"

Nils supposed Dommy might see it that way. He didn't.

"And she tells you what this is about?"

Bly inched closer again to Nils. "He doesn't know much. Not enough to be trouble."

"But to be helpful, maybe?" The hand came away from Dommy's jaw and pointed into the air with two fingers out like a gun. "So?"

"He doesn't know where the flash drive is. We looked."

The fingers came down and pointed to Nils. "I speak to you now. So you know this is important?"

Nils had no words. He'd seen the helicopter. The men at the top of the mountain. The men who had taken him in the van. That seemed important.

"You know we must be sure?"

Now words came to Nils. "I don't know anything about what Jimmy took from you or where he put it."

Dommy's gaze shifted to Bly, then to one side to Zeke and to the other to Petey. Then to the men behind him. Something passed between them that Nils didn't understand.

Then Dommy's gaze came back to Nils. "So you know enough."

"Daddy, no."

"Warbly, my little—"

"I'm not your little girl."

Dommy stepped forward. "Warbly."

Bly steadied herself against the ferry deck, the pistol still at her side. "The flash drive is lost. No one will find it."

Dommy came forward again. "If that is true, then we can resolve all of this—" the hand with the fingers made a tight swirl in the air— "very quickly."

Dommy gestured to Zeke and Petey. Zeke looked resigned. Petey looked excited like bacon on hot grease. Both men moved toward Nils. Petey cackled. "Roo-ooo!"

"Daddy!"

"This will not take long."

Dommy stepped behind Zeke and Petey.

Bly pushed Nils behind her and stepped back, moving them along the ship's rail. "Leave him out of it. He doesn't know anything."

"The boys can make sure of that."

"Daddy!" Bly pushed Nils harder down the rail.

"Little Warbly, we will not hurt you."

Dommy stepped forward. Bly and Nils stepped back.

"It is this man we want."

"You can't have him."

"Warbly, be reasonable."

Dommy and the men stepped forward. Bly and Nils stepped back.

"Daddy, I like him."

"Wait." Dommy stopped. The other men with Dommy stopped. Petey danced uncomfortably, the wolf ready for the chase. His eyes lasered on Bly, revenge lurking in them.

Dommy spoke. "You like this man?"

Bly nodded once.

Dommy's eyes dropped, almost imperceptibly, then re-leveled. "This I regret very much." He gestured to Zeke and Petey. "We will be quick. Strike fast and the pain will be over."

Bly's pistol came up.

Dommy stepped from the other men and faced his daughter. "Little Warbly, we will not hurt you. You must step aside."

"Daddy, you already have hurt me."

Dommy's eyes changed. Harder, set, resigned. "No. We will hurt you no more after this. It must be done."

Bly stood true, the barrel of her pistol up and riveted like an extension of her body. "Daddy, please listen."

He did not. Dommy's face no longer showed the look of a father. It showed the look of a man who wanted Nils, and he would have him now.

Petey cackled. His arms came up and an image of a horned wolf appeared on the shirt beneath his jacket. A holstered gun hung at his waist.

Bly shoved Nils back. "Jump."

They had reached the girder. The beam where Nils had hung when this started for him. When he first saw the woman and child. He looked over the rail at the dark waters below. Would the woman have jumped? Would she have asked her daughter to, if that was all there was left to do? And could Nils jump now?

Bly called to him. "Nils, I'm with you."

He reached up.

"I'm making the call. Jump."

His vision clotted and his senses swam. Something beyond the rail called him. Was it the orcas, singing from the deep?

A gunshot rang out.

"Warbly!"

Bly stepped hard back into Nils. His hands gripped the steel beam and he pulled himself up, fast, high, tight, curling his body into a ball.

Another gunshot.

Nils swung out from the beam, arcing over the rail.

"Nils! Jump! Jump!"

He already had. He spun, arced, turned in the air, and grasped at a fleeting glimpse of the sundress as he fell.

"Nils!"

"Ahhh-rooo-ooooo!"

Then it was only darkness as Nils plunged toward the cold, cold Salish Sea.

22

NILS REMEMBERED to suck air, force his lungs to fill to avoid the sharp intake of breath that hitting the cold water could bring, a reaction that could be fatal. He tried to scissor his feet apart, hold his arms out in a cross, and bring his feet together and his arms down to limit his descent in the water.

Then he hit hard. And cold. Cold cold cold.

Deep into the water. Nils' body twisted, his feet coming up, his head down, spinning. He slowed. Cold. Dark. Up. Which way was up?

He opened his eyes and found dim light. Kicked, pushed, swam toward the light. Keep Moving. Move. Don't stop. Kick, push, arms. Don't stop.

He surfaced, found air, breathed.

Cold. Swim. Move. Don't stop. He was near the ship. Swim from the ship, from the engines, from the water that would churn. Swim from the smaller boat. Swim. Don't freeze. Don't stop.

His shoes dragged and Nils kicked them off. His pants sucked at his legs and he uncinched his belt, struggled for his wallet before the pants floated away. Wallet clenched in his teeth, swimming.

He dove and swam, dove and swam. Kept moving. Don't freeze. It was unbearable and interminable. Maybe the last thing he would do. Don't stop and maybe it wouldn't be.

It was endless until it wasn't. Until Nils found ground. Mucky, soupy, slick ground. Mud flats. Old piers. A lost dock. Lots of mud. Cold.

The mud reached his shins. He waddled and ran, reached firmer ground, peeled the destroyed socks off.

Then a road. Nils ran in bare feet and underwear, a ruined shirt. He wanted warmth. Cleaned of the muck. He wanted Bly. Nils wanted, he wanted. He ran.

And his mind slowly emptied, only a few thoughts left. Not frozen. Not drowned. He ran through the streets like a dog.

If ever asked what he'd done, if he would tell, Nils might recall a few key elements.

Boots left in a carport.

A laundromat, clothes left unattended while their owner smoked a cigarette outside.

A city park, a maintenance door left open. Warmth. Rest. Longing. Where was Bly? What had happened to Bly?

Lord, how he ached. Lord, how he longed. Lord, how things had changed in an instant.

He slept a little or not in the maintenance building and rose before daylight. He had wet money to buy a few things. Shoes that fit, socks. Pants, a belt, clothes. Then walking, coffee, food.

He hitched a ride to Sequim.

Then walking, walking, to the storage unit. The key to his lock on the unit gone, swallowed with his pants by the Salish Sea.

Nils waiting a long time for someone to arrive at the facility. Then he convinced that man to call the owner. Waited again, until the owner came and remembered Nils, took the lock off Nils' unit with bolt cutters.

Nils in his storage unit. With his things. What he had of things. Some money left, tucked above the door. The last of his savings. He would need that.

Then a place to crash. Friends. An unused tent on a wooden platform. Alone in the trees at the edge of a lavender farm. Some work. Some cash. Some food for meals.

Alone. Lots of time alone. Company up at the house if he wanted it, if he would walk there, leave the tent on the platform in the trees and interact with humanity.

Nils opted instead for a hot plate and a single lamp. Electricity from a long extension cord run from a small outbuilding used occasionally by the farm. A mattress in the tent on the plank platform floor. Wooden apple crates to hold the hot plate and house the few belongings Nils had purchased.

They were good friends and knew Nils' ways, and they let him be. The folks who owned the land, owned the farm. Nils had helped them out of a jam a few years ago. Their son, some locals, the authorities. Nils had helped the kid make restitutions. It meant a lot to the family, and Nils had stayed and worked for a while. Returned again for a few brief stays.

He'd said this time simply that he needed a quiet place for a while. The friends had pointed to the tent in the fields. If they knew he'd jumped into a car on Orcas Island a week before, they didn't mention it. They asked no questions. They were that kind of friends.

Nils had seen the recent news. A federal agent killed on a Washington State ferry bound for Anacortes. Others overboard and assumed drowned. No one was named, not even the number of people involved. The story ended with the traffic back-up, the snarl of delays from the late and cancelled ferries.

It was the plural that got to Nils. *Others* overboard and assumed drowned. He was one. How many others, and who were they?

Now, eight days out from his swim in the Salish Sea, Nils was still numb, his mind not yet working right. Alone, and waiting. For what?

His days were slow, his thoughts slower, moving like brackish water in the bayou. Cottony thoughts that wouldn't fully form, that slipped away when he tried to grab them, fluttery things that would not become concrete and sensible.

Nils' body was preserved, but his mind was loose and rambling. He was good at being alone, but wondering if he would have to stay hidden forever was unsettling. Wondering what had become of Bly was unbearable.

Now, trying to gather his thoughts, to find some grounding, Nils sat on the edge of the wooden platform that held the tent. The tent was behind him, the platform larger than the tent, and Nils rested at the edge of shade, in dappled sunlight. Today, he would gather himself. He would begin to plan how to move on. Today.

A shape appeared in the field, approaching. A figure, thin and lean. Graceful. A memory.

Nils didn't rise. If he had, the ground may have rushed up too fast to meet him.

He sat, quiet. Waited, while something began to resurrect within him.

Bly approached through the sunlit field and crossed into the mottled shadows to Nils. She wore long pants and a lightweight, long-sleeved shirt. A large-brimmed sun hat protected her face and neck. She carried a small day pack on her back.

Bly stopped in front of Nils and looked at him, and Nils at her. Then she sat on the platform beside him so they were thigh to thigh, her legs dangling where his legs dangled. Bly removed the hat. "Nice place you've got here."

"It's for the seasonal workers."

The hat went down to the wooden deck. "Is that you?"

"No. There's no one here now."

"Just us."

Nils figured that about summed it up. "How did you find me?"

Bly looked out on the fields. "Do you know how many lavender farms there are up here?"

"A lot."

She let her eyes come to Nils' now. "I remembered you talking about it. A place you'd worked. Like it meant something to you."

"It does."

"I couldn't find you. I didn't have anywhere else to look." She reached to Nils' face and tucked a strand of sandy hair from his forehead. "Have you seen the news?"

"Some. A week ago."

She released the strand of hair. "You're not dead."

"No."

"Everyone else seems to think so."

Nils' head turned slowly, very slowly, until his face lined up exactly with Bly's.

"They've called off the search."

He tried to nod, but he just wanted to look at Bly. "I wondered about you too. How'd you know to look for me?"

"You weren't dead."

"How did you know?"

Her eyes crinkled, some deep thought or feeling passing behind them. "I didn't want you to be."

Bly could do that. Will things into being. She'd willed herself to find Nils and snatch him from the agents on the mountain. Willed Jimmy Cheek's key to be real and for them to find it. And now it was as if some part of her had helped will Nils into surviving the jump from the ferry and for her to find him. He wondered what she could will into being next.

The crinkle faded from Bly's eyes and she smiled. "Look at us. Both not dead."

They sat together for a moment, both just being alive, knowing the other was too.

Then Bly said, "I'd just about given up trying to find you. But there seems to be some sort of connection between us."

She didn't have to try to explain it. Nils felt something lighter inside him where there had been something heavy. A weight lifting from his mind, trying to float away. "I have some questions."

"And I have some things to tell you."

Half a minute passed. Neither of them asked a question or told the other anything. Nils lifted himself from the deck. "I don't have much. I could make coffee."

"Coffee would be nice."

Nils moved his feet and went into the tent. He could do that now, he could stand and walk and function, his mind assured that Bly was no illusion, that she was real and solid and not a chimera conjured up by the sunlight and lavender.

Bly got up and called into the tent. "Is there a place to freshen up?"

Nils shook his head. "Sorry. Just an outhouse."

"No worse than what we've done before. I really just want to clean up."

He pointed with a thumb. "There's water at the pump. Soap and a towel."

"I'll manage."

"I know you will."

Nils put water in the kettle and set that on the hot plate. He scooped grounds into the coffee press and waited.

The tent was tall enough to stand in, and the front flaps were open and made an upside-down *v*. Nils watched as Bly reappeared through that aperture.

The coffee was ready. There was a chair inside the tent and the tops of the side-turned apple crates he could use as a table, but Nils carried the coffee and a porcelain cup outside. He set the cup on the decking and poured. "We'll have to share. There's only one cup."

Bly grinned. "I know how to share." She let the coffee sit and cool. "You look like you're feeling better."

Nils straightened.

"When I walked up. You looked a little…"

"Bit of a surprise when I saw you."

"Yeah. I was going to say down in the tooth."

"It's down in the mouth."

Bly put an elbow very gently into Nils' rib. "See? You're already feeling better."

"I guess I am."

Bly tested the coffee, a small sip. Too hot.

"Sorry. No cream." Nils pointed to the outbuilding where the extension cord ran to the tent. "There's a little fridge in there, but I don't keep much in it."

"What would you keep in there if you did?"

"Beer."

"Got you." Bly set the cup back down.

They sat, not side by side now, but facing, with the coffee press and cup between them. Bly with her legs crossed.

Nils dangled one leg from the decking. "I heard gunshots. On the ferry, before I jumped."

"Yes."

"You fired?"

"Yes."

The coffee cooled. Nils ignored it. "One of the FBI men was killed."

Bly looked very serious. "Yes."

"You killed him?"

"No." Bly kept her gaze very steadily on Nils. "Petey."

"Hmm."

"The agents and daddy disagreed. They wanted you gone. Daddy is more flexible."

"Your father seemed like he wanted me dead."

Bly placed a hand on Nils' knee. "I'm sorry about that. Since then he's become…more open to options."

"Why is that?"

Bly's eyes said something Nils couldn't read. "You don't know?"

"What don't I know?"

"I jumped."

A cold stone sank through Nils' chest. "Jumped?"

"Off the ferry. After you."

Nils recalibrated. "I didn't know."

"I couldn't find you. In the water."

"I swam away."

"That was smart. They found me. Zeke pulled me out."

Sunlight filtered through a movement of the trees and warmed Nils' face. He felt grateful for that. Warmth.

"I don't think I would have made it if they hadn't pulled me from the water. I don't know how you did."

"It was cold."

"Very. I was in there a long time."

Nils thought about it. "Because you were looking for me?"

"Uhm?"

"You were in the water a long time because you were looking for me?"

"Yeah."

"And I wasn't there. I swam away."

"You didn't know. That I was looking for you."

He hadn't. "So your father took that as…"

"My daddy's thinking has shifted. He saw that I trusted you enough to risk my own life."

Nils tried the coffee now, for a thing to do. It was still a bit warm and he took a swallow. He set the cup back down. She trusted him enough.

Bly's hand came from Nils' knee and she settled it into her lap. "I risked both our lives. You trusted me enough to jump. I owed it to you to follow."

"Okay."

"My daddy thinks you're dead. But if he knew you were alive, he would think differently from before."

"I guess that's good."

"The FBI men think you're dead too."

"And that's good?" Nils felt a breeze on his neck. Warmth on his face. Mixed messages. "Everyone thought I was dead but you."

Bly looked down at her hands. "It wasn't real until I walked across this field and saw you sitting there. I believed, but now you're real. Now I can touch you."

Nils touched Bly's shoulder. "Same."

"There's more, now that I've found you."

"Listening."

"Daddy has offered a deal. I'll look for you. He has no problem with that. He thinks you're dead. If I don't find you, this will end."

Nils thought it over. "That's not much of a deal."

"There's more. If I can't find you, I'll come back home. I'll stay with daddy."

"And become part of the business."

A sad nod of her chin.

"Is that something you'd really do?"

"I don't know. But it's a deal I had to make to look for you."

He turned that over. "You father's paying for it? For this." He gestured to Bly being there, her presence with him at the tent in the lavender field.

"I don't have much of my own without him. Daddy wouldn't let me."

"It keeps you close to him."

The tilt of Bly's head said yes.

"And if you find me?"

"That's more complicated. You can stay disappeared. You can run away and create a new life if you want, hope not to be found. That's what you wanted before."

That's what he had here, in the lavender field. But this was short-term. After here, Nils didn't know what he had.

"Or I can help you try to get your life back. Then you can do what you want."

That possibility hung between them like fruit on a limb just out of reach.

Bly wasn't done. "There's another part of the deal I made with daddy. If I find the things that Jimmy took from him, if I return those, he'll let me go. This has nothing to do with you. Daddy thinks you're dead. But finding that flash drive is still a way out for me."

"You believe that?"

"Daddy is a man of his word. Especially with family."

With his Warbly.

"And since you aren't dead, it can be a way out for you too."

"And if you don't find it?"

"Then I'll go to daddy and make another deal. If I can't find the flash drive, no one can. It's lost forever. He can let you go."

"He'd go for that?"

"He doesn't think he'd have to. He thinks you're dead." She took up Nils' hands in hers now. "Listen, we won't find the flash drive. We just have to show that we tried. As hard as the agents or anyone else could. Eventually, that locker will be opened. It might be a while, but time will expire and that locker will be opened. Someone will find the flash drive when that happens or not. They'll look at what's on it or not. These are all assumptions. We don't really know that Jimmy put the flash drive in a locker and the key from your backpack fits it, but what else could be the truth? And if someone looks at the files, so what? They'll be financials. Numbers, spreadsheet accounts. They could be for anything. Daddy is already switching over his accounts. He has people for that. It's a protection. The details are coded. They don't say what the transactions are really for. Those files would only be meaningful to daddy, or someone who knows what he's doing."

"Like the agents your father is working with."

A nod. "And if someone else ever found those files. If they ever looked at them…"

"They wouldn't know what they were."

"Exactly. Or be interested."

Nils looked at the coffee they hadn't drunk. It was surely cold by now. "It's a long shot."

"This whole thing has been a long shot. I think there's something happening between us. There was. There still could be. I want to find out more about that. I'm not good at this, but how good do you have to be? If you want to be with someone, how perfect do things have to be to make it work?"

True. Nils took in the things around him. Trees, lavender farm, tent, coffee cup, woman. Bly. "Not perfect at all." This was plenty good enough.

They let their hands go. Nils adjusted himself on the deck. "So where does that leave us?"

"Same as before. We have to show that the files can't be found."

"Your father believes I don't have them?"

"Jumping from the ship was a convincing move. Being dead is even better."

Nils supposed so. "How long do we look?"

"Long enough to convince daddy."

"That will have to be your call."

"I have some money. I can use my ID. Daddy will track that. If we're careful, he won't know you're with me."

So Bly had already decided. Nils would go with her. He stood and picked up the coffee press and the cup. "Let's get planning."

Bly's hand went to Nils' arm. "Leave the coffee. First, there's something we should have done a long time ago."

She guided him into the tent, turned him around, and sat him on the bed. "Nils?"

"Yeah."

"You're not dressed for the beach."

"We're not at the beach."

"No." Bly stood in front of Nils, in front of the upside-down *v* of the tent flaps, with the sunlight and lavender fields behind her. She pulled loose the sun shirt she wore and stretched it up over her torso and from her arms. The fabric was very light and floated over Bly's head like gauze.

She wore nothing beneath the shirt and Bly's slim figure glowed a very light tinge of golden brown under the sunlight. Her smile was quizzical, her black hair brushing the tops of her breasts as if inviting them to dance. Her breasts were small and firm with dark little nipples, as Nils remembered them. Better.

Bly held Nil's gaze. "I saw you pretending not to look at the beach." She put a hand to the waist of her hiking pants and with the other took hold of the zipper. "You were being such a good boy."

"Uhmmm."

The zipper came down, and the pants came to rest atop Bly's boots. She deftly stepped from the boots, then from the bunched pantlegs. "I have a confession." Her runner's legs were sleek, the muscles firm at the calf, defined at the thigh, and slipping tautly under white cotton panties. "I looked too."

"Uh huh." Nils was getting on board now, heavily.

"It's one way to gauge a man's level of interest."

"I hope you didn't look when we came across the woman with the dog."

Bly's smile was genuine, sultry cut with surprise.

Nils had his shirt off now, working to catch up with Bly. Tugging at his shoes, getting ready for the beach. "Or when we came out of the water."

Bly's smile cut from sultry to smoking. "Nils?"

"Uh-huh."

"Are you still interested?"

He stopped tugging at a shoe. "I've had a mental hard-on for you since you chased me down the mountain." He touched the fingers of one hand to the opposite wrist. "Since your fingers touched my wrist."

"A mental hard-on?"

"You know, in my mind. Nothing weird."

"A little weird is okay. I've wanted to jump your bone since the beach."

"Bones."

"What?"

"The saying is jump your bones."

Bly ran a hand up one of her runner's legs, over her runner's thigh, under the white cotton to the inside of the runner's hip. "It's just the one I've been thinking about."

She stepped closer. One leg hooked inside Nils' knee. "Hold your hand out."

He did, and Bly reached for it and turned the hand over, palm up. She stepped into the hand and pressed the white cotton against Nils' touch. "Nils?"

"Yeah."

"No more teasing, okay? Let's do this."

They did, Bly leading and Nils following. Then the lead changed, and changed again. For Nils it was something like a very erotic series of dances he vaguely knew the steps to. A gentle waltz to start, just getting to know you. Then a tentative foxtrot, elbows and limbs searching for angles and direction in the close space. Then the quickening rhythm of a salsa, steamy and with a lot of hip. Sliding to something of a jazz riff, a central theme with some testing of the edges, stretching and bending of the notes. Exploring for new harmonics. He might even have believed something of a disco was involved, a wild spinning of sensations like the mattress had become a swirling ball.

When they were satisfied, Nils lay with Bly's head on his shoulder, the scent of woman and of lavender hanging over him.

23

THEY MAY HAVE DOZED. Then Nils felt Bly's legs wrap into his. "Well, we seem to be compatible."

It was a strange feeling for him, going from alone, alone, alone to Bly, Bly, Bly. It was a feeling he could get used to. For more than a week he'd thought Bly was gone. Now, love was more than just in the air. It was in his bed. It was a good day at the lavender farm. "Was that a concern?"

Bly moved now to open some space between them, letting air in where it had gotten warm. "I wouldn't call it a concern, but it's a good thing to know." She rolled off the mattress to the plank floor and stood. Stretched, and walked around the mattress to her clothes.

Nils watched silently.

Bly reached for her shirt and smiled. "Is the view here as good as it was at the beach?"

"Better."

She pulled her shirt on.

Nils admired that. "You still have the dress?"

"Sadly, no. I'll get another if you'd like."

"I would."

Bly pulled on her pants and zipped them. "We never drank our coffee."

"No."

She stepped out of the open tent flap and bent to the coffee press and the cup where they sat on the decking. "Okay if I make fresh?"

"Sure." It was a luxury they could afford now.

Bly brought the press in and made coffee as she had seen Nils do, heating the water on the hot plate and pouring that into the press over grounds.

Nils dressed and came behind Bly. Space was close in the tent and he was unsure of protocol. So much had changed in one morning.

He rinsed the cup of old coffee and set that by the press. "What happened to the truck?"

Bly watched the coffee in the press. She and Nils were very close. "That's what's on your mind? Right now?"

"Uhm."

"I'm making coffee."

"Uh-huh."

"We're talking about the truck."

"Yeah…?"

"Normal things."

"Well, I don't think most people would consider it normal to get a truck the way we did, then abandon it on a ferry by jumping into the water."

"Setting that aside." She made a little motion as if picking up a small thing in her fingers and moving it out of the way. "The truck was probably impounded, reported stolen, and returned to the guys at the garage, just like we arranged."

"Okay."

Bly wrapped her arms around Nils. "What do you want to do right now?"

He hugged Bly back. "Have coffee?"

"Good answer. With me?"

"Of course with you. With the one cup. Like we did on the trail."

"A normal thing? Coffee?"

"Yeah."

"Our way, with one cup?"

"Yeah."

"That's what I want too. See? Normal."

"Uh-huh?"

"Nils? I told you this is the part I'm not good at. After. But look. I'm making coffee. I'm here. I don't want to run away."

"And you don't want me to run away either?"

For an answer she squeezed him tighter.

"So it's not awkward?"

Bly released the hug. "I didn't say that. It's a little awkward, but it's what I want to do."

And it's what they did.

They sat on the planks in front of the tent, shared coffee from the one cup, and watched sunlight on lavender.

After they'd had their fill and the coffee had begun to cool, Bly said, "This is nice. And I'd like to stay here but..." She leaned back on her hands. "I have to try to give you your life back." She picked up the cup. "I'll have to plead my case to daddy. I could do that now. We're not going to find the locker. We don't have to pretend to look for it. Daddy will decide what daddy decides."

"And what does that mean?"

"I want to get this over with."

Nils raised an eyebrow.

"This thing with you and daddy. And the agents. I want you to be clear of all that."

"I want that too."

"But..."

Nils waited.

"I didn't expect to find you. But I did. And right now nobody else knows you're alive. Just me and your friends there in the house. And I don't think anyone is going to come looking for you."

"Probably not."

"I have you to myself. And I like that."

"I'm with you."

"But let's go. Let's get this done. I don't have to hide from daddy anymore. I have a rental car and I can bankroll. Let's drive down the coast and *look* for that locker." She used air quotes at *look*.

"Just you and me."

"You and me. And then I'll jump into the fire. I'll figure out how to make my case with daddy, and I'll do it. I'll get you clear."

"Done."

They cleaned up the coffee pot and the cup. Nils packed a few things. Then they walked out of the fields to Bly's rental car and drove.

They made a game of it. Where would the key fit? Where do *you* think it would fit? Making funny suggestions. And they went and tried some of them. Others were just part of the game.

They started in Fort Bragg. Drove back down the coast, taking their time, stopping when they wanted and driving when they felt like it. Little motel rooms. Diner food. Keeping it breezy, trying not to think about what would happen when they reached Portland. That's where Bly knew that Jimmy had flown into, and it's where she had determined they would stop looking and she would decide how to talk to her father.

They found no match for the key in Fort Bragg and started back up the coast in no hurry to get to Portland.

If asked to recall what that week with Bly had been like, Nils might reply that he'd felt like a kept man. And an invisible man, except to Bly. And he'd had no problem with either of those.

They drank a lot of coffee. They did the things that came before coffee. They did the things that came after coffee. They were compatible on all counts.

They ran along the beaches. Did isometrics on the sand. Yoga, plank, squats. Bly showed off with handstands. She did some kind of fighting maneuvers while Nils watched, Bly's form sure and exact, quick when she moved. Nils found monkey bars on a playground and did lifts. Both of them staying in shape.

Not once did Nils feel like he wanted to be alone.

When they reached Portland they slowed it way down. The game of finding the key got more attention, not because they thought they would find the locker but because neither of them wanted this time to end.

They rehearsed what Bly might say to her father, nothing sticking, nothing feeling right. They checked the short-term lockers at the bus and train stations, knowing these wouldn't likely be a fit. They found a luggage storage place near the airport that didn't use keys. That didn't work.

There wasn't much left before Bly would have to go back to her father. They walked and ate at the food trucks and drank coffee. The game was almost over. Nils got quieter, and so did Bly.

At a street corner near the car, when they were out of ideas and headed for the airport and Nils could hear the fat sizzling in the fire that was coming, Bly stopped and set a hand on top of what looked like a row of oversized dog cages. "Are these what I think they are?"

"If you're thinking bike locker."

"Let's say I was." She took the key out. "Doesn't seem like Jimmy, but this may be our last chance." She kissed the key. "Maybe if I click my heels three times."

"That's for going home."

"I thought it was for making a wish."

"Only if you're wishing to go home."

"Huh."

"Have you even seen The Wizard of Oz?"

"Heard of it. I know there's witches."

"Just put the key in."

Bly Bent to the nearest lock. "But no heel clicking. I don't really want to go home." She casually slipped the key into the lock.

Nils stared.

Bly inhaled. She gave a little twist and the key didn't turn. But it went in. "Nils."

"I see it."

The key came out. Bly turned it over for a closer look. "There are numbers."

Nils was already looking at the other lockers. "Read them."

They tried all of the other lockers. None of them matched the number on the key. Bly tried the key in all of the locks anyway. None of them opened, but the key slipped into every one.

Then Nils took Bly's arm and drew her around the corner. "That looks suspicious. Checking all the locks."

She had her phone out. "Are there other bike lockers anywhere else in the city?"

"No idea."

Locations for other bike lockers popped up on a map on Bly's phone. Nils was looking at them and checking street signs against the map.

It didn't take long from there. The next set of lockers had a matching set of numbers. The key went into that lock and turned. There was no bicycle inside.

Bly crouch-walked into the locker. A few seconds later she came out with a small manila envelope in her hand. The envelope had a rectangular bulge in the center. "Nils."

"I see it."

"I can't look."

"You can."

Bly opened the envelope and tipped it. A flash drive dropped out into her hand.

24

BLY GOT SERIOUS. She bought a laptop computer and took that with Nils to a hotel room near the airport where they holed up.

She worked the laptop, navigating the set-up with intensity and focus.

Nils watched. It was Bly's game.

She thumbed the flash drive from its casing. "What are the odds we'd get this far?"

"So very long."

She fitted the drive into the port. "Saddle up."

The storage device was neither encrypted nor password protected. Folders appeared. Bly selected financials and drilled down. An Excel roll-up appeared, then another, and individual files. "Cost centers." She scrolled through columns and subtotals.

"You know this stuff?"

"My daddy has guys with degrees. They taught me some things." More columns and rows and numbers rolled by. "He was preparing me."

Nils tried to see Bly in a business suit, big mahogany desk. Running a board meeting? Sending Zeke and Petey out on errands? None of it fit. But she seemed comfortable with the numbers.

Bly backed out of the spreadsheets and selected other folders. Documents opened with account names and numbers. Transfers, balances. "Some of this is dark web. Money changing, fungibles. Some crypto."

"So these are the files Jimmy took?"

"Yeah. A hundred percent." Bly's fingers danced, then they stopped. She zoomed in. "You see that?" Her finger went to a name.

Nils leaned closer. Read the name.

"That's daddy's main guy. The agent. The one that pulls the strings at the FBI." She did a search in the file, found the name again. "I know him a little. He says crazy stuff. Like hell from a wildcat."

"Come down on you like hell on a wildcat."

Bly stopped.

"Whatever that means."

"How'd you know that's what he says?"

"He's the one I talked to on the phone. On Orcas."

"Before the van."

"And the guys with the guns, and the bag over my head."

"That makes sense, but I don't like it."

"Why not?" It sounded silly. What was to like?

"He doesn't like people to know who he is. He wouldn't like knowing his name is on these."

"I guess that's good to know, but it seems like it makes the problem a little harder?"

"He might not know his name is on here. Maybe we can use that."

Bly opened the snipping tool and took a screenshot. Saved that and took another.

Nils watched her work. "That's how you found me. The first time."

Bly's finger stopped. "Yes."

"You knew your father's guy."

"Nils…"

He put a hand up and waved her off. "Nah, it's okay. That's how you knew I was going up Mount Constitution. Then you double-crossed this FBI guy when you…"

"When I took you for myself."

Plucked him right off the mountain. Nils turned from watching Bly at the laptop.

She looked back. "We okay?"

"Yeah. I'm good with that."

Bly went back to the Excel files and the snipping tool.

Nils crossed the hotel room to the sink outside the bathroom. He switched on the light and looked at himself in the mirror. He needed a shave.

A hand went to his face, ran over the stubble on his chin and cheek.

Cheek. Jimmy Cheek. This whole thing had started with a last-minute addition to a hiking trip, an addition that should have meant nothing. Just another walk in the woods. Not a life-changing event.

He put a hand on the counter, then used the other to turn the cold water tap and splash water on his face.

"Nils?"

Water dripped from his chin.

"Nils?" Quieter.

"Yeah."

"You okay?"

"Sure."

"I can tell him now."

"Who?"

"My father. I'll tell him I found the files. He doesn't know you're alive." She looked over from the little desk in the hotel room. "We'll have to tell him, to try to make the rest of the deal."

"I know."

"There'll be some risk for you."

"We knew that."

"I think this should be your call. It's your last chance to…"

Nils looked in the mirror, saw his own reflection and Bly's farther behind. Waiting for him. He grabbed a towel and dried his face. "Do it."

Bly went to the window and took out her burner phone. She hadn't used it. No one would recognize the number. She opened a text and attached an image, added simply *from Warbly*. Nils watched her send that, then another image.

Then Bly opened the camera and took a shot of the two of them. She smiled at the photo, then sent that too, adding, *Nils is here*.

They didn't have to wait long.

The phone rang. "Daddy—"

"My own daughter!" The call was not on speaker. Nils didn't need it to hear.

"I found the files. You should be happy."

"Happy! This is treachery."

"Not my treachery, daddy. Jimmy's."

"You should not be involved."

"This is what we talked about. On the boat."

"When you jumped to your death."

"Daddy, I'm not dead."

"Such treachery."

"Daddy."

"My own daughter jumps to avoid facing her father."

Bly breathed, heavy. "That's not why I jumped." She breathed again. "And you know it."

"We will not talk of this."

Bly cradled the phone. "We will."

"You were not supposed to find anything. You are supposed to come home."

"You can be safe now. I found what Jimmy took from you."

"You have not made me safe. Before, this man, he knows nothing. Just that something was taken. Now, what has he seen?"

Bly held the phone from her ear and looked at Nils.

"Warbly, what has this man seen?"

Bly studied Nils. Nils mouthed *I'm in.*

"Nothing. Nothing that matters, daddy. He doesn't want to know. It means nothing to him. We can make this work."

There was silence for a moment. The room seemed to get larger.

Dommy's voice filled the space again. "It is unexpected."

"It's like we talked about."

"We talked because this man was not alive. You sent him to his death."

"No."

"You sent him into the water. He should be dead. This should be over."

Bly paced in front of the window. "It's not over, daddy."

"It is not possible. To find the thing that Jimmy took. To find this man."

"It wasn't easy."

"Impossible."

"Yet I sent you pictures." The pacing stopped. Bly turned from the window. "Daddy, I love him."

The room grew immensely quiet.

"He knows this?"

Bly's raised her eyes to meet Nils'.

He nodded.

"Yes, daddy. He knows."

"Such a thing."

"I want you to let him go."

Quiet.

"It will not be easy to convince the others." The call ended.

Bly pocketed the phone. "I think he needs some time."

"To convince Zeke and Petey."

"No. They'll do what he says. That won't be a discussion."

"So the FBI guys?"

"That's my guess."

Nils wanted to wash his face again. Why, he didn't know. "What do you think will happen?"

Bly was looking out the window again. "We'll have to see."

The phone rang. Bly took it from her pocket and looked at the screen. The phone rang again. She answered.

"You will come home. Now. I will send a ticket. You will bring the materials. You will not bring this man. He will stay behind."

"We're a package. Nils comes with me."

"The man will go with Zeke and Petey."

Bly ended the call. She jammed the phone into her pocket, crossed the room, and yanked the door open. "I'm going for a walk." It wasn't an invitation.

Nils stayed behind. He tried to see his future. He could not.

Bly came back to the room. Nils didn't know how long she'd been gone. It didn't matter. Bly had left. Now she'd come back. He wasn't alone.

Bly was sweaty. She reached for a hand towel. "We're going there. Home."

"Both of us?"

"Yeah."

"Your father agreed to that?"

"Not exactly. He's softening."

"Softening? How much?"

Bly held one hand out with the thumb and fingers stretched apart. The fingers moved in a fraction of an inch.

"That's not much."

"Sometimes it only takes one crack in the ice for the whole floe to break loose."

Sometimes.

"Sorry I was gone so long."

"I didn't notice."

"I ran off a little steam."

"I can see that. You talked to your father?"

A nod. "And Zeke."

Nils had questions. Where did allegiances lie? How far would Dommy have to soften before Nils could stand up in front of the man? What about...? He settled on that one. "What about the fed guys?"

"I don't know. That's daddy's business. He'll have to handle them."

"I don't think those guys like me very much."

"Neither does my father. He uses them because it benefits him."

"A couple of those guys probably like you even less." The men she'd zip-tied to the van's steering wheel.

Bly hung the hand towel over the bar. "I handled them before. I can handle them again if I have to." She turned on the bathroom ceiling fan. "I'm sweatier than I thought. I'm going to take a shower. We can talk more when I get out."

When Bly got out she was naked and clean. That led to a delay on the conversation. It also seemed to improve Bly's mood.

When they were finished, Bly rolled out of bed. Nils watched in the mirror as she crossed the room to her clothes. Yes, better than the beach.

"The key to this is my father. If we can get him to…" She looked at Nils. "Sympathize, we can make this work."

"You seem optimistic."

Bly pulled a shirt on. "What are our options, Nils?"

"Run away?"

"We've talked about this. You want that?"

"It's better than being dead."

Bly pulled on pants. "I'm still his daughter. He'll listen to me."

"What about those other guys?"

"Nils."

He was quiet.

Bly straightened. "Talk to me."

"I'd be more comfortable if your father would soften a lot more."

"What do you want me to do? This is going to take some time."

"I understand that. But when you talked about risks, that's now, isn't it? And those risks are mostly for me."

She zipped abruptly. "And not so much for me."

"You're his daughter."

"I know that."

"And I'm…"

Neither of them finished it. Bly reached for her shoes.

Nils sat up in the bed. "We might need to explore other options."

Bly snugged her laces. "We might. Maybe. If you want to give up. But I don't. And right now I'm going for another walk."

This walk was a lot longer. Nils didn't have to time it to know.

When the door opened again, Bly was sweaty again. "New plan."

Nils had been to the hotel gym and had a long workout, then a hard ride on a stationary bike. He'd showered and shaved and put on fresh clothes.

Bly closed the door. "We're—Oh, you're looking dapper."

Nils laughed. "Dapper?"

"What? People still say that."

"As if it's a good thing."

"It is the way I meant it."

Nils got up. "Good. We're bandying."

"We are not."

"People bandy. It's what we do."

"Bandying is not a thing."

"It's our thing."

"Nils."

"Bantering, then? Maybe we're bantering?"

"We can be bantering, but this is not the time for it."

"I thought it might help to lighten the mood."

Bly's expression slipped. "Oh, Nils. I'm sorry."

He stepped closer. "For what?"

"I got you into this."

"No, Jimmy got me into this."

Bly wiped an eye. Just a gesture, maybe, or grit from her walk, but Nils had never seen her do that before. "I really want to get you out of it."

"I want that too."

Bly had composed herself. "They're coming here."

"They?"

"Daddy and some others. He's tired of waiting. We're going to make a deal."

"What deal?"

"The best one we can. This is the far end of the chessboard. It was improbable that we'd ever even get this far. But we have, and now we have to play it out. There aren't many squares left to move on, and if we can't win on this board we're going to have to look for a different game."

Nils imagined a chessboard floating on water. A king and queen at the far edge, clinging to each other, rook falling to its side. A knight tumbling into the ocean. Pawns scurrying, looking for shelter.

"Nils?"

"Great metaphor."

Bly went to the window and pulled the blind back. "We're going to give the flash drive to daddy. That part is hammered out. The rest, he's working on that."

"Okay."

"It's the best I can do."

"If that's the best, that's what we'll do."

"Quit trying to convince me."

"Who's trying to convince you?"

Bly let a quick breath go. "You're the one who was worried."

"I'm still worried. There's a lot to worry about. But this is the best we can do. We'll do it."

"What are you trying to say?"

"I'm saying I'm ready."

"I'm ready too." Bly set her phone on the counter.

"When?"

"A day. Maybe two. We're working out some details."

"So we have a little time left."

"A little."

Nils considered that. "So where do you want to start?"

They started with dinner. Then sleep. In the morning Bly took her phone and went for another long walk. Nils knew she was planning, and he let her go without any questions.

When she came back, Bly closed the door carefully behind her. "Tonight. And we have to go now."

Nils reached for his shoes. "Where?"

"Anacortes."

"All the way back up there. Whose idea was that?"

"The agent. He wants to use the same men from the field office near there."

"He would." The same men who had grabbed Nils. "You're okay with that?"

"The federal agents aren't our concern. Daddy is."

They checked out of the hotel. Gassed the car and got sandwiches and coffee. Then Nils drove them in Bly's rental car back up the Northwest coast again, Portland to Anacortes. There was no time to stop. They didn't take the scenic route. Nils was getting more familiar with the I-5 than he wanted.

Bly's phone bleeped occasionally with messages. There were some back-and-forths. She was coy with the details but passed some updates to Nils.

Not long after they crossed the Columbia River Gorge, she said,

"They're in the air."

When they'd cleared Olympia, Bly engaged in a long exchange of messages, her fingers working the phone as Nils drove and waited. Finally, Bly lowered her phone. "Daddy wants you there."

"At the handoff?"

"He says he won't respect you if you're not there."

"And we want him to respect me, right?"

"That will help. A lot."

Nils squeezed the wheel. "Are there any downsides?"

"Nils…"

"I know. If I have to ask."

"You can say no. I can go on my own and try to make this work."

"No."

"It'd be safer for you."

He squeezed the wheel some more. "What do you think?"

She took a moment. "Neither my heart nor my head wants you to be there. But my heart does a little. So…"

"So I can be a man to your father."

She sighed, long, hard, heavy. "I don't know. Your call."

Nils tried to see it, how it would play out. No scenario seemed real, none that he could imagine. He just didn't know. So… "Okay. I'll go."

In the thick of the Seattle traffic, Nils' mind was still trying to play out scenarios. "Do we know where this is going to happen?"

"I didn't tell you?"

He managed a blank look.

"I guess not. It's going to be at the ferry terminal."

"Ferry terminal? Why there?"

"I suggested it."

"You want to tell me your thinking on that?"

"It might give us a way out if we need it."

Nils adjusted in his seat. "I don't like the way that turned out last time."

"I'm not thinking of a swim. I'm thinking somebody gets on, somebody doesn't." Now Bly adjusted in her seat. "I hope it doesn't come to that."

They cleared traffic and reached Anacortes in good time. Instead of letting him drive to the ferry, Bly said, "Let's go to town."

"Why not the ferry? What are we waiting for?"

"It's going to happen late. After dark."

Nils gave a look with a question in it.

"I wanted it to be late. They'll be on East Coast time. More tired than us."

"You think that will help?"

"It can't hurt."

Nils slowed for a light. "Is there anything else I should know before we get there?"

"You know as much as I do now. We buy walk-on tickets. We'll meet on the pedestrian bridge. We give daddy the flash drive. He makes sure you're cleared."

"Cleared?"

"Of everything."

"He can do that?"

"We don't have other options for this particular play. End of the chessboard."

He again imagined the chess pieces clinging to each other, trying not to fall off the board into the ocean. Sometimes you had to play it as it lay.

Instead of town they went to Cap Sante and walked the park and looked at the water. Bly took Nils' hand. "If we get out of this—"

"When…"

Her hand squeezed his. "When we get out of this, I'd like to ride up that mountain with you."

"If that's a metaphor, I like the way it sounds."

"It can be a metaphor if you like. But we never biked up that mountain on the island. I'd like to."

"It's one of the few things we haven't raced at yet."

She laughed. "It doesn't have to be a race."

"You say that because you know you'd win."

They walked some more, up on the rocks, looking down at the bay below. Bly said, "It feels good, this bantering we're doing that you know so much about."

"Bandying."

They sat at the gazebo for a long time. Eventually Bly got up. "Nils? It's time."

She drove them to the ferry terminal. Vehicles hunched under the lights in the boarding lanes, campers, trucks, and cars waiting for a late ferry to the island. Bly took them around the queue to the public lots and the pedestrian entry. In a dim corner of the far lot, she parked and reached behind the seat for her backpack. Nils watched as Bly extracted the pistol and checked the load in the clip. "I hope we don't need this."

"You and me both."

Bly reached into the pack again and pulled out the slim runner's belt she'd worn when she'd run Nils down on the mountain. "You might need to help me with this." She pushed the seat back, raised her shirt, and slipped the belt on underneath at her waist.

Nils leaned over and snapped the clip on the belt closed, wishing their intimate position was for a better reason.

Then Bly checked the safety lock on the pistol, reached with the gun behind her, and slipped it under the runner's belt. She opened her door and stepped out, and the shirt fell down over the pistol at her back. A quick step to test, a pinch at the fabric of the shirt to tighten the belt beneath, and Bly leaned down into the open door.

Nils knew what she wanted to say. She wished they didn't have to do this. He wanted the same thing. Before either of them had to find words for it, Nils opened his door and got out. "I'm ready."

And they held hands lightly and went together down the walk to the pedestrian bridge. Travelling light. Just Nils, Bly, and passenger fare. No luggage. But for the flash drive, and the pistol tucked behind Bly's back under her shirt.

They entered the covered catwalk ramp alone. Vehicles still sat in queue in the lanes, not yet boarding. Bly squeezed Nils' hand once very gently. "Quiet."

He'd noticed.

They reached the top of the ramp and turned into the high, covered span of walk that crossed over the boarding lanes below. Still no cars moved onto the ferry.

At the far corner, where the walkway turned again to angle toward the ship, there was shadowy movement. Bly squeezed Nils' hand once more. "Here we go."

What looked like a group of men stepped around from behind the corner. Bly walked steadily toward them. Her hand slipped from Nils'.

It was clear now that this was not one group of men hunched together, but instead two small groups of men hunched separately. One group was Dommy Milkov with Zeke and Petey. The other group was not a clear memory to Nils, but he guessed two of the men to be those who had taken him in the van by the Orcas airport. The third man he guessed was Dommy Milkov's agent in the hole, the man Nils had talked to on the phone before he was abducted.

All eyes faced forward. Two sets met before any of the others. Father and daughter.

"Daddy."

"Warbly."

Dommy was a square figure in a crisp gray business suit and tie. Old school. Petey was the wolf in waiting, beside Dommy with his hands on his hips, watching with vulpine eyes. An image of a hairy-faced animal peeked from a t-shirt beneath Petey's sport coat, and a pistol grip jutted from his hip. Big Zeke morphed out from the group in his Giants jacket and warm-up pants, angling toward the second group of men.

The three federal men all wore dark clothes and dark shoes and had dark moods hung on their faces. They could have been interchangeable but for the leader who stood in front and was taller and frowned more deeply than the others. More for him to lose here.

Nils looked behind him to an empty walkway.

Dommy waved a hand. "No one else will come. We have seen to that."

Nils stopped a half-step behind Bly, the two of them facing the others across just more than arm's length.

Dommy looked to Nils. "You have seen me before. You know who I am?"

"Dominykas Milkov. Bly's father."

Dommy put two fingers together in the shape of a gun and tipped them toward Nils in acknowledgement. "And you have seen Zeke." The fingers moved to the big man. "And Petey." These weren't questions. They were acknowledgements, and Nils accepted them without comment.

Nils felt Zeke's eyes roving over him, the man solid like a block of stone, the linebacker before the play, sizing up the field. Petey rocked almost imperceptibly on the balls of his feet, the wolf ramped and ready.

The G-men could have been dirty clay, each pressed from the same lump of earth into the dark shapes that faced Nils and Bly.

Dommy's fingers went to the three federal men. "These associates will go unnamed."

Nils crossed eyes with the two who had taken him in the van. The one who'd hit him with the gun grinned back a challenge. Nils paid no mind. It was the tall man in front he focused on. The man who's eyes fixated on Nils like a fox on a rabbit. Nils wanted the man to speak, to reveal his voice as the man from the phone call before he'd been abducted.

Dommy stepped from the others and put his nose close to Nils. "We start with a show of good faith. Let me see your hands."

Nils raised them. "I'm not armed."

"Lower. Hold them out."

Nils looked to Bly for help.

Bly returned a blank stare.

Nils lowered his hands.

Dommy grabbed one hand and drew Nils in. The grab was not a shake, exactly, but it was something very awkwardly intimate. "You touch my daughter with these hands?"

Nils looked again to Bly.

She blinked, tipped her head once very slightly.

Nils' hand was still caught in Dommy's. He held Dommy's grip firmly. "Yes, sir."

Dommy's eyes moved slowly to Bly. "And this pleases you?"

Bly looked like she would faint or throw up. Nils suspected she would do neither. Instead she surprised him and blushed. "It does."

"It is like you said? This word you used. It is strong. The one I used for your mother."

Bly's blush threatened to swallow her up. She breathed deep and the pink retreated. "It's true, daddy."

Dommy's grip inched Nils closer. "My daughter says she loves you. Do you believe this to be so?" Dommy's thick, dark mouth came close to Nils' ear and the words came just above a whisper. "Or does Warbly say this only to get something she wants?"

Nils felt as if everything slowed just a step, a tick down so slight that only he could perceive it. In that tiny void, words came to him. "I believe it's true."

"And what makes you say this?"

"You saw. She jumped into the water."

Dommy kept Nils pulled in close. "Yes. And..."

Nils' heart beat. Once, twice. Things slowed again, too slow. The void expanded. He looked to Bly.

Dommy put his mouth to Nils' ear. "Not from her. From you. And...?"

Nils didn't know.

"Warbly says she loves you. And..."

Nils thought he got it. They hadn't said it, he and Bly, neither of them to the other. But it was the easiest thing in the world to do. He tried to look to Bly. Dommy wouldn't let him. "Yes, and..."

Bly's voice came in a whisper. "Your call."

Nils said the words. "And I love her too."

Dommy released Nils, stood back and nodded. "And how do you demonstrate this to be true?"

Nils stood square, toe to toe with Dommy. "Because I'm here."

"Ah." Dommy reached once more for Nils and drew him into a quick embrace and release. "Now, we can move on."

One of the feds behind the tall agent snickered. Dommy threw a look at the man and he quieted. Zeke remained a stone. Petey was coiled energy.

Dommy laughed once, sharply. "Bah." He held a hand out. "Now, my daughter. You have something for me."

Bly reached to a lanyard around her neck and pulled it from beneath her shirt and over her head. Hanging from the lanyard was the flash drive.

All eyes moved to the dangling object. The federal man in front licked a corner of his lip as if he'd found a morsel lingering there. He put a hand out for the flash drive. "Dominykas."

Dommy moved a hand in front of the federal man's and stopped him. The flash drive hung in the air. Dommy turned his head to his daughter. "It is as you say?"

"Like I said, daddy. Jimmy's files. From the key he left with Nils. No copies. No one else knows. This can end here."

The tall agent's eyes flicked greedily. "It's not going to be as simple as that."

Bly pulled the flash drive back.

The agent's eyes followed the lanyard. "This ends here, but not like you think."

Bly looked to her father.

Dommy had the hand up again, making the fingers into a gun. He pointed them at the agent. "We have an agreement."

"No, Dominykas. You agreed. Not me."

Dommy's eyes darkened, as if a cloud had settled there. "Do not mistake my patience for acceptance. This is family. My daughter. We will do as we promised."

The agent had no cloud over his eyes. They were sharp and piercing. He spat once on the floor and spoke with the cockiness of a man who carried a badge and a gun. "Nilson Garner isn't leaving here." His glare cut to Dommy and Bly. "Not with you, anyway."

Bly signaled to Nils with a look and mouthed a single word. "Go."

Nils turned, but the agent stepped around Nils and blocked him. "I should have had them finish you when I had the chance."

Nils looked at the tall man. This was the man he'd talked to on the phone. The man who'd sent the others to take him in the van. The name he'd seen Bly point out on the files. He looked this man in the eyes. "Gregory Colbert."

Colbert snapped. He pinched Nils' chin in his hand. "What? You do not say my name, you hear me?"

Nils wrenched back, freed his jaw from Colbert's grip.

"I will come down on you like—" He pushed Nils aside and lunged for the lanyard that still dangled from Bly's hand.

Bly pivoted and jerked the lanyard back and swatted Colbert's hand away.

Colbert reddened and grabbed again for the flash drive.

Bly stepped to the side, let Colbert lunge in front of her, then placed a foot in front of the man and a hand on his back and pushed hard.

Colbert spilled to the metal floor and one knee thunked down with a sickening crack. "Mother fuck—"

"Errrooooo!" Petey's howl completed the man's yelp.

Bly stood over Colbert. "Like hell on a wildcat."

The two federal men jerked, hunched at their knees, hands to the holsters at their waists.

Petey spun and kicked and a foot whipped into one agent's hand at his holster. The fingers popped and crunched and the weapon broke free and skittered away.

The agent bent and cradled his injured hand.

"Aaarroooo!"

The second agent froze, hand on his holster, eyes on his boss still on the floor.

Zeke stepped in front of Nils.

Petey squared in front of the agent with the hand on his weapon, the wolf daring the man to move.

Dommy straightened himself in the middle of the melee, one hand up in a signal to stop, the other reaching down to the man Colbert on the floor. "Gregory, this must end. Get up."

"I get up, this man dies."

He didn't have to say Nils' name.

Dommy shook his head. "No, my friend."

Colbert clenched a fist and grunted, the rage showing in his movements. "He knows my name." He tried to put weight on the damaged knee and grunted more deeply.

Dommy's hand no longer extended to help Colbert up. "He will not do anything. That can be arranged."

Colbert gritted his teeth and pushed up. "That's not enough, Dominykas. I'm exposed here."

"This is something you will have to work out."

Colbert had his weight mostly on his good knee now, halfway up, still trying to rise. "I'll work it out." His hand moved up under his jacket.

Dommy motioned to Petey and Petey jumped to Colbert before the man's hand could reach the weapon holstered under his arm.

Colbert held. His eyes swiveled to the agent who still had his gun. "Shoot him."

The agent cleared the weapon from its holster and swung the barrel to Petey, pivoted to Dommy, and then back to Petey.

Cobert screamed. "Nilson, you idiot. Shoot Nilson Garner. Kill him."

Bly was a blur, raising the back of her shirt with one hand, drawing the pistol with the other. She jerked the weapon up and leveled it on the agent. In the same motion her leg came up and a foot crashed into Colbert's wounded knee.

Colbert howled. The wolf howled. "Aaa-rooo!"

Colbert rolled over.

An orange flash exploded. A sonic boom. Everything too loud in Nils' ears and then a ringing and deafening quiet.

Another flash. Petey moving, the wolf swirling and wild. The berserker freed.

Another flash and a boom. Nils going down, the world tilting. He couldn't right himself.

Nils catching snippets, sound and sight not working right. Bly's hand on her gun, the weapon at Colbert's head.

Nils falling, slipping sideways, trying to right himself. Trying to hear. Trying to get to Bly. Reaching, trying.

A heavy thing on Nils' back, forcing him to the ground. He tried to move, crawl forward toward Bly. The heavy thing became heavier, crushing Nils down, and then the sensation reversed and he was up, rising, lifted into the air. Everything stale and dirty and ringing and not making sense, and Nils riding on Zeke's shoulders, the big man carrying him away down the catwalk.

25

NILS TRIED TO PUSH free. Big Zeke clamped Nils down hard on his shouldered and muscled down the entry ramp.

Nils' ears still rang and he could not distinguish the sounds behind him. Then they were out of the covered walk and Zeke dropped Nils to the ground beside a sedan, opened the rear door, and shoved Nils in.

Zeke got in and drove fast.

Nils righted himself on the seat. They exited the ferry terminal and the sedan whined and picked up more speed.

"Zeke, slow down."

"I promised Warbly."

A red light flashed by overhead. Tires squealed and a horn sounded. "Slow down."

Zeke slowed. He turned onto a side street and stopped at the curb. Zeke jammed the gear selector to park and spun in the seat, his big frame filling the space over the headrest. "If things went bad, I'd get you out of there. That's what I promised."

"Is Bly okay?"

Zeke's big head sagged. "Lord, I hope so. I ain't want to leave that girl." He reached for something. A big hand came over the headrest. "We didn't have much time to set things up. I ain't supposed to talk to her without Dommy knowing." In the hand was an envelope, bigger than the one he and Bly had found in the bike locker. Thicker. "She told me to give you this."

"What is it?"

"Open it."

Nils did. There was money and a phone inside. "What's this?"

"It was all I could do. There wasn't much time."

"What do I do with it?"

Zeke cocked his head like he'd heard something stupid. "Lord, what I do for that girl. If Dommy find out…"

Zeke faced forward in the seat and reached for the gear selector. "Where you want me to drop you?"

"I don't know."

"Well I got to drop you somewhere. I got to get back."

Nils looked at the phone and at the money. "She didn't say anything else?"

"She said to tell you you had to get up that mountain with her. I don't know what it means, so I didn't want to say it. Now where you want to go?"

"I don't know."

"Then you'd better get out."

Nils did.

The sedan sped away.

Nils turned on the phone and checked for messages. Nothing. No contacts entered, no record of calls, no voice recordings, nothing on the notes apps, no bookmarks in the browser. No browser history.

The battery was at full charge. That was something. There was no charger.

He walked. Just Nils. Alone. It was a familiar feeling for him. No belongings, nothing other than what he was wearing and the money and the phone.

He walked to where he and Bly had left the rental car. There was no car and no Bly. The line of vehicles queued for the ferry still sat on the mainland, waiting. Some people had exited vehicles and were leaning against fenders and looking at phones.

Red lights flickered in the distance. A lone wail sounded, then another.

Nils moved away quickly and with no real direction but with a vague sense of hope, he walked the darkened streets to the same city park where he'd found refuge before, after his swim in the sea. He found the same maintenance building and the same unlocked door.

Nils tried desperately to ignore the absurd repetition that seemed to be swallowing him up. Life on repeat. Alone, not alone, alone. Not alone, alone again. Up the coast, down. Up again. Down and up again. Chased, forgotten. Back in this same building again trying to pass another long, terrible night.

Spinning, drifting. He checked the phone. He checked again. He tried to sleep. The night passed unbearably slowly. There were no messages and the phone did not ring.

Nils was out of the building when the sun was still thinking about coming up. He walked to a coffee shop where he absorbed coffee and ate what he could get down. No messages or calls arrived on the phone.

The barista pointed Nils to a bicycle shop. He walked there, waited until the shop opened, and used some of the money from the envelope to buy a used bicycle. He rode that to a gas station. In the convenience store there he bought water, snacks, a sandwich, and a nylon drawstring bag to carry them in. He hung the bag on his shoulders by the strings and pedaled to the ferry terminal.

The phone was close in his pocket. It held a charge but showed no other life.

The early ferry had been canceled and there were long lines of vehicles backed up waiting to board. Nils got a walk-on for the mid-morning ferry. He pushed his bike up the pedestrian bridge, and when he came to the turn where he and Bly had encountered Dommy and the agents the night before, fresh rugs had been spread over the stained flooring.

Nils pushed dark thoughts away and boarded the ferry.

He left his bike in the storage area on the lower deck and went up to the top rail, to the girder where he'd dangled when the woman and child had come to him. Where the woman had asked him to help her. Where he'd stood with Bly. Where he'd jumped into the sea. The deck was quiet, the wind was quiet, the sea was quiet, Nils was quiet. He reached up to the girder and lifted himself once in a chin-up. The pull was smooth and his muscles felt strong, but Nils didn't feel like doing it again.

On the island, Nils rode. He pedaled past where he'd ridden on top of the Civic, past where he and Bly had found his backpack and the key Jimmy had left behind. He rode the bike, wondering. Was Bly here? Would she be?

Nils pedaled to the pottery shop and there he purchased the little coffee mug that Bly had held, the mug with the orca and the ferry painted on the side. He tucked that into the drawstring bag, holding onto it like a promise or a hope.

From there Nils pedaled through Eastsound, where Bly had found him at the solstice parade. He pedaled down the far lobe of the island, to Mount Constitution Road. He stopped at the turn-off and the view there, the stretch of blue sky, blue water, islands humping from the sea like the backs of big green turtles.

He had encountered nothing unusual. No helicopters, no black vehicles and men with dark clothes and guns. No one chasing him. The island was quiet.

But Nils listened. It was too far away to be true, but he believed he could hear the orcas, swimming the Salish Sea, singing. What were they telling him to do?

He started up the mountain. What else was there?

Nils pedaled, the road growing steeper. Birds chirped, cars passed, a breeze blew, something beeped.

Nils braked and stopped. The phone had beeped. He extracted it from his pocket. A message appeared.

Nils?

He grinned. *Yeah*

You're OK?

Yeah

We're in the clear

Nils stared at the message. *What does that mean?*

Colbert is no more

Nils stared harder at the words. *You killed him?*

No. Petey. But I would have killed him.

Nils let that settle for a moment, then his fingers moved. *That's what you didn't want. To do the things your father would do. For the business.*

This wasn't business. This was you.

Nils' fingers moved again. *What now?*

The agents are dead. All of them.

Nils breathed. He thought. His fingers paused over the screen. A long message from Bly appeared.

Daddy has a new man inside. There's no case against you. They have a new story. Colbert was working with Jimmy and used you to try to cover his tracks when Jimmy went on your trip. Dommy's not part of it.

Nils read it twice. *That's not what happened…?*

Daddy fixed it

So that's it?

There will be some fallout. But it's something. An opportunity.

I don't completely understand

Nils waited a minute. Then Bly's reply came. *I'll explain when I catch up*

Nils looked up from the phone. The road ahead was empty. The road behind, the long slope down, was empty.

Another message beeped in.

I'm with you. Look behind.

Then Nils saw it. A lone, slim figure in the distance, down the mountain road below him. A figure on a bicycle, phone tucked into a holder on the handlebars, head down and riding sure and true and hard up the grade. To him.

Nils pocketed the phone. He got on the bike and pedaled, rode hard up the mountain. He was strong, he was fast, but he knew Bly would catch him. Nils could pedal as fast and as hard as his body would let him, and she would catch him.

He rode hard anyway. That would make it more fun when she caught him.

Thank you for reading.

If there's something you liked about this book, will you please consider leaving a review on Amazon, Goodreads, or somewhere else where readers might encounter it?

You can also follow me on Amazon and/or sign up for email notices at scottgeisel.com. I won't send more than a few emails per year – only to announce new books or other big news.

Thanks again.
Cheers!